Life On Mars

by
Michael J Dawson

Copyright 2015

Sour Grape Productions Limited

first printed 2015 : Lulu Edition

ISBN 978-1-326-37877-6

Sour Grape Productions Limited
www.sourgrapeproductions.com
info@sourgrapeproductions.com

"This is what I was really doing"

Special thanks to Sid for having a great thought and Blossom for helping make it happen. Your encouragement and support shows no bounds.
An honourary mention to Choppy Slater, Billy, Ollie and Ramirez for all the smiles.

Table of Contents

Forward : by John O'Neil AKA Absolute Bowie

Authors Note
About the author

Foreword

John O'Neil A.K.A Absolute Bowie

Over the last ten years I have had an incredible time traveling the UK and Europe with our Absolute Bowie show. Meeting some incredible human beings who are so often bursting to share their stories about how David Bowie has influenced their lives as much as he has mine. Despite his chameleon persona his fans remain loyal and come back again and again. David Bowie is a genuine cult icon. His music runs much deeper than just the sound and the story of Ziggy Stardust is one of his finest examples. I am honoured to be in a position to pay tribute to his art. The make up and costumes are always a challenge but it's essential to make the experience as close to the real thing as possible for the audience. David Bowie fans are a demanding lot and they have high standards. I am lucky enough to have an outstanding bunch of musicians behind me. I intend to continue with the tribute act as long as the adrenalin rush is there which should be a while yet.

Michael approached me some time ago with some trepidation when he came up with the idea of writing the book. He felt that fans would reject it 100% or go with it provided it was good enough. I felt the latter and it has proven to be the case. As I said earlier whether it's a stage tribute, book or cover song the Bowie fans expect quality.

The story touches on so many of Bowies works with subliminal references to albums, videos and characters. I am pleased to be writing this forward and I am convinced that the book and stage show will be a huge success with fans.

John O'Neil

www.absolutebowie.net

CHAPTER 1

My Death

"My death waits like a bible truth
At the funeral of my youth
Weep loud for that - and the passing time"

Jacques Brel

Vic Jones had never been a sentimental man. Cold logic and reason had always driven his decisions. The towering success of his business endeavours was in stark contrast to that of his personal relationships. In later years the questions about his death were quite redundant. When they asked him what it felt like to die he had no satisfactory answer. It was just a process, a means to an end. Included in that process was the underlying certainty that he would indeed be resurrected at some point.

These unique circumstances had eliminated some of the things that made most people's demise so difficult. Growing old for one, ok he was 68 but still of sound mind and body, if you didn't include the terminal cancer. Some might be concerned about what pain could be involved, but in his case there should be none. The shadow of uncertainty had been removed because Vic had known for some time exactly how, when and where he would die. It was to be right here in this room and in around two minutes time.

Inserting a cannula can be tricky at the best of times but when you have to do it yourself, one handed it's a stinker. He was eventually successful but it had resulted in a thick stream of blood pouring across the back of his hand, dripping from the tips of his fingers onto the carpet. Mrs Barnett from housekeeping was not going to be able to get that stain out if he didn't deal with it. The hastily bandaged right hand would not win any first aid awards but it stemmed the flow for the time being and allowed him to get back to the business in hand. There was a burning sting below the reddening bandage but he still had enough movement to press the button on the remote control that would release the chemicals.

The crows sounded agitated outside in the grounds as the rising sun broke through the grey overcast sky. He wondered for a moment if the damp autumn morning may brighten later as it had yesterday, knowing that even if it did he would be long gone by then.

Vic looked at his watch, it said 9:25. He expected to hear Nathen's Jag purring its way up the gravel drive at any moment. Once inside he would make his way to the grandiose conference room to find his friend sat peacefully in the tall leather chair. Noticing the tubes and equipment around him Nathan would quickly make sense of the situation and find the note.

The grandfather clock ticked away the last seconds of Vic Jones present existence. With a clunk the chimes whirred into life and without a seconds hesitation Vic pressed the button. Watching the chemicals pour down the tube and into his veins a triumphant smile spread across his face. By the sixth and final chime Vic's head had slumped onto his chest and he was gone.

4

Doctor Algeria Touchreik hadn't slept a wink. He hoped today would provide some closure, some kind of explanation. Ironically at the precise moment he genuinely began dozing off he started to see golden light behind his relaxing eyelids. He kept them closed, rolling away from the brightening dawn. The sky lit up in a slow explosion of golden sunlight casting long shadows through the treetops. In response a relaxing dawn chorus of tropical birds and animals began to build. The warm sun rays cast across his face interrupted every few seconds by a cool breeze. He enjoyed the moment without stirring, smelling the moisture in the air and hearing the familiar soft rumble of thunder in the distance. He needed to move.

He stirred beneath a heap of thin silken material by a sandy riverbank. The waters swirling eddy currents fractured the golden light whilst the dense jungle engulfed every other patch of dry land. Tall branches reached out across the river, desperate to shake hands with their counterparts on the other side. The growing sunlight turning the treetops from deep green to autumn gold. The Doctor stirred at last sitting up as he stretched and rubbed his eyes.

The storm and rain would be here in around four minutes.

"Close please," he said in a loud clear voice and was instantly back in his own bedroom. Duke shut down the holographic imaging program and lit the room to 70%. For a second the room was in bare mode, revealing its shimmering silver walls. Duke illuminated the holograph for the living space and the room appeared to decorate itself. Algeria now settled on the edge of a huge circular bed with layers of luxurious fur coverings. Gigantic artworks filled two of the walls as the space seemed to triple in size in front of his eyes. Imitation sunlight burst through a two story window at the bottom end like a searchlight illuminating the bed. He felt the warmth of its glow on the back of his neck.

Algeria had friends who used the same wake up programme every morning but he liked the variety of a random setting. Some days it might be a tropical beach, a jungle scene or even an interstellar sunrise as observed from Jupiter. One thing that seldom changed was the sound of his ancient caffeine generator. An expensive museum piece that Ramona had given him as a gift to celebrate the millennia back in 2499. Of course it was a copy but it ran well and was supposed to give caffeine in a way utilised by organic coffee beans, at least that's what the designers claimed. In honesty it probably didn't taste much better than a 4D version but he loved the ritual, the noise and the smell.

He sat up and swung his body around running his fingers through his hair. Reaching out he blindly snatched a robe with his right hand without lifting his gaze from the floor. He gestured with a wave and the wall in front of him changed into a mirror. He observed himself for a moment, disappointed that the events of the last seven days or so were beginning to tell on him. Scrubbing his cheeks vigorously he strained to his feet and padded into the food prep area.

Mumbling something abusive to himself Algeria whipped the waiting caffeine off the table in a single motion before turning back towards his life room. He ignored the small spill he left on the black marble worktop.

"Hell Duke, tell me it's not 7am." he groaned.

"Good morning Doctor Touchreik" said a cheerful disembodied voice. "Yes, I am afraid it is 7.07am".

Algeria tapped a small augmented reality device on the back of his neck to initiate the intelli 3D display and his daily itinerary appeared floating in the middle of the room. There was one activity in his personal stream flashing in red. It just said 'meeting'. There was no detail or time or place, no additional files or attachments, just one word.

Twenty minutes later Dr. Touchreik had donned a yellow slim fitting suit and white shirt with high collar. His straggly dark hair still hung irritatingly over one eye. At 37 he was still a young man to hold the position of research director for pre shutdown analysis at the National Science Institute. His speciality being history reaching as far back as the Moonage. Long before the Dome had ever existed. No one remembered why Heathen was nicknamed the Dome because it was far from being one. It was a towering supercity built from steel and glass. After the shutdown any survivors or scavengers from societies 'outside' as they were called had eventually broken down and been welcomed here. A stable and peaceful environment for hundreds of years under the management of 'Mother'. Mother being the 'Saviour Machine' a data cloud system based on Mars.

Once dressed Algeria Touchreik collapsed into a large white leather armchair, slowly gaining consciousness. The living area was a cavernous bright space with large shrubs and trees in gigantic pots almost blending with the panoramic holographic green views through the three story windows.

Algeria reached out and touched a few menu's and brought up some ball sport news. Two holographic people appeared from nowhere, sitting on the settee opposite him they began chatting about the latest V-event in the dome. Algeria spent five minutes abusing the proud athlete as he discussed his victory with an interviewer. He was convinced that players in the team had been taking 'Nutritions' and it would all come out in the end. They continued chatting with no reaction to the Doctors remarks. The Doctor sat in his chair leering at the player on his settee looking for any signs he was lying and occasionally heckling the man without response. The interviewer finished speaking and then looked up at Algeria as he stood to walk away. He drained the last of his caffeine whilst avoiding the black grains in the bottom of his cup, ignoring her eye contact as he passed.

"Coming up soon Pierrot with the latest entertainment news but first lets take a break."

As Algeria walked towards the bathroom a tall handsome man came out wearing a chefs outfit and carrying a tray of sweet smelling 4d food gels. As the man picked one up to offer it to Algeria he reached around and tapped the back of his own neck and the man disappeared.

"You seem very convinced they are influencing in that team Doctor," said Duke softly.

"Dam right they are, you wait and see," he mumbled.

Duke gave a soft cough and attempted to change the subject. "I see the latest fantasy movie has signed up a million actors on it's first night," sparkled the cheerful electronic voice of the Duke.

"No," said the doctor without looking up. He was no big fan of immersive filmonic experiences anyway unless they were history based. The Duke carried on regardlessly offering interesting titbits of media like a hospital visitor at a bedside.

"Caveman to be regenerated," he piped expectantly. "Go on," said Algeria pausing at the mirror to pull down an eyelid with a finger as if counting the veins in his bloodshot eyes.

"Mother is pleased to announce the exciting news that a 23 year project is finally coming to fruition. The last remaining cryogenic man from pre shutdown will soon be ready for release. The man nicknamed 'the caveman' was discovered amongst samples kept by the Major Tom expedition to Mars and so has incredible historical significance, scientists believe he dates back from as early as the Moonage. Initial fears that the man could harbour harmful and ancient bacteria similar to those outside the dome have been allayed," cried the Duke excitedly. he paused for reaction, getting none he continued.

"However, it's only after a series of stringent tests that 'Mother' will feel it safe to allow the caveman to have contact with organic life forms. As the man is from pre shutdown it is felt his knowledge of organic human history will be a useful addition to our historic data banks. From his records it seems he entered a cryogenic state in the late 20th Century, possibly as early as 2012. However scientists have confirmed that his poor physical condition has delayed the project for over two decades."

"Keep me up to date with that," he said acting as disinterested as he could.

"I certainly will, sounds very interesting doesn't it?"

Algeria ignored the comment, but he was right. It did sound very interesting under the circumstances. He picked up the piece of paper he had found on his door yesterday and stared at it intently. A stranger accosting and threatening him last week,

the note and now a cryogenic caveman regenerated at the Institute? Could there be a connection of some kind? Later today he was going to be blackmailed, but for what?
Certainly not money.

CHAPTER 2

Vic had always imagined coming back to life was going to be different to being born. No one can remember being born and for very good reason. They'd have nothing to reference it with. No power of deduction, no intelligence or experience on which to gauge what is going on. Vic had expected that it would be a very different experience for him when he was brought back. He was after all an intelligent and articulate 68 year old man. To his surprise the opposite was true. Just like a baby being born his initial understanding was zero. He heard voices. He wasn't sure what they were at first. Not who they were, but what they were. No concept of anything which fortunately included fear. Then he felt a warm dizzy feeling as if someone had opened a sluice in his head and torrents of liquid were crashing around inside. It would only be later that he could put words to what he felt right now. Was it Knowledge, water or drugs? It made no difference, he had no words for those things yet. He was waking up in ultra slow motion. Over time Vic became aware of himself, his own body. He started to become aware that he could have these thoughts. Feelings and sensations started to arrive before finally he could hear his own heart beat. He had planned on being dead for a very long time indeed and yet emerging from an indescribable blackness he was concerned, he had a realisation of the passage of time now. It felt like maybe ten minutes since his last conscious though, since that smile, seeing the chemicals running into his frail diseased body. It was like finally getting off to sleep and then being disturbed.

He still had no control and could not command his body to do anything. Then memories, not real memories more realisations. Realisations that he existed, that the universe existed. Within his own universe were all the objects of everyday life. Everything he knew was entering his world like players on a stage. Once everything existed on his stage he could start to build his own story and existence around it all. He needed time to start adding in consciousness. He quickly ran through some strange dream like scenarios, the needle which was as tall as him with deep scratches he could put his fingers in and then the wheel inside a wall, Hidden. A man who was a shadow and then a smell that he could hear? Existence was returning. Consciousness was returning and he was now becoming aware. Vic started to remember that things existed and as a consequence so did he.Yes, so did he. Now it was all quickly falling into place.

"Can you hear me?" The voice again but this time he knew what it was, a voice.

It was another person and yet he didn't recognise it. This was not Nathan, but who else could it be? It sounded whispered and urgent. Of course he could hear but had no way of responding. Having replayed the scene many times in which Nathan would find his old lifeless body. He would find the note and probably cry, holding him. He hoped so. He hoped lots of people would cry. It pained him to choose Nathan and yet he needed someone strong and someone who cared. If all had gone according to plan then he could be, well his body could be dealt with very quickly. Vic had left clear instructions that his body was to be preserved in a cryogenic state indefinitely. He could not pass the responsibility to any individual and so had made his survival a company matter. After all, he knew that companies could very easily outlive, friends, family and employees. By the time he was thawed everyone he knew including Nathan would probably be long dead. As for the company? That would still be there, he hoped.

Another voice more distant "Everything is proceeding normally, vitals are excellent."

"Is he alright?"

"Don't worry its quite natural, it's going to take some time but it's possible his senses are returning."

Vic was now whole again, complete. He could feel everything, every part of himself. He started to remember, very recent thoughts. That's when the fear hit him, just for a moment and then the pain. Every part of him ached and his head felt like someone had inflated his brain.

All the planning had obviously failed, they had resuscitated him. It had failed and yet he had gone to great lengths to ensure everything was in place. There was no way his body could be found until his alarm was raised shortly after his death.

What could possibly have gone wrong? The dosage or something may have been miscalculated or an unexpected visitor had raised the alarm? Without opening his eyes he was aware of a green blinding glow on the other side of his closed eyelids. The chatter continued around him. Voices whispered in his ear. Metal was being placed under his eyelids, cold and yet not painful. He felt his eyelids prised open but he saw nothing but a blinding watery light.

He was in a chair and although he could not move he knew his wrists were fastened to the arms. Vic started to see again as water streamed down his pupils. A blur of bright lights and movement presented itself. He was indeed in some kind of hospital. A strange place, like some kind of communist state. He certainly wasn't at Nathen's place anymore. What appeared to be the very latest medical equipment was all around him along with several medical personnel. Although this seemed incongruent with the room which resembled an old tube station or warehouse. Ten minutes ago he had died and somehow he had ended up several miles away. He had to assume he was in the Royal London or even London Bridge Hospital.

"Welcome," said Blue softly. "How do you feel?"

Faces started to come into focus but all the voices seemed out of sync with the mouths. "Mr Stardust, are you feeling ok?" said another voice. No he wasn't feeling ok, he felt like he had been hit by a truck and who the bloody hell was Mr Stardust?

Were they talking to him? He saw a face come into focus and was aware of a pleasant odour, maybe aftershave or perfume.
"Hello Mr Stardust. Welcome. My name is Blue."
Vic opened his mouth to speak and then everything went black.

CHAPTER 3

Doctor Touchriek's apartment block was typical of most in Heathen. A tower of preformed 3D printed accommodation, clad in glass and steel, plain with plush holographic interiors. Dr Touchreik was unusual in two respects, one that he had a job of work and two, that he actually attended it physically from time to time. A combination of V-world and Mother ensured there was no real need for either. The fully automated robotic system controlled by the Saviour machine ensured a plentiful supply of pretty much everything. Food, clothing and other resources were plentiful since the shutdown. There was no need for any physical labour unless it was through choice. There were those who enjoyed the challenge and experience that monotonous, repetitive work provided. This could be experienced through virtual reality inside V-world. Users are able to create either private or public 'Sims' and live their lives within them. Because V-world tapped directly into the human nervous system it was in effect real anyway as far as the brain was concerned. Rules could be defined by the user or the sim itself. It provided limitless experiences from laborious labour intensive tasks to space adventures and wars. Since Mother had made so many DNA changes to the pool over the years, V-world had eliminated the need for physical intimacy. In lots of the latest generations of humans the useless organs of reproduction had been removed. Even socialising and sports were mainly experienced within V-world. It was for these reasons that the Doc was unusual in attending his workplace physically.

Naturally his apartment block and work environments were secure, as was the transport system. However, the apartment foyer between the transporter and entrance was effectively a public space. A paved area outside the block which at some time may have been designed for socialising or more accurately 'it was designed to look like it was designed to socialise in'. A paved square with benches here and there, small amounts of rubbish had accumulated through years of apathy. It was reasonably well lit but he would seldom find himself out after dark and even if he did his Augmented Reality Device could be switched to infrared. In all the years he had lived here he could never remember meeting a single individual, that is until last week.

He had been returning home from the Museum as he had done many times. The transporter had already pulled away as he headed towards the main door. That was when he first noticed a figure walking towards him, at first he presumed from his own block. As they passed under the light the downward beam gave the man a sinister appearance as it deepened the shadows across his face or so he thought. But on closer inspection he was sure that the shadows had been painted onto the man's face, exaggerating his features. On his head he sported a shoddy improvised turban which revealed greying sideburns. The man was tatty and disheveled, definitely not from this sector, if he was from the dome at all. He was dressed in rags pulled around his body and what looked like similar improvised shoes on his feet. The man strutted, purposefully and arrogantly past him. The Doctor quickered his pace and caught the man's grin as he tried to avoid making eye contact. The Doctor walked through a trail of pungent odour. Dirty, an earthy smell he recognised. The Doctor's job took him to the outside on occasion and that was it, the smell of the 'outside'. The man could have been a humanist. He certainly looked the type. He put his head down and quickened towards the sanctuary of the main door.

Humanists were a particularly unsavoury group of extremists. They shared an insane belief that society should relinquish the help of machines, including the Saviour Machine. Not content to stay on the outside and live like animals they chose to remain amongst civilised human beings, on the fringes of society. Spreading their filthy germs and ideas amongst decent people. Their activities causing power shutdowns, grid disruption, software problems.

"These fucking people," he thought.

His heart rate was racing now and just thinking about them made him angry inside, making him almost wish for a confrontation.

He got one.

As the man passed him he felt the hairs on the back of his neck bristle, daring him to look round. He had intended to continue on his way.

"Doctor Touchreik," a voice from behind him said sarcastically, as if greeting an old friend. The man knew his name? He was certainly not acquainted. The doctor took a few more steps taking him closer to the secure entrance before turning around. His eyes darted nervously looking to see if there was anyone else to offer any moral support, more importantly whether this scumbag was alone.

"Do I know you sir?" he said.

"Do I know you, I know you. DOCTOR Touchreik." The man repeated mockingly, stressing the word Doctor. "Oh you will know me Doctor, in a few years, your looking well for your age," he approached Touchreik and put an arm up high on the streetlamp, watching him intently. "Incredible," the scum whispered to himself studying the Doctor like a specimen in a jar. The Doctor opened his mouth to speak but the man placed a finger on his own lips. "Ssshhhhhh!"

The man took his arm off the post and stood with his hands on his hips revealing his twisted yellowing teeth in a grin as he looked the Doctor up and down. "Old school shoulder surfer, you don't look the type. I know about you and," he paused to lower his voice, "and Ramona."

The Doctor's heart skipped and he felt the blood draining from his face. He felt physically sick. Ramona.

Maybe he heard wrong, surely not, only he knew. "Ah, Ramona A Stone, night of the female good time drone," sang the scum.

"I have no idea what your talking about," said Algeria his guilty tone clearly indicating that he did.

"Neither have I," Giggled the stranger. "But I was told it might get your attention and I see it has."

Touchreik frowned, furrowing his brow. He had to think fast. Someone knew about Ramona. "Who, who told you to mention that name, how do you know my name for that matter?"

"That's not a conversation for now, but let me tell you what is." By now the stranger was circling him, hands on hips and walking on his toes. Without realising the Doctor had backed off towards the door a little further but the man was closer, intimidating. "This is important. I will be dropping you a little note, when we're ready for you," laughed the scum.

"Who's ready for me?" he said.

"Like I say, a conversation for another day but the message is clear. I wanted to see you for myself, make sure you were not lying. Well I have seen yer!" he had stopped circling now and looked as if he was turning to leave.

"Don't fret over Ramona, it's our secret. I will be in touch Doctor Touch-reik," he enjoyed that rhyme. Spinning he snapped, "OK?"

"There must be some mistake," the Doctor shouted after him, his voice trailing off as the man turned to approach him once more.

"Are you Touchreik?" pointing angrily into his face the smell stronger now and beads of sweat on his forehead. Deep shadows cast across his face, some by the dim light and others painted on giving him a devilish appearance.

"Yes but."

"Well there's no mistake, I'll be in touch," again he stressed the word touch, turning quickly he walked away, before he disappeared the Doctor heard him shout.

"We are going to save the world at last." His words echoing across the empty courtyard as he skipped away. That was all last week. It was too risky to have contact with Ramona until he knew what this scumbag was after. Then last night, the note telling him when and where to meet. Interesting because it was hand written which indicated a level of intelligence he wouldn't attribute to the scum he met last week. There could be more than one blackmailer? He had demanded a physical meeting, close to the Doctor's place of work. The meeting place was well inside the Natural Selection Reserve which was off grid. So he knew where the Doc worked, he knew about Ramona and then this morning the news about the caveman.

Dressed and ready to leave he felt a bit more alive, passing the hallway table the door slid open. "See you later Duke."

He felt for the note that had been left for him the night before and pushed it deep into his pocket. It gave instructions to head for a section of the dome in a corner of the Natural Selection Living Specimen Museum. It suggests that there has to be a reason for discretion. Not only that but it was going to be very convenient for him to visit unnoticed. He didn't know whether that mattered but it was a hell of a coincidence, his meeting was right next to his physical workplace. Blackmail, he was almost sure it would be blackmail. Perhaps he was a soft target, certainly not a man of means. Sending that little message about Ramona, letting him know that they knew everything and if they knew he was having a physical relationship with a drone, then they did know everything.

He picked up his bag and doubled back to grab a meal gel from the fridge on his way out. "You are aware of your meeting this morning Doctor?" Duke sounded concerned. "I have no details on file, do you need any assistance?"

"Oh I am fine thank you," said the Doctor with a twinge of guilt at keeping a secret from a machine. Although Duke was not technically Mother it felt the same as lying to her too. Even though the cloud or 'Mother' as she was known controlled everything, was everything, Duke was independent and could be trusted with just about any personal data. Well most personal data, even Duke didn't know about Ramona, the only person who knew about Ramona was the Doctor himself, that is until last week. He stepped outside and climbed into a transporter as it slowed to meet him. Settling into a large suede armchair for the short trip to the Institute. The pod was an egg shape lay on its side with the bottom part flattened. As it approached it looked like the entire front half was transparent. Pulling away the grim grey view through the windows was replaced by a colourful holographic display. The whole system moved about 6 inches off the ground on an invisible magnetic field.

He voiced his destination and settled down with his tablet to flick through some data relating to the days events. The transporter pulled up to a crawl outside the National Museum and he picked up his case and stepped onto the sidewalk. There were wide green spaces around the expansive building complex. The three story C shaped structure was clad in gold reflective glass and as he approached it felt like the building was reaching out and embracing him. Scanning his DNA at the unmanned security station he was at his station in minutes, albeit a couple of hours earlier than usual.

He took a look around before removing his security chip. Then he reached around to the back of his neck and removed his augmented reality device and placed them both in a draw, quietly sliding it shut. Five minutes later he was outside on the sidewalk again walking briskly towards the Natural Selection Park, a 15 minute walk at a sharp pace. The Park was a kind of electronic national park which is open to the public throughout the year. There is a complete ban on any kind of modern communication equipment, location chips and apps. It's frequented by students and old school organics who love the idea of being off grid for long periods of time. Lots of museum piece transport systems, natural plant and animal species are cultivated. It's meant to represent the 'outside' as it used to be. A time when species including humans relied on random DNA selection and physical reproduction.

The hired 21st century transporter was waiting for him on the parking area. It was an accurate replica of an old wheeled self driven transport. Inside was the the optional map he had ordered, a real map on paper which he was going to need to locate his expected meeting point. He fingered through the cumbersome piece of paper and got his bearings using the signposts outside the reception and hire. Without his augmented reality device he felt exposed almost straight away. He had no access to cloud data or location, he felt naked. The transport had no navigation or automatic drive system either. He pressed the accelerator and nothing happened until he remembered gears. He pulled the gear stick into drive and jerked off into the wilderness in a cloud of dust.

Like most people the Doctor very rarely had an opportunity to drive himself and was enjoying the thrill as he wound down the window and enjoyed the air. This area had been climatised by Mother to have seasons even though they were false. To serve everyone's tastes an entire year took around 4 months so there were ample opportunities for visitors to catch winter, spring or summer. After about half an hours drive he pulled off the main highway and spotted the old service station up ahead. There was no carbon fuel needed, the vehicle he was driving didn't have an internal combustion engine. The whole thing clunked and puffed out fumes just for effect. Underneath the bonnet was a regular solar generator. However the service station served as a landmark, there should be an old track almost cutting back on itself about a mile ahead. Pulling into the imitation fuel stop he found it deserted. He spread the map on the seat and fingered his route down the narrow lane to a small mark he had made earlier. The paper slid off the seat as he pulled out and headed off again and almost missed the turn, breaking hard. He reversed slightly and then used some of the opposing lane to swing the vehicle round and guide it down the dusty, bumpy track through some trees. Weeds were growing up the centre of the track and got higher as he passed a few large gateways to either side. He felt invigorated by the smell of warm damp air as it wafted through the window. Perhaps those simulated odours were accurate after all and were appealing to his primeval past. In a fraction of a second he almost cried out for the vehicle to stop before he remembered to press the brakes. One more quick look at his map and he was pretty sure this was the place.

Just gateposts but no gates, he pulled into the driveway and made his way up towards an old dilapidated but grand 21st century house. Three stories high and still in reasonable condition though clearly it was uninhabited. He was real nervous now spinning the vehicle around the redundant fountain and stopping with it facing the exit. He switched off the engine and looked around, considering his escape should he need it. What if the driveway is blocked by an oncoming vehicle? There was an expanse of land around him and he imagined this vehicle would at least get him to the woods to his right if he needed to escape.

It felt like dusk even though it was morning but the climate inside the reserve bore little relation to the outside. There was nothing but the sound of nature. That warm summer evening glow, the low sunlight was bright and yellow. He sat up sharply when he thought he heard a vehicle, no nothing. His own vehicle crackled and cooled in the imitation evening air.

He waited about half an hour and was thinking about heading back. Watching the road ahead he was distracted by a movement in the corner of his eye. Something moving across near the woods. No, maybe mistaken. Wait? There it was again. A flash or reflection off the low sunlight. He watched, squinting. It was a man.

There was a man coming out of the woods and heading across the field towards him. He was slow and appeared quite old, could be a renter or something, maybe even a Marshall. It certainly wasn't the scumbag from the other night. The Doctor stayed put, reaching for his AR before realising it was back at the office. The man was definitely heading his way. Keeping his hands out of view he pushed the button down on the door to lock it as the lady had instructed at the reception and hire.

The man took an age to make his way through the long grass, maybe it wasn't his meet? As he approached he could make him out a bit clearer and he felt a little more at ease seeing that he appeared older. He was dressed a little strange, walking unaided but with a stick and a rucksack over his shoulder. Red woollen loose fitting trousers with a green patterned shirt. The collar of his thick woollen overcoat pulled up around his bearded face. His expression was further hidden by his large but thin rimmed dark glasses and a tan fedora hat. He trampled across the gravel and reached the passenger side of the vehicle and peering through the dusty glass, he smiled broadly beneath his scruffy beard. He looked pleased and relieved. The man seemed to sigh as the Doc wound down the window a couple of inches. Placing his wrinkled fingers either side of his eyes as if wanting to pull the glass down further the man peered through the gap.

He stared for a moment and the Doctor struggled to see what was going on behind his dark sunglasses. "You made it then?" said the stranger. He sounded so familiar, did he know him? For a second he felt all this mystery would be for nothing, just a prank.

"What's this about? Who are you?" said the Doctor as confidently as he could.

"Look, there's no easy way to say this so I'll come right out with it. I'm..."

The man paused glancing down in thought as if he might want to go back and reword the sentence but he didn't. Taking a step back he simultaneously removed his hat and sunglasses. With an item in each hand he spread his arms as if to take a bow.

The Doctor could not believe what he was seeing behind the grubby glass window. The pair stared into each others eyes unblinking for a moment. The stranger stepped to the slightly open window and spoke into the gap.

"As you can see, I'm you." he said.

CHAPTER 4

What else could he have said? There was no doubt once he saw the eyes, heard the voice. This was no elaborate hoax or joke. The man before him now was an older version of himself. He was a lot older maybe 106, 108 years old and had known 70 ish years of an existence that the Doctor had no knowledge of, because it hadn't happened to him yet. The Doc had clambered out, legs like jelly and touched his face. He sat himself down on the stoop step of the house to catch his breath.

The Professor laughed raucously. "Amazing ain't it, just as crazy for me too." The Professor had given a quick summary of his story but who knows whether it would sink in.

It transpired he had lived his life until some time around the year TVC90 or so and then travelled back in time to be here today. Right now it was TVC15 so that made him around 75 years older. The Doctor was still dazed, sitting on the front porch of the house with a stick drawing in the dust. Yes, his future self was now Professor Algeria Touchreik, no longer a Doctor.

"So you lived my life, our life and then came back here, back in time to meet me?" muttered the Doctor to the ground. Struggling to make sense of the facts, there was so much information, so many questions. The fact that he was here with a man who had lived his future and his past was odd enough but all the other stuff, the time travel stuff? At least now the Ramona thing made sense because he was right, no one else did know about Ramona. His future self would be the only one who knew.

"So you will know lots of things about my future, about Ramona, everything?" said the Doctor glancing sideways up at his own weaker, older body. The mention of Ramona seemed to demand some kind of justification from his older self. "I have been here for around a week, I couldn't just walk up to you in the street. I understand that Jack may have startled you a bit but I needed your attention and I needed you here, alone." The Professor stood with his arms across his body, one hand on his chin straightening his beard. "The future I know could just be the one that happened to me. It's important to keep it as close to that as possible for now. That's why there are some things it might be dangerous for me to discuss with you," he said staring out across the landscape as if he was referring to something out there.

"What about Mother or the group, we have to tell somebody?" said the Doctor.

The Professor was slowly pacing up and down in the yellowing sunshine. He stopped, turning on one heel and rushed towards the Doctor. "We have to tell no one. No one. It's too dangerous." Seeing the shocked expression on the Doc's face he stepped backwards.

The Doc sighed realising the implications. "You know about my future, how things are going to be." He had learned a tiny detail about his potential future already or at least the future he could have had if the Professor had not come back in time. From the way he understood it, he was of course to become a Professor, this was clear because he was standing right in front of him. At the moment the future was relatively untouched but like the butterfly flapping its wings in a forest the implications will get bigger. For example the meeting. Where would the doctor have been had he not come here? What lives had been effected even slightly by this meeting?

"I've been careful to watch events in the past week and it really does seem like everything is happening as it last did. I take it you were impressed with the South Sector Virtual Ball game results?" said the Professor grinning.

"Oh I was alright, I have been impressed all season." said the Doctor, eyes widening as he slowly realised what the Professor was saying. "Wait a minute." he said pointing.

"Yes I still remembered, I remembered being right about that and I also remembered oversleeping that morning. That's why I picked today to meet with you," smiled the Professor.

"You know you and me could do very well out of this?" grinned the Doc, "You kinda know things before they happen." He smiled, "Maybe, you may not realise it right now but we are not the same person, not anymore, people change with age more than we think. It's slow, subtle. There would be no use me telling you to grow up and out of it. You'll get there. We are different." His eyes narrowed, he looked sad. "Your future changed me," he said "The future you haven't lived yet. I think it will change you too in time." Their eyes remained locked for a moment and in a way the Doctor could see he was probably going to be right. "Which reminds me, time is getting on we have to get back."

"Back where?" questioned the Doctor standing up. "Home," said the Professor reaching down to pick up his rucksack. "Don't you see that we have to stay close. It's vital that we keep my impact to a minimum."

He had explained this was a one way ticket and there was no way back for him, but home? So what were they to do now? Forever tied together like a pair of Siamese Twins, pretending to be one person so as to avoid any impact on future events? They couldn't live like that forever. The Doctor didn't know it yet but that was not what the Professor had in mind. The future will now be different regardless of what they did, but how different? That was the question, a question the Professor was praying he already knew the answer to. Because that was the exact reason he was here, in the hope he could change the future he had just come back from.

"For the time being we have to share meals, a bed, our home," he said.

"Our home?" said the Doctor. "It's not 'our' home its my home. Your home is 70 odd years in the future. What about Duke, my work? Do I leave you sat in a chair everyday whilst I go out?"

shouted the Doctor raising his arms in the air. He stood up and threw the stick across the courtyard as he walked towards the transporter.

"It's temporary, I have a plan, trust me?" the Professor called after him. The Doctor swung open the door of the 20th century transporter, noting the creak and imitation rust in the metalwork. Jumping in he dropped into the torn leather seat, sponge exploding through the tear, slamming the door shut with a hollow rattle.

"Trust me," he said to himself with a slight nervous laugh. The Professor swung the passenger door open and peered inside as if waiting for an invitation. The Doc opened his hands in a gesture on his knee whilst raising his eyebrows and the Professor climbed in beside him. The Doc sat for a moment with both hands gripping the top of the steering wheel, staring across the horizon at the reddening sunset.

"So what?, we go back a few years and then there's three of us?" said the Doc at last.

"Honestly?" said the Professor shaking his head. "I have no idea. I have a spare belt with me. I just brought it. I had to anyway. These are the only two in existence and I couldn't leave one behind, besides I am not sure how many jumps can be made with these things."

"Well surely there are others?" he paused "Who will come after you," said the Doc twisting in his seat to gauge his response. The Professor looked away scanning the landscape. He sighed. "It's very unlikely for a number of reasons," he said. "Start driving and I'll explain."

There were certain things the Prof still didn't know about time travel but it seemed there were huge limitations. Most didn't matter right now but there was a need for some explanation. As there were only two time travel devices in existence when he left, and he had them both with him then it was unlikely there would be others for now. The second was the obvious dangers, not only attempting the leap but the dangers of actually changing events. The third reason was perhaps the most profound.

They pulled into the transport and equipment hire reception and the Doctor turned a key and the engine spluttered to a halt. The Professor looked across waiting for eye contact. He stared for a second then looked down dropping the large floppy hat onto his head. Finally as he looked up the Doctor saw the look of dread in his eyes.

"At the moment there's a single reason why no one will be coming back from the future," he said twisting himself round and resting his elbow on the back of the seat. "Unless we change something, one very important thing here, in my past, your present then there will be no future for anyone to travel back from."

"What!" The Docs eyebrows dipped as his jaw hung open. The Professor looked away out of the transporter window and his eyes followed a family group with chattering excited youngsters heading into reception.

"That's the reason why I am here," said the Professor turning and slapping his younger self on the shoulder. "Lets go," he said. "I need a caffeine, that machine of yours is gonna breakdown forever next year so lets enjoy it while we can."

CHAPTER 5

Vic exploded into consciousness and a powerful burning light stung his eyes. Instinctively he tried to cover them with his hands but his wrists were restrained by lightly fitting straps on the arms of the chair. Squirming, he attempted to hide his face beneath his flailing elbows. Mercifully he was wearing sunglasses which reacted rapidly to the light and the scene before him slowly came into focus. For the first time since his death he felt mentally alert and yet the same could not be said for his physical condition. The act of just raising his head took an almighty effort and it was only now that he felt a third belt loosely placed around his waist. As intended it was preventing him falling forward out of the chair onto the tiled floor. He was on a stage in what looked like some kind of lecture theatre, instead of seats there were glass booths up to five or six levels high. The place smelled clean, sanitised like a hospital. He could see movement behind almost all the panes but the reflected light inhibited any detail. Dark shadowy figures, jostling for position behind the tinted reflection. They were like royal boxes but without the pomp and gold. Instead this theatre was almost completely white and so bright not a shadow was cast. He saw oblong patches of light inside some of the booths. Doors sliding open or ajar as more figures poured in from the back. Possibly standing in open doorways and on tip toes to see through into the room. Were they here to see him? Was he still unconscious? It could be some kind of reality based illusion caused by the drugs? He was sure he was in one of the local hospitals, there had been little time to take him elsewhere. But what was with the freak-show? His neck muscles burned with the effort as he heard an electronic Ping, similar to what he heard in foreign airports before an announcement. This was followed by the sound of enthusiastic applause and cheering from another room nearby. Vic's chin dropped once more under a strained effort and he saw his bare knees protruding from a crisp white hospital gown. He realised the muffled applause wasn't coming from another room after all, it was from the glass booths. The sound of cheers and clapping slowly died down and there was a long silence. He could hear his own heartbeat and then there was a loud electronic thump followed by a seconds ear piercing feedback. A clear male voice began to speak.

"Good Morning Mr Stardust," the voice echoed around the cavernous space, the man speaking paused to clear his throat nervously. "My signature is Burroughs."

Stardust? That name again, who the hell was bloody Stardust?

"Entree to Heathen," a slightly less enthusiastic ripple of applause followed. "We are very pleased to have you here with us," he continued. "I understand that you may be a little unsettled and we hope to make things as tranquil as possible for you. Please be assured you are quite cherished and free from danger. Your present condition is robust and healthful. You are going to need some time before you are fully roving again. You will be transported from here to a familiar household where you can spend the next 7 days getting able bodied." The speech stopped and he could hear some whispering as if a hand was over the microphone. This was one almighty cock up that's for sure. It was essential he speak to someone as soon as possible to sort this mess out. It just didn't make any sense. Even if they had mixed him up with another patient, this Stardust fella, it still didn't explain why he was here. No matter who bloody Stardust was. He felt dread, what if he had died? What if he was in some kind of coma? Shit they might start cutting him open, right here. The panic gave him the strength to lift his head long enough to make out a door sliding open to his left. A tall figure entered just outside his peripheral vision. God he had to move, had to let them know he was alive. The figure approached moving lightly, cat like with purposeful steps towards him. The echoey clatter of footsteps stopped abruptly behind the chair. He felt a jolt like maybe a brake coming off.

The voice spoke again. "May I acquaint you with Blue who will be looking after you and I am very much looking forward to meeting you individually very soon. Thank you."

He heard the mic click off followed by more muffled enthusiastic applause. They must know I am alive, they are speaking to me? His chair spun, whipping his head to one side and it felt like someone had tugged on his hair. His wheelchair careered towards the side door which slid open again as they approached. Vic was still too weak to lift his head for very long, least of all look around. He was pushed along wide corridors which appeared to have once been quite clinical although this was hardly the case now. The floors and walls were grubby and stained and yet it still smelled clean. The air was cool but stale, like an air conditioned building. He watched the floor whiz past under his bare feet before the chair stopped once more at a pair of dented, scratched elevator doors. Once inside the chair was spun round to face the exit. Feeling motion but unable to judge whether he was going up or down. Vic caught sight of the person pushing him via the brushed metal elevator walls. Certainly no national health orderly for sure. Probably female, tall and wearing what looked like white leather pants? She smelled good too. He recognised the smell, of course yes, that was it. When he arrived at the hospital, it must be the same. Could he have ended up in some private institution, an ambulance crash maybe? They were not going to let him die in the street just because he wasn't in bloody BUPA? Still it was like no hospital he had ever seen. The lift doors opened and a warm gust of air greeted him. It no longer smelled of drugs and bleach, instead, clean and perfumed like a musk smell. This was even less like a hospital and more like the Hilton or some other high class hotel. He stared down at his bare feet as they hovered silently over deep red carpet down oak panelled corridors. The chair halted sharply, the waist belt doing its job admirably. A burst of light from his right indicated a set of double doors had been opened. His chair was whisked round and he was pushed inside feeling the sharp tug on his scalp once more. Vic struggled to look up again, this place really was plush. To his right he could see another set of open double doors which housed a luxury king size bed. In this room which was some kind of lounge area there was a glass door, half slid open with a white net curtain gently blowing in the breeze. Then, thank Christ, yes it was. He could see the London skyline through the gap as the breeze blew the curtain gently inwards. The London eye, the post office tower, not too far away.

Blue clicked on the chairs brake and came around to the front. Crouching down in front of him she began undoing the straps whilst occasionally stroking his cheek with the back of her fingers. Her voice was crisp, masculine but kind. "Now do not concern, everything is going to be fine. I hope that you find items to your satisfaction."

He summoned his strength once more to look up into her eyes or at least he thought, she was a she. It wasn't easy to be sure if she was a boy or a girl.

"Where am I?" he whispered in a dry hoarse voice.

She looked at him with large kind eyes, the make up, even to a man looked crude. The bright whites of her eyes made her look youthful. Mid twenties or possibly older judging by the tiny crows feet. She had a natural shimmer to her skin, eyes lined with deep blue eye shadow indicating youth. Her mousy brown hair was cropped short, natural yet pasted close to the scalp. She had on a white leather outfit with a military style double breast jacket and it complimented the muscular physique. As she crouched down the material across her thighs and shoulders strained and creaked. Stretching to bring her head lower than his she stared up to meet his gaze.

"You are in Heathen, at the science institute," she smiled kindly. "Please do not concern, I am sure you will find everything to your contentment. I am here to care for you, be assured of that," a reassuring air hostess grin followed.

"Look, listen to me," he groaned. "Who knows I am here? I need to get out of here."

Blue stared up at him, embarrassed or unsure how to deal with the situation. Without lifting his head he stared down at her, his bloodshot eyeballs straining, summoning all the strength he could. He spoke purposefully. "Get me someone in authority so I can find out what the bloody hell is going on," he growled. Blue stood quickly, lips quivering. Physically she was tall and well built, masculine and yet he had clearly upset her. At the very moment Blue regained her composure Vic caught a glance of his own reflection in the full length mirror behind her. Blue began to speak again but the words meant nothing, they were just a background noise. What he saw set his heart racing and threw him into a state of utter shock.

"What the fff?" he croaked hoarsely to himself. He was aware that Blue was still speaking but he heard none of it. He tilted his head to try and see around her legs but she was still chatting away about the facilities and the importance of him as a guest. How he needn't worry and all that kind of crap. Vic summoned all the strength he had to scream. "I said, fucking move!"

Blue stepped quickly to one side, silenced by his outburst.

"Oh my God," he said each word individually and slowly as his mind absorbed what he was seeing. He looked down at his hands, then his bare feet. He looked weak as expected but, he was not a weak 68 year old man as he was maybe an hour or two ago. What he saw in the mirror was not that at all. What he saw was a weak young man, clearly in his mid twenties. Just as he remembered himself when he was that age. Of course he was thin, pale but absolutely not 68 years of age, more like 22. Albeit he was completely bald. Not just his head but eyebrows, everything. Some kind of swimming cap of sorts with tubes attached was attached to his scalp. The tubes passing over his shoulders like plastic dreadlocks. "What year is this?" he whispered without turning away. There was no reply.

"Miss, er Blue I asked you a question," he said a little louder as calmly as he could. "The year is TVC15," she paused, realising he would not understand she bit her bottom lip to make the conversion for him.

"Twentieth Century, V for 500 plus fifteen years. That would be, yes, to you that would be the year 2515."

CHAPTER 6

Arriving back at the old apartment a couple of days ago had been the Professor's first real feeling that he was a time traveller since he arrived. So far so good, he had thought. He was here in TVC15, alive and well. His time travelling expertise was strictly 'learn on the job' seeing as he knew of no one who had ever done it before. He was well aware of the theory that if no one had ever announced themselves as being from the future then that in itself was proof it was never going to be possible. What they had failed to take into account was that it just does not seem feasible to travel outside of your own lifetime. Certainly for no measurable amount of time, his early experiments with animals had proven that. Secondly there was the very fact that anyone who travelled back in time made such an announcement would be most foolhardy. A mistake he had no intention of making, at least for now. Of course even small changes could have catastrophic effects, the fact that he had returned to make a huge change was as far from his mind as he could push it. Nonetheless it had required that the Professor stay close to his younger self at all times and when he couldn't he should make as little impact as possible. Now that the first part of his plan had been completed and he was actually here it was starting to feel that travelling back in time to meet himself, might just be the easy part. There was a huge task ahead with his younger self and by putting that to one side he had never realised how bloody annoying he had been at that age. The bad taste in entertainment systems, untidiness and ignorance. Perhaps nature had given us all the ability to forget how obnoxious we were as youngsters. The Doctor's place was exactly as he remembered it and even though it had been knocked down many years previous in his memory it felt like walking into an exact reproduction. He had to remember that it had not been condemned yet to make way for the transport upgrades, that would be some way off. One of the most eye watering things was hearing the familiar voice of 'Duke'. It was a voice he had relied on for many years and he hadn't heard it for decades. Having upgraded him around about TVC34 and although he uploaded all the memories to his new assistive software he had upgraded the voice and personality. The Doctor had tried setting his older self up as a separate ID Commander for security and access but the Duke had been unable to deal with that. It was the DNA and voice indents that had been the problem for him. All that information was identical in two life forms and so the two were indistinguishable to Duke. The problem was resolved with relative ease in the end. It seemed that Duke's software ident package had no problems at all as long as it treated them as the same person with identical security rights. And so that's what they did. After all that's what they were, what did the Doctor have to hide from his older self? They were the same person and knew everything about each other as had already been demonstrated, the Professor knew all the personal secrets too. It had not gone unnoticed that the Doctor had casually asked about Jack Halloween the man he had sent to set up the meeting.

"Who was that man?" the Doctor had enquired suspiciously.

"A messenger, that's all," the Professor lied. He knew what the Doctor was hinting at from his tone. "That man?" Almost questioning his humanity, he didn't say but he strongly suspected he could have been a Humanist or at least associated with them in some way. Knowing his younger self, he could probably smell a Humanist at a hundred yards.

After travelling back in time the first thing the Professor had done was head up to the Manhattan Chase area on the edge of the city and make contact with them. In particular he had sought out a young fellow called Jack Halloween. By nature he still held a deep mistrust of the rebels but his knowledge of the future assured him that Jack was a safe bet. He had met him in the future.

The Prof knew he was going to need to stay out of sight for a while. There was also a need to confirm that significant events he remembered were happening again, exactly as they did the first time. Once he had confirmed that, and so far this seemed to be the case, the timing was crucial. Having outlined his plan to Jack Halloween he had no trouble persuading him to set up the meeting, in fact he was sure he wanted to see the Doctor for himself as a way of confirming the whole ludicrous story had any truth to it.

"No red hair, no lightning stripes ok?" the Professor had insisted. "Turn up with any Humanist symbols and we have blown it."

Jack had reluctantly agreed and gone along with it for now. "He's gonna find out what company you are expecting him to keep sooner or later," Jack snarled as he wrapped his head in rags.

"I know him remember, I was him. It will take time. Believe me he hates Humanist rebels."

"And you?" said Jack facing the mirror and tucking the rag into a kind of turban shape. "What about me?"

"Your the same person right, your just older."

"Human existence is at stake, you will turn out to be right after all. Is that what you want to hear?" The Prof walked towards the door glancing over his shoulder he added. "Incidentally, no I don't like you."

A broad smile spread across Jack's half painted face as he stared the Professor down. He scrubbed the symbolic lightning stripe from his face and applied tanned flesh coloured make up which looked like shadows across his face. Spreading his hands at the Prof who stood in the doorway now. "I don't want to be recognised do I?"

The Professor knew that Halloween was exactly the kind of person he would have found obnoxious as his younger self and now, he found him a distasteful necessity. With what was at stake and the reason he had come back Jack Halloween would be the perfect ally. Here he was actually planning to cooperate with a Humanist, he would never have believed it. As his young self would he ever have believed that Jack and these savages might one day be right, might be the ones who have preserved the skills of survival long enough to save mankind? Never in a million years, yet here he was.

The Doc was not entirely satisfied with his answer but Jack was not mentioned again and the Professor preferred it like that for now. Perhaps to pursue it further would have brought up the subject of his physical relationship with a drone robot called Ramona A Stone? A subject neither of them wanted or needed to discuss now, if ever. Professor Touchreik had some advantage over his younger self but they both knew that the dark thoughts that everyone holds would remain in the dark. Tucked away and never to surface, even with yourself.

The one topic of repetitive conversation was the reason that the Professor had come back. He had made it quite clear that it was essential to the survival of the human race. That was not a subject that could be dumbed down and it was that simple. Humans or no humans.

"You can't tell me? Are you serious?" the Doc said. "The end of humanity, you came back to stop it and you can't tell me?"

"Trust me, it's vital that things happen as they did the first time around for me, for us," the Prof corrected himself again. He knew if he was going to execute his plan then he was going to have to tread very carefully. He had long realised how people change over a lifetime as youthful abandon succumbs to stoicism and maturity but this was going to be different. This was not going to be like trying to convince his younger self to give up rock/tech for sonic/opera. It went much deeper than that. He still remembered vividly his passion for Mother and the world order. Even more now he had spent a couple of days with his younger self. He knew in the coming weeks he was going to have to change everything the Doctor believed in, turn it on its head. To convince him to kill the one thing he loved above all else. It was going to break his heart, that much he was sure of and yet he could only hope that reason would win through.

"We should go to Mother, put a message out," The Doctor said.

"Absolutely not, we must not discuss this in the cloud. Besides, 'Mother' would utilise all its inputs to try and solve the problem and that's the last thing we want."

The last couple of days had been a strain, the Professor would occasionally drop in comments about this and that. How the Doctor might cough without covering his mouth or how he was so critical of others at times. The Professor would comment on his diet and how it could lead to medical complications in the future. Yesterday he was enjoying a soda drink. "Another one?" the Professor commented "You know you could get joint problems with that stuff?" he said. The Doctor was growing more and more impatient.

"What do you mean could?" he said staring the Professor in the eye. "Either I will or I won't."

The Professor knew what he meant. "TVC40," he said looking down humbly. "Nothing serious but still, I am only trying to help."

The Doctor finished the drink in a single swig and launched the empty container in the general direction of the disposal. The battered can bounced off the lid and across the floor before a small droid the size of a cat began its slow journey to the can. Finally pushing it against the skirted wall where it disappeared into a slot.

"I don't suppose there's anything nice I can look forward too?" he said storming into the food prep area to grab another. This was a perfect opportunity, he hated to hold back crucial information but here was a chance to move the plan forward. Time was running out, he thought it was going to be easy to manipulate his own young mind. Not so.

"There's the new project," he said loudly as he went into the life area and sat down. The Professor placed his calves on the settee and flamboyantly cupped both hands behind his head. He closed his eyes as if he might take a nap. The Doc wandered in casually, soda in hand. "New project?" he said, collapsing into the huge L shaped sofa. "What new project, when?"

The Professor opened one eye.

CHAPTER 7

Vic picked up the dining chair and hoisted it above his head, stumbling towards the balcony. As he swung it over the barrier the momentum was almost enough to pivot him upwards and drag him over the edge. His bare feet squeaked on the marble floor as his outstretched toes kicked backwards. Steadying himself Vic clung on to the chair grinning as he surveyed the London street 15 floors below. The pavement was a shifting mass of exposed heads and shoulders. He wasn't sure how much longer he could hold on, if he didn't let go soon he would surely go with it.

"Zigg!" said Blue marching purposefully across the room towards him. Being called Zigg still sounded a bit odd but it was growing on him. He had no intention of rocking the boat just yet, after all if they found out he was not Zigg Stardust, who knows? They might be really pissed and just throw him back in the freezer, like when you started thawing steak instead of chicken. He thought it best to play along for now and get the measure of them. In his own memory Vic Jones had died a week ago and here he was 500 years later, no sign of the cancer that had been eating away at his frail body. Even better he had acquired a brand new 22 year old version of himself. He was being reasonably well cared for, if a hamster in a cage can be counted as well cared for that is.

500 years is a long time and there were just as many reasons why he could have ended up in a cryogenic pod with the wrong label on it. The pod must have been moved around a lot over time and maybe the label fell off or something, who cares. If it turns out they only want to experiment on him in this futuristic human zoo then he might tell them the truth. Heck he thought, I might want to go back in the freezer anyway. Over the past few weeks Vic had become aware that even in the year 2515 putting people in new bodies was a breakthrough. He still wasn't sure how far their experiments would go though. Even

in his own time he knew bringing back the wooly mammoth didn't mean to set them free to roam the plains or whatever they roamed. It meant sticking them in a cage so we could all gawk at them. Was his destiny to become the star attraction at a freak show? There's no need to piss them off just yet. It had crossed his mind that they might not even be human, he could be anywhere. Go along with it, be a good boy and see what happens. At the end of the day who gave a shit about Zigg Stardust. He didn't know him and even if he did he wouldn't like him. What sane person calls themselves Zigg or Zowie or whatever? Let him stay in the freezer for now, get a handle on what's going on first.

It was testament to his growing strength that he was able to hold the chair for a few moments before letting it go. He watched as it tumbled towards the passing throngs below, catching on a protruding ledge sending it spinning madly downwards. Then, slowly as it got closer to the bobbing crowd of exposed heads below, it disappeared. Vic shrugged disappointedly and wandered back into the apartment. It had been a weeks since he was thawed and as his strength grew so did his boredom. A childlike attention grabbing boredom. An illustration of his will to be set free, to explore the mysterious new world he found himself in.

It wasn't any kind of threat or sense of being in-prisoned, that wasn't it. If he wasn't in a prison then he was certainly in some kind of quarantine. Over time it had become clearer that the 'Futures' as he called them were keeping him in a kind of human zoo. He called them futures because although he knew they were human beings they seemed different to him. A bit like foreigners or aliens, from a very different culture. Weeks had gone by and he still had no real idea what the outside world actually looked like. Blue had been a daily companion or maybe a guard depending on how you view it? Either way she had proved to be kind and considerate as well as being, well just pleasant company. In the early days she had tended to him physically but as he had grown stronger he had become more independent. Blue became more of a mental help, explaining what she could about how things had changed and what he could expect. She was like a kind of ambassador to the futures, passing messages and facilitating his development. At night she would leave him and return the next morning.

It was during these long night hours, particularly as he had become stronger that he had tested the security. He felt no need to escape yet, he just wanted to know if he could. He soon discovered, he couldn't.

Not a window, door, or ventilation shaft would show a hint of budging. Even the flimsiest window catch or air conditioning shaft was only designed to look flimsy, none of it was. His most realistic chance of escape appeared to be the balcony until he learned it was purely a hologram, all be it a very real hologram. He passed off his testing of its impregnability as just childish pranks by throwing items over the side for fun. If it was a hologram then perhaps there would be a screen or projector which may be a way out, should he need it. Instead items that were dropped or thrown simply disappeared as they fell, putting paid to any ideas of taking a leap of faith in the hope he might land on some kind of screen. Anyway this thing never gave even a hint of projection. It was beyond an illusion and it would take nerves he didn't have, to jump and hope for the best. For a couple of nights now Vic had been fooling around with the lock on what seemed to be an adjoining door. Amazingly when on the brink of giving up, the lock clicked and the handle gave way. Slowly he pulled the door open to find that he was correct, it was a doorway into the next apartment. Eyes wide Vic pulled both doors open and glared into the darkened room. Lit only from the light in his own apartment it appeared to be a mirror image of his own. Buoyed by his success he bounded forward cracking his forehead on what he first thought was a glass door, but it wasn't glass. It was similar but invisible, like a force field. Vic was sure he could feel the air coming in from next door but his fist could not penetrate the barrier. He felt his way around it like a mime artist, detecting what appeared to be a join in the middle. Forcing his fingers into the gap and pulling it outwards like an invisible bull-worker. It would shift just a little yet it soon became clear it was not going to budge more than an inch. Every time he got some purchase on it the force would spring the invisible door back together and threaten to trap his fingers. He closed the existing wooden adjoining doors and went back to bed, if nothing else he had peeked into the real world without depressurising the place or setting alarms off.

Vic was becoming stronger and more confident by the day and was keen to get out, and if they were not going to let him go out why have a hologram of London? Blue had explained how they had tried to help him feel at home so as to adjust to his new surroundings. Why not just open the window and let him see the future, it would be so much more exciting. He couldn't help wondering if they were hiding something from him.

The 'futures' had certainly done their best to help him feel at home and whether he chose to admit it or not, the quarantine cell disguised as a hotel suite had certainly put him at ease. The holographic view of the London skyline from the balcony was incredibly realistic, along with interior fixtures and fittings which resembled a 20th Century hotel suite. Discovering in time that all of it was in the main, false. Light switches didn't work and draws didn't open. The TV didn't work either, there was just white noise when he switched it on. On the balcony he could experience the sounds and smells of the bustling city below. He had naturally assumed it was real at first and it made him feel closer to home, to reality. Even now he found it comforting. Discovering it was just a hologram he tried to work out where in London he would have been by checking out the buildings he recognised on the skyline. It was only then that he realised how bad it's geography was. Everything that you would expect to see was there but in the wrong places. Yet it was so real, he could feel the cool city breeze, smell the mixture of fresh air and car fumes. He wanted to go downstairs and run out into the street. Sadly he knew that the street wasn't there, even if he could open a door. Everything had been designed to their very best interpretation of how things were 500 years ago in or around the year 2014.

He would shout obscenities at passers by below, they always ignored him. On the third day he dropped a cushion off the balcony and watched as it fell, slowly disappearing. In other ways he had been kept comfortable. Every kind of food he could wish for in any quantities was provided by a kind of room service. He never saw anyone else, just the trolley outside the door. Over time though Vic had come to realise that every meal he ordered would arrive looking hot and appetising yet always tasted the same. His eyes tricked his brain into tasting different things but deep down he knew that chips tasted like peas and peas tasted like steak. In order to confirm his suspicions he ordered something he hated, squid. Squid was the vilest thing he could think of and it would have turned him green even if he managed to keep it down. When it arrived it certainly still looked vile but guess what? It tasted like chips and steaks and peas.

Growing more and more restless every day his curiosity about the outside grew, at least in prison you knew what freedom could be like. He slumped back into his chair, picking up the remote he repeatedly opened and closed the curtains. Staring across at Blue out of the corner of his eye, trying to look deeper into her soul whilst her attention was elsewhere. He was realising how quickly he had become fond of her. Blue had an incredible knack for saying or doing the right thing, a master at managing his mood or feelings. He had spoken to other futures over the last week but only on screen. That Burroughs guy and a few others had been on, assuring him he was safe and important and all that kind of thing but she was the only one who seemed to be civilian. The only one who was ever physically here with him. The others had that official, medical tone, not Blue? It was like she cared, really cared and he probably needed that right now. A 22 year old body, a mind with 68 years of experience, in a world where he had no experience at all. It almost seemed dangerous, like a baby with a shotgun. He was embarrassed at his growing infatuation and interest in her, particularly in light of her sexuality. Technically she was neither male nor female, purely androgynous. He hadn't stopped to bother about that, yet.

Blue and the other futures had reassured him that he would not be confined here indefinitely. They had to ensure he was safe to meet their population and visa versa. There were natural concerns about ancient germs, viruses and such like. Not just ones he might transmit but what he may receive too. There was also the vast gap in culture between him and them. That was how he came to understand that he was quite a big deal around here. Vic or Zigg as they called him, was being groomed and educated before being introduced to the general population. He felt like he was training to be an ambassador to 2014 and they didn't want him making a fool of himself or them.

He had considered the analogy and it made sense, imagining bringing someone back from 500 years ago? There's definitely going to have to be some adjustment. They had given him a new young body, he was going to be a younger version of himself. With all his memories and mind intact and he was physically around 22 years of age. Feeling lighter, stronger and virile once more. Physical feelings had returned that he had forgotten existed because he never noticed them go. Sex drive, strength and power all slipping quietly away in the night, bit by tiny bit unnoticed over so many years. Until 500 years ago in his late 60's, weak and diseased he had committed suicide and waited. Inside this new body all those things had returned in an instant and he felt like a pubescent teenager struggling with his boiling hormones and emotions. Now he was out of his bubble he wanted to party and most of all he wanted sex.

Does being in an enclosed environment mean a person will sexually gravitate to anything human? From what Blue had told him she was neither male nor female, like many people these days. That was believable looking at her right now. The male part of her features and her strength was what gave her the machismo with enough feminism to attract him. Still juggling with his teenage emotions he felt there was something more to it, being attracted to Blue in a non sexual way. He shrugged it off as dependence, like a kidnap victim who falls in love with their captor. But Hey, he thought, it's been five hundred years! He tried the old fashioned approach, asking about leisure, parties and partners but she struggled with that concept. Whilst he struggled with their concept of sex, boy, girl, male and female.

He had a lot to learn before the concept of sex, male and female in the future would make any sense. Staring back blankly at the wall Vic's eyes glazed over as he considered his time here. What had felt to him like ten minutes had turned out to be hundreds of years. His plan had been to thaw out when there was a cure for his illness.

"Cured? Oh no we can't do that," Blue had explained matter of factly on the day he first saw himself in the mirror. His illness was not only very old but was age related. The reason humans had died of such things in his time was because the breeding was done very young. These days it was much older and by all accounts less physical and whilst degenerative illnesses still existed they would appear much later in life. What they had successfully done instead was to reset his body clock by using his existing DNA to create a younger body. What they had failed to do, up until he had seen himself in the mirror was to actually tell him. Clearly they were expecting him to be pleased, like a surprise, as if someone has valeted your car or decorated the front room while your out.

"Surprise! What do you think of the new body? Yes that's you in the mirror! While you were frozen we took your brain out and put it in a new 22 year old body. Great huh"

"Aw a new body," he should have said. "22 with eyes of blue! You shouldn't have. I love it. Thanks guys."

To be fair he had adjusted surprisingly quickly over the last week and it had been made easier as he felt physically better every day, in fact he was close to full fitness now which only added to his frustrations. It would be some time before he understood the significance but Blue had gone to great lengths to explain that his legal age was actually 22 years old. There was now some kind of legal lifespan allowance of 130 years before euthanasia. Being used to a life expectancy of 80 ish years it seemed fair enough. In the year 2515 however it was a different matter all together. The act of euthanasia being cause for celebration these days. A way of giving something back to society, making space for others.

"How come everyone doesn't just get a new body, like I did?" enquired Vic.

"That would be very unfair and selfish," said Blue abruptly. "Why would anyone do such a thing, Euthanasia is a special time for everyone?" she said in a quizzical way as if the very idea of cheating the system to stay alive was an alien concept.

"How old are you?" asked Vic casually. Blue stopped and thought for a moment, he was used to her being very decisive and it seemed like a long moment. Finally she blinked and ignored the question completely, that's a ladies prerogative he supposed. She continued to explain how in order to manage the gene pool the computer thing that ran the place had decided that 130 years would be the limit. By being 22 again he was cheating the system but he would go with it for now. From the way some of the futures had treated him it was never going to matter, he was special. Either way it would be over a hundred years before he was expected to stick his head in the oven so until then he would be happy to flout the rules. The main concern right now was what that hundred years had in store for him. He felt young, fit and agile. Was he ever getting out?

Blue sat next to him and had been oblivious to his stares. She was surprised when he spoke her eyes widening as if broken from a trance.

"So is this it?" he sneered angrily.

"What is your implication?" Blue folded the tablet computer she was using and swung her legs around looking concerned. Her brow furrowed above her deep blue eyes like a nurse who had suddenly noticed a blip on a patients monitor. Sitting up and turning her complete attention to him he chose not to reciprocate, continuing to stare at the constantly opening and closing curtains.

"I feel fine, why am I a prisoner here in this fucking zoo?" He gazed up at the ceiling. "Are they watching me right now? Like a panda! Maybe they will want to breed me and get some more cavemen to experiment on!"

Vic stood up glaring down at Blue as if waiting for an answer, there was none. She looked up at him hurt and confused. Like a mother who had been told she was a failure by her only child. She had no response, the lip quivering again. He paused a second too long and spun around fists clenched with his own nails biting into his palms. He stormed into the bedroom and slammed the door throwing himself on the bed. Blue watched him go, jumping as the door slammed loudly. With a shocked and worried expression Blue reached for the tablet she had set down beside her. Vic launched himself onto the bed closing his fists around the silk sheets before picking himself up on all fours kicking and punching the pillows in frustration. On the other side of the door Blue calmly tapped and stroked the screen once more whilst hearing his muffled screams over the low hum of the city outside. Vic jumped off the bed and put his fingers behind a high walled dresser to topple it. Realising it wouldn't budge he screamed and turned his frustration on a small table which was similarly fixed. Crazed he ran around the room pulling and heaving at items of furniture. Nothing would move, everything was completely immobile. Not a single item of furniture would budge. He would not even get the satisfaction of trashing the place. Vic went back to the bed with tears of frustration running down his face. Screaming into the pillow like a child until he could hardly breath. A mixture of snot and tears across his reddened face soaking into the cloth. He thought Blue would come to comfort him, he wanted her to. Desperately he wanted her to come so he could scream some more, tell her to leave him alone and blame her, but she didn't. After about an hour he had cried himself to sleep. When he woke up the room had darkened as the simulated sun had set across the city outside. Vic slid off the bed and staggered over to the bedroom door and slowly opened it. Looking around the empty apartment, aside from the low hum of the city outside there was silence. Blue was gone, calmly closing the door with a click, he turned and went to bed.

CHAPTER 8

The next morning Vic came out of his room, shielding his red eyes from the glare of a bright summer morning bursting in from the balcony. He had been pretty upset last night and still was. He couldn't help thinking that the summer morning was just for him. That the futures had programmed it to cheer up the caveman. Maybe they thought the caveman would like that kind of thing, after all they were used to living outside when they were hunting buffalo, they might say. Blue knocked and entered as usual bringing in his breakfast. Pulling his nightgown around him he shuffled across the room without making eye contact. She placed the cup and plate in front of him as he sat at the dining table. It was becoming a pointless ritual now that he could clearly bring his own meals, not least cook them. He looked down at the plate of steaming sausages, eggs and beans along with brown toast and mushrooms. He felt his blood boiling with anger, he had to make something happen, he felt like a rat in a cage. He must refuse to perform for his captors. Without thinking he slipped his hand under the warm plate and launched it across the room sending the food splattering down the gold leaf wallpaper. Blue flinched at this explosion of anger and looked at him, the tiny residue of food droplets running down her face and clothing. He stood up breathless with anger, his chest and shoulders heaving up and down, his eyes demanding a reaction. He regretted his actions immediately. The pain in her eyes made him feel like an angry father who had just lashed out at a playful toddler.

Shit, he thought. He could read her mind, she was stunned by his act of aggression. He suddenly felt pathetic, he was a caveman after all. That's what she was thinking, and he didn't want her to think it. He wanted to take away what he had just done and wipe it clean but he couldn't.

"I have a surprise for you today," she said holding back tears and smiling, dabbing her face clean with the back of her hand.

He looked away to the floor in shame. "It's time for us to explore and for me to show you our history, your future. The future you missed."

Her voice was croaky like an abused wife trying to reason with the animal she still loved. The double doors swung open and a couple of futures came in. Both were dressed in white lab coats and wearing hospital face masks. Vic wondered if they had been outside and heard the commotion yet they didn't look at him once. Both he and Blue looked away embarrassed like a couple who had been caught rowing at a party. One of the futures pushed in a trolley with a suitcase size device on it and then left, gently closing the door behind them with a click.

Blue composed herself. "Today we are going into V-world so I can show you our past, the part of our past that we know about." She looked down at him with that smile again. "It will help you understand things," she paused. "Why things are different now," she was struggling for words, wringing her hands together but he knew what she meant.

"Hey caveman we don't run around raping and killing each other anymore like you did. Why not come with me and find out why life is so much better without people like you. I can show you why you really do belong in a fucking zoo you animal!" but she didn't say it. She was too kind to say it.

"V-world?" he whispered to the floor. "Is that it, my quarantine is over?"

"Not quite, but soon. We all want it to be soon." Her palms were forward as if she might have to ward off a blow. This made him feel even more pathetic. She had spoken about a great many things during their time together and she had mentioned V-world a lot. He shrugged looking to the floor again avoiding eye contact.

"V-world is a computer generated, er place. A three dimensional environment. I have created something special for you. To help you understand," she paused "us," she finished. He got the feeling that V-world was much more than any computer game he had known and understood it to be a very important part of life here. V-world was the futures answer to virtual reality but the technology was way beyond anything Vic could have imagined. V-world was real as far as any brain might be concerned because of how it worked. Blue explained once more. "Imagine you put your hand near a fire or you see the colour green," she said. "How do you know that?"

"I suppose," he thought about this a little more. "My nerves tell my brain, my eyes tell my brain?" He wasn't sure if that's what she had meant.

Blue grinned. "So if those nerves told your brain you were cold or could see orange?"

Vic thought for a moment "I would be cold and see orange I suppose." He shrugged. "That's exactly how V-world works."

Blue reached into the case and held up a helmet not unlike the leather flying helmet that second world war pilots would wear, complete with goggles. "By wearing this device it can intercept all the inputs that are coming in from various nervous systems and disable them at the base of the brain. It then inserts new ones dependent on which sim you are in," she said. "So as far as my brain is concerned V-world will actually be real?" This sounded scary. "Almost, you can't die and there's a finite limit on certain inputs such as pain whilst other emotions can be accelerated," she stated handing him the helmet. "All you need after that is a world to visit called a sim, you can decide on the rules within this world, like whether you can fly or not and anything else you want. So when you are in a sim, and enjoying adventures then you can do so in complete safety."

"I see," he said thinking that they obviously had some different ideas about safety these days, intercepting and disabling brain function was considered rudimentary now. Blue continued. "Sims can be public places where others around you are real people or private where the other people are in fact A.I. bots, theres little difference in the experience."

For years V-world had gone beyond a game. By setting certain rules people could not only socialise but, for those who chose to, experience a cooperative work environment. Vic was astounded to find that because life was so leisurely many enjoyed the challenge of a group task with high demands or monotonous time conscious duties. In effect their job was now their challenge and pastime. In the same way as they achieved nothing in a game the same was true in work type environments, it was to experience different worlds. V-world allowed humans to work, play and even have sex from their own armchairs. Physical travel in the real world had become less and less of a requirement. Blue continued to bring him up to speed as best she could and assure him it was safe. There were moments he felt like a caveman being coaxed into an aeroplane. It took a few minutes to get things ready with Vic being overly polite at appropriate points as if it might lessen the effect of his savagery earlier. There was no mention of his recent outbursts and soon they were ready to go.

"This is your first time in V-world so it can be very disorientating," Blue explained. "First of all let me explain that nothing you see is real, it's easy to forget that. Everything you experience is through the helmet. If at any point you want to leave just do this," she raised her right hand and with the thumb protruding outwards and placed it on her chest whilst using her left in a similar fashion to flick her forehead outwards in a single movement. He mimicked her. "Good," she said, "that's it." Blue seemed a little nervous, more nervous than he was. Blue proudly explained the entire simulation was designed by her, with a little help. She went to great pains to express that nothing is real and that most of the time they would not be with the general population but in a private simulation. There were various methods of experiencing V-world but the gear they had was the absolute top of the range with the very best receptors.

"Sounds good, kinda like having the latest Xbox with a wide screen TV and quadrophonic sound." she looked at him puzzled as he sat down next to her.

"Ok," She said making the escape move once more "Take these and put your helmet on." He looked at the four green pills in his hand with his palms still open. "Nutrients, sugar and protein," she said and dropped her goggles. He swallowed them in one gulp, put the helmet on and dropped the goggles over his eyes. He sat silently for a moment, completely blinded by the glasses through which he saw nothing. "Are you ready?" she said excitedly.

"Ready," nervously adjusting himself.

"Here we go."

CHAPTER 9

Without further warning he felt an immediate rush of panic as the air was being sucked out of his lungs and his skin tightened. Then as quickly as it came there was a release of pressure which was replaced by a breeze, a calming breeze like he had been pushed out of an air conditioned building onto a hot street. Then he could see, it felt like he had opened his eyes but he realised they had already been fully open. They were now both stood on what looked like a busy London street. Vic looked down at himself to see he was wearing a green silk two piece suit with bright red shoes. A high collar shirt and garish tie hung neatly around his neck. Nothing she had said could have prepared him for the reality of what he was experiencing. Next to him was Blue, he could tell it was her but she looked different. She had on a dark blue business suit with her hair flowing down her back. It was a different colour too, it was much darker. She looked over at him. "How do you feel?" she said smiling.

"Where are we?" he asked looking around. Realising what was incongruent about the situation. Mainly it was colours, bright hair, suits. The fashion was wrong but other than that he was standing in a London street. Actually standing in a London street, he could feel, hear. Just like that hologram outside the window only now he was actually in it. He reached out to touch a table at a cafe they were stood outside and he knocked on it. He smelled the calming waft of perfume as a woman brushed past him on the walkway, the smell of a city returned as she disappeared into the crowd.

"I created a simulation to help you understand, it's London, what do you think?" "Amazing," he said, Blue beamed with pride jumping and then stopping herself, wrinkling her nose in a smile. He didn't mean the street but just the reality. This was reality in every way but she clearly misunderstood his compliment and he allowed her to.

"I had a little help," she said, "but I will tell you about that later." Blue pointed across the road. "Let's sit there," beckoning him over to a park bench on the other side of the street. She ran across and he followed darting between slow moving cars, having to dodge a speeding bicycle in the lane between them.

"This is a good simulation of what Lon-don may have looked like around 2045," she said pointing around at the throngs of people and pronouncing London in two broad syllables. "We're not sure where you were at this time but it was the next stage in the technological revolution," she shouted above the city bustle. "It was as a result of the light-age." "The light-age?" He questioned, his heartbeat rising. "Hundreds of years ago, even before your time a man called Albert Einstein claimed.."

"Yes, I know Albert Einstein!" interrupted Vic excitedly. Blue looked at him raising her eyebrows. "You know, I didn't know him. I knew of him." Vic corrected himself.

Realising that 500 years had introduced some misinterpretation, even in the same language. "Well of course he was a famous scientist, centuries ago," she continued. "He had put forward a theory on how light could possibly be treated as a particle, something unheard of in your time. By applying Planck's theory it could.."

"It could be used to develop light processors," said Vic finishing her sentence for her. She trailed off giggling and squinted at him curiously. This was all so elementary to her, probably learned it all in school. Here she was trying to explain it to him, like explaining an iPhone to a caveman. She reverted to a more basic translation. "If light could be used in computer processors then we would have optical computers. This idea was perfected around 2045 and was the beginning of a revolution in processing speeds and artificial intelligence."

"2045, that would be about 30 years after they put me in the freezer," he said gazing into nowhere as he absorbed the scene around him.

Blue looked back at him nervously. "Er, yes," she said slowly. He knew quite a bit about light technology but was pretty sure Zigg didn't. Still, to hear they had done it stunned him for a moment. Vic was busy picking out the differences in this London to the London he knew. There were still numerous old buildings, Georgian, Victorian or whatever they were. Were they genuine? Who knows but he wouldn't have been surprised to see so many of them outlive the twentieth centuries lifeless glass monoliths a few times over. The vehicles and cars didn't roll on wheels, they looked like they did but they hovered. The thing that was really timeless was that hustle of a big city. The chill of a busy Monday morning in the air and people who had places to go as quickly as possible. The traffic was calmer, not calmer drivers but the traffic was actually calmer as if every vehicle was going to get where it needed to go. Could cars look more relaxed?

She pointed across the street at a bright red London bus which had no driver, it was clearly of a more futuristic design as if inspired by its original. To the left some humanoid cleaning robots were busy sweeping the pavement.

"Can you imagine how that effected technology?" Particularly Artificial Intelligence and the field of automation and robotics exploded. Manufacturing, food production and everything else became artificially intelligent. Everything was efficient and connected to everything else. Your fridge could predict its requirements and talk to every other machine in the food manufacturing process right back to the field or factory. In time output and efficiency were so high the tax system became pointless and was turned upside down. Gainful employment went the same way and it was the system that provided for everyone. The days when you were slaves who worked for your government were over and so went government too."

"No government?" This was sounding better and better to Vic. "No taxes?"

"By 2068 what used to be called the World Wide Web now became intelligent and autonomous. It had access to millions of other experiences and data. This meant it would not only search but think and provide answers much quicker than organic life forms. It would have been super intelligent because it had experienced every problem and could come up with an answer much quicker. Around this time the Web started to manage more and more of the data, food production and management of resources. Along the way it made more and more decisions."

Vic watched as people walked faster and faster in front of his eyes until they became a blur of reds, greens and blues, clearly symbolising the passing of time.

"Communication and technology peaked as A.I. and robotics advanced at an incredible rate. There was nothing that humans could not dominate and control. Soon it was technology creating technology and artificial intelligence could actually theorise and deduce. Humanity eventually had the technology to reach out to its nearest planet, Mars."

Like a theatre stage curtain the streets of London collapsed to the ground and disappeared. The bright city colours turning into the empty blackness of space. Vic watched in amazement as he stood on the surface of the red planet. He crouched down picking up a handful of dust which ran between his fingers noticing how some of it was on his shoes. They were both still dressed the same, in street clothes. As Vic looked up an enormous spaceship the size of a medium office block silently landed a hundred yards in front of them. Blowing dust in its wake as it came to a halt. Vic's eyes widened as Blue continued her commentary "By the year 2110 the new World Wide Web has intervened in global debate and is starting to make decisions. Along side this it made sense to take all written data and digitise it, making it available to everyone. Paper data became redundant. This data and art archive was stored across the web, it is around this time that we think it happened."

Blue's voice seemed to crack a little and she may have had a tear in her eye as she turned around. Vic followed her gaze and had not realised there was a space station about another three hundred yards behind them. It looked like a small city covered in shimmering red and green neon lights which flickered and went out for a moment before coming back on again. Like an office block might burst back to life after a momentary power failure.

"A self sustaining colony was being established on Mars led by Major Tom. It was during this time that the data crash happened, we are still not sure how or why but it could have been some kind of electronic weapon or virus. Perhaps in your time you had wars which were fought with bombs or armies. By 2068 that would have been pointless and the people or nations who owned the data were much more powerful. Whatever happened in those weeks would have been the technological equivalent of a nuclear bomb. In stages across the world from South America, Australia, France, Germany, UK and all around the world. Every single electronic device burned out and failed, destroying the data of the entire world and disabling technology. In a matter of weeks it would devastate the planet and leave the colony on Mars stranded.

Vic heard a voice in his ear like he was listening to a radio transmission. The voice sounded distressed, urgent. "Ground control to Major Tom, can you hear me Major Tom?" There was white noise then further voices, garbled but undistinguishable. He could not make out anything being said, just the tone. Similar, urgent. Then the first voice once more. "Major Tom, there's something wrong, your circuits dead. Can you hear me Major Tom?"

Blue interrupted. "The entire network across the earth was shut down. Every single piece of electronic equipment ruined and unusable. Human beings so dependent on technology left in the darkness with no way of fending for themselves. All historic data destroyed and very few humans survived the aftermath."

Vic could see lots of activity around the space station as figures came and went through a large air lock. Loading and unloading items onto a waiting craft. Much smaller than the other one and not quite so sleek, it was different and he soon found out why.

"What about those guys?" he questioned.

"Yes," she said respectfully. "Major Tom and his team were stranded on Mars with as little hope of survival as anyone else. As it turned out they were to be the ones who saved the human race from extinction. They would be the ones who created the world we have now. A world with the City of Heathen."

"Are you telling me they survived up here," he said tailing off, noticing his use of the word here. Remembering he was not actually here on Mars.

"From what we know they did much more than survive. An ancient space race was turned on its head, Major Tom and his colony spent years developing a way of returning to Earth to create the Heathen project," she paused again. "I am telling you this so that you know the truth," said Blue gravely.

"Why would I not believe you?"

"Not everyone believes this version of events, when you go out and meet the people of Heathen you may hear other stories about the Major."

Blue looked deep into his eyes. "They are not true," she said seriously as if it was a command instead of an opinion.

"What was to be a colony using some of the earths brightest minds to populate Mars actually ended up returning to repopulate earth. In the time it took them to return to Earth there was devastation. The most advanced society in the universe as far as we know, reduced to a medieval existence."

Vic felt like a ghost watching the general goings on around the space station with figures coming and going, busy moving items to a waiting launch pad. Blue continued. "Meanwhile on earth there must have been devastation and mass starvation with a return to a tribal existence. Far worse than in your time. That's why we need you now, why you were regenerated."

Vic's heart skipped a beat. "Need me?"

"Yes," she said "You come from a time before the digital age, a time when there were written records of human history. By the time the shutdown hit everything was digitised, pictures, photos, historic records, the names of presidents. Virtually every piece of human knowledge was in the web and when that was destroyed, so was our history." Vic drew a breath and brushed some Martian dust from his sleeve.

"So the only knowledge that was left, every invention, event, life was lost? The knowledge of the entire human race now consisted of what was in the heads of Major Tom and his crew?"

"That's exactly it. Thousands of life samples had been taken to Mars for storage, a kind of life blueprint backup. Amongst those samples you had remained undiscovered for hundreds of years. It was miraculous that eventually your existence came to light. When you were found we were so excited that we could regenerate you, that you could teach us so much." Vic scratched his head. "Yeh," he said as confidently as possible. "That's just amazing."

"By the time Major Tom and his team had returned to Earth the human race had been almost completely wiped out," said Blue raising a hand in a pointing gesture. She lifted off the ground and pointed towards earth. "This way," she said.

Vic mimicked her hand movements and found that he too was floating next to her high above the planet. He followed as they both soared towards earth at a speed so fast the planet tore towards them increasing in size. He felt like a character from the Snowman or some kind of superhero film and yet there was no gushing wind or resistance. It was more like they were pulling the earth towards them. At last they approached the earth soaring over mountains and oceans until finally they approached a large city skyline. The pair swooped effortlessly between tall dark buildings that could have been the financial centre of any modern city. They settled slowly to ground level amongst the scenes of desolation. A horrific apocalyptic sight presented itself amongst the tumbled rubble of a once towering city. They stood in the middle of what would once have been a busy thoroughfare. Long abandoned cars burned and rusting, smouldering piles of rubbish littered the street. The breeze sucked battered blinds out of the broken windows of tower blocks which once stood as corporate monuments, now just depressing skeletons of depravity. From the tops of these black monoliths came the faint glow of flame, camp fires maybe? Perhaps the last remaining humans seeking safety high above street level. Starving dogs scurried amongst rotting corpses competing for the dead flesh with huge rats who could almost match them for size if not ferocity. Battered shutters, half open rattled and hung from shops looted and stripped bare long ago. Vic shivered inside feeling the piercing red eyes peering upon him from the darkness. Small tribes of humans scavenged and fought amongst the debris. Filthy and disheveled they looked pathetic, wearing what would once have been expensive mink and fur coats, matted in blood and dirt. Items that were once symbols of opulence and wealth now just a worthless piece of improvised survival equipment. Two starving emaciated dogs, once so pampered fought angrily over some scrap of food, so thin they looked like they could have easily slipped out of their diamond encrusted collars.

"This is what was left of our planet by the time Major Tom and his crew arrived." Blue held out a hand and began strolling amongst the debris, kicking empty cans and stepping over chunks of concrete and broken glass. She seemed calm and unmoved like she was strolling in a park. Remember that nothing is real he thought. He had to convince himself of that, difficult as it was. The stench of death and piss, the rotting flesh. None of it was real. He felt the heat from the fire as they passed a group of survivors warming their frail thin bodies, eyes empty, staring and unresponsive. One of them muttered something to him as they passed. "They set up Heathen for those that remained and decided that from then on they would never make the same mistakes again. Over population, wars and the battle for resources. They answered all of these problems over time. That was when the Saviour Machine was designed."

Vic heard a loud bang coming from an ally to his left followed by a scream. Skipping to keep up "What's that?" he said.

"A kind of advanced algorithm, it was designed to love humans, to manage resources. We call it Mother."

That wasn't what he meant, he strolled closer behind. "Isn't that dangerous to give so much power to a machine?"

"Of course not," she looked puzzled, he was embarrassed at saying it having clearly watched too many science fiction movies.

"The resources were plentiful as long as the population could remain stable, the Saviour machine would eventually see to that. Sadly the population was tiny and there was no need to mine steel, cooper or any precious metal. All that had been done long ago."

Vic surveyed a city street full of burned out cars, computers and twisted metal. Blue stopped and turned towards a shop doorway. "Come," she said stepping through.

She disappeared into the darkness and Vic paused to make a choice. Stay out here or step into the blackness after her. He looked around at the tribes of humans around him, they seemed curious, eyeing his plump flesh. "Nothing is real," he muttered under his breath as he skipped through the doorway. Once inside they stood back in his suite where they had started. "I think thats enough for today," she said as if addressing a toddler who might become over excited.

"Another thing, that sim, the one we were just in. You said you had some help?"

"That's right, I had some help from you, that's how it works. I was able to adapt some of your inputs, we are learning already," she said triumphantly. "That's why nothing we saw is literal. The sims can be contaminated easily with fantasy, dreams and wishes. Usually we would have spent more time cleaning up the environment before going in."

She slipped her helmet off and helped Vic with his, throwing them both to one side. There was a knock on the door.

"The timing is perfect today," said Blue. She skipped over to the door and swung it open. In walked a tall skinny man wearing a bright yellow suit. The man peered at him throwing his straggly hair out of his face only for it to instantly fall back. He gave Vic that look again and it was becoming familiar. It's probably the kind of look that very famous people are used to seeing. It's a facial expression that seems to say, 'Oh my god it's really you but.... I am going to pretend your just an average guy'. Vic noted he didn't look medical at all like the others. The fact that he was here in person was a novelty in itself.

"Zigg." said Blue proudly and shot a gaze between the two of them. This gentleman is one of our foremost experts on ancient history and he is going to be working with you.

The man stepped forward. "Mr Stardust," said the man confidently. This time his left hand stayed on his head holding the hair in place whilst he held out his right. "I am very pleased to meet you. My name is Doctor Touchreik, Doctor Algeria Touchreik."

CHAPTER 10

The Doc came bursting through the door, rushing from room to room. He had kept calm all day even though he was physically shaking when he met the caveman for the first time. Throwing his tablet on the chair and running around until he found the Professor. "I met him," he started. "I kept calm but I tell you a real living.."

"No," the Professor had said the minute he had mentioned it pushing his palm upwards to silence him. "We cannot discuss it, remember I was there?" he pushed past him into the life room. The Professor continued "I have already experienced it but if we discuss it and I influence your work it could change his attitude or yours, there will be time for that later."

He turned away and closed the door to his room. At the time he said that, the Doctor had assumed he meant 'time later' for discussing, not a time for changing attitudes. He'd soon discover he was very wrong about that, and very wrong about a great many things. He felt utterly deflated that night, his excitement had built from the moment the Professor told him what would happen. That he would soon be offered the chance to work with the Cryogenic caveman. In the meantime he had decided to let it go, put his head down and enjoy the progress he was making with Zigg.

It was a long but fascinating process and in the previous week he and Zigg worked very well together. Doc felt the pressure, it was one hit. The information had to be gained and catalogued correctly. It was vital and important work and an opportunity that would not come along again. Returning one evening he was crossing the square and paused under the lamp to look up at the silent shuttered building where he lived. There were hundreds of people inside that dead empty looking place. Locked away in either V-world or the real world experiencing as individuals but with no physical interaction. Such a difference to the times that Zigg had told him about when the planet was teeming with human life. Billions of people all mixing, touching and walking the streets. Interacting, sharing space and most interestingly having physical acts of sex and love. Physical relationships were commonplace with humans and even a necessity in and around the 20th Century. Without it they would have never been able to produce offspring, there was no 'Mother' to do the task for them. He had often thought it might perhaps be a natural thing. If animals did so, why not humans? There were many people like him who shared that belief but were afraid to speak out. He thought of Ramona for a moment, it had been such a long time. He dare not see her since that night and since gaining this position it was even less likely. She would understand he was sure but imagining the scandal made him shudder. Regardless Ramona was in his mind even while he slept. In his loneliness he felt like the caveman may understand that there could be real physical feelings for Ramona. The Professor would, but there had been no mention. What if something had happened in the future, what if the Professor had changed and lost those feelings for her? When in love do you really want to be reminded that it will ultimately end? Nothing is more certain in any relationship but those thoughts are always buried deep in the conscience. If any of that was true he'd no wish to find out just yet. A couple of days ago, almost telling Zigg his secret he pulled back and came to his senses. Although it was tough in the days that Zigg came from, the past had some benefits and one of them was the acceptance of physical relationships.

The hiss of the transporter pulling away flicked a switch in his brain and pushed him back in time. To that day, four or five weeks ago which seemed a million years now. When the Humanist had accosted him here and threatened him. There was no point denying it anymore, he must have been a rebel. The Professor was no closer to revealing his intentions and the Doctor had conceded to trust him. What the Professor had failed to consider was that they were the same person and thus it would be easier to second guess him. It was a simple deduction based on what he knew already.

He had not admitted as much, yet his older self had clearly associated with Humanist rebels. He had in fact befriended one of them and sent him to set up the meeting. If he assumed that the Humanist was still involved with that organisation then somehow the Professor had gained their trust. But why? 'Mankind was under threat.' That was a hell of a statement to make without any qualification but it was obvious where any such threat would come from. The Professor would never end up in the same camp as the Humanists. His opinion of them was just too strong to imagine buying into their bullshit ideas. Secondly it would be no surprise to find those lunatics would eventually become a threat. Was he working on a plan to destroy them once and for all but he can't reveal it until the time is right? He would make sure all the vermin were in the trap first, he was convinced that must be it. The Professor was cunning and cautious, he was him and that's what he would do. This being the case it stood to reason that the plan must be to infiltrate their organisation. The Prof must have found a weakness. We were going to put them out of business before they got lucky and harmed Mother. If that's the way it had to be then so be it. For too long they had been left out there on the city's fringes, living off Heathen whilst wishing her dead.

The Doctor had begged for clues and got nothing, finally giving up. Supposing the Professor would know he would guess his plan instinctively. Why not just tell him? It was becoming obvious anyway, if he was going to get a chance to get rid of that scum forever. If they were to infiltrate the Humanists then he would assess any physical dangers when the time came. One thing was for sure, a threat to mankind had to be a threat to Mother and if that's the case the Doctor's mind was already made up. Deep down there was always a chance that the Humanists would go too far and someone, someone like him might have to step forward. Psychologically he was ready to do whatever needed to be done for 'Mother' and for humanity.

If it was to be him, he thought letting out an involuntary laugh, both of him then so be it. He stepped through the security door and decided to take the stairs for a change. Leaping joyously, two at a time until he reached his floor.

CHAPTER 11

It looked like the places he had seen on space documentaries about Cape Canaveral. Everything pointed towards a huge screen on the left hand wall. There was too much data to make any sense of. Numbers cascading down and across a map, blips, lights. There were fifty or so unmanned desks laid out in rows each with its own myriad of data, buttons and switches. The place hummed with energy and the temperature was stable, air conditioned. The smell of a cool, clean office environment. In the centre was a huge high backed chair turned away from him. Seconds ago Vic had been stood in his suite but still couldn't get used to that outrush of air when he entered V-world. He stood for a moment to catch his breath as lights blinked and various instruments beeped. The chair spun slowly round to reveal its occupant. Blue had her hands clasped and her elbows on either arm looking like a bad guy from a bond movie. "Remember, I said nothing is real?" she said. Vic was looking round and nodding at the same time. "Well this is not real within not real," she smirked.

"It's to illustrate the Saviour Machine, the Saviour machine does not exist in any single place but if it did? Every input, every experience and every answer. Like an algorithm and search engine combined that no longer answers searches but answers questions," she stood up and stared up at the screen. "The fact is, there is no control room, no authority. The Saviour Machine or Mother as it is commonly known is everywhere. Its us really. Its a little bit like an internet of thought," raising the notation as if to ask if he understood.

"Ok," whispered Vic still taking in the idea. "With no government isn't there some authority? Police or something?"

"There are citizens of Heathen, we are the authority. Citizens are able to take care of anything unforeseen but I can't imagine what?" Blue seemed puzzled by the concept of authority. "You must remember that Mother does not exist in any given place but...Her servers are on Mars." Blue noticed his eyebrows furrow.

"Then how can it work things here?" said Vic.

"Its not a server in the sense you might remember. Any instructions from Mars are more global whilst instant decisions happen locally."

"Let me give you an example," she stopped, waiting for a response. Vic stopped scanning and turned to her. "Imagine that enough people wanted to build a transport system through your living area? In your time that might have involved decision, authority, agreement and of course disagreement. Yes?" Blue beckoned him to sit down opposite her in a noticeably much smaller chair. He nodded slowly. "Well imagine if all the opinions, expertise and past experience was already there? Imagine if all that input could be correlated to show how it could be done, who would like it done and at the other end?" There was a ping as a small slip of paper slid out of the console in front of her. She leaned over and tore it away, holding it up with the word 'yes' printed clearly on it.

"Of course it does not work this way, there's no control room like this one but in principle that's how Mother works. The Saviour Machine does not need input because that happens instantaneously. That's why we love her, that's why we trust her. What you said about it being dangerous, that it would hurt humans? Thats why it will never happen because we are part of it. The Saviour machine was able to solve the problems that had bothered primitive humans for centuries. War, famine, over population and pollution were now managed by everyone who exists. Even though they have no need to consciously consider or vote for anything." Pleased with herself Blue stood up becoming more animated the background lights blinked across her features. She really is a very attractive person he thought. Noting how his mind had used the word person.

"Everyones choices and experience are taken into consideration in every decision, if they want them to be. There is no need for government or leadership. Robotics are so advanced that food and resources can be harvested, because of the limited population the materials are all around us. Steel, glass and stone that used to supply billions of people before the shutdown are sitting around on the surface of the planet."

The screen above them burst into life showing images of robotic trucks collecting scrap cars, clearing cities, smelting and recycling components. Mountains of electronic equipment being turned into light processors and robust utility robots. There was no sound but he could see the film was being presented by an unusual clown type character who seemed to be explaining what was going on. He casually walked through devastated streets, followed by huge bulldozers gathering the Earth's waste. Then flyby shots of fields that stretched as far as the horizon, filled with what looked like wheat and green healthy vegetables. It showed what looked like environmental clean up operations as filthy discoloured seas and desert landscapes gave way to blue oceans and lush countryside. It was like an almighty planetary promotional video showing happy residents, youthful and good looking, enjoying the fruits of robotic labour. Like a car assembly line goods were filtered into conveyors and directly into homes. The whole process was seamless with what seemed like no human intervention.

"In your time most people had to work for their government. Now there is no work because there is no need, if you want something you just order it and it arrives, most times it arrives anyway."

Vic was mesmerised. "But, how many people are there, what do they do?"

"We are in V-world right now but this is a private sim created by me. But in the grid, V-world is everything. It's where most people work, meet and compete." The screen sprang to life once more showing epic battles, operating theatre drama, plane crashes and high powered race car collisions.

"V-world has always been much more than a game and now it's becoming life itself. Imagine the pride and excitement we feel when one of us reaches their time to euthanise. To break away after 130 years and leave room for their race to advance, it's an amazing privilege," said Blue excitedly. "That's all changed now because those whom we have known and engaged with in V-world and the real world can now still know us thanks to the Salvation project." Blue raised her hand and brushed the screen to one side. "After Euthanising a person would have been gone forever, or at least they used to be. We now have the Salvation project, a way of euthanising and still existing without depriving your comrades of resources. Isn't it amazing?"

Vic stared past Blue at the blank screen. "I am not sure I?"

"At 130 years of age our Euthanasia is the time when a person in Heathen celebrates their demise and prepares to make way for others. But Mother seems to have solved a problem we didn't know we had. At age 130 citizens celebrated their euthanasia, but now it's possible to have both. To die and then upload every part of your personality, memories and wishes into V-world and be there permanently."

"You mean you could live forever in a computer game, in here?" said Vic stunned. He said it louder than he intended and hoped he hadn't upset her by expressing his shock. "Yes, isn't it just wonderful?" she jumped up and down again, he clearly hadn't. I want you to meet someone, come."

Blue marched across the room towards a pair of out of place gothic double doors. Vic was frozen in place for a second before stepping towards her. Clasping a handle in each hand she stepped forward thrusting them both wide and opening her arms as she did. They walked through onto a high wide balcony overlooking what looked like a busy fifties dance hall. It was crowded and people were dancing, drinking and chatting. They stopped as if they had been waiting for him and indeed they were. The music stopped and everyone stood in silence staring for a moment before a spontaneous round of applause broke out. Blue stepped out onto an upper stairway balcony which overlooked the crowd below. "Ladies and gentlemen," cried Blue. "Please carry on your fun, don't let us disturb you," she beckons for Vic to step forward. In a low voice she proudly whispered. "We are now in the grid, all of these people are part of the Salvation project." Vic cautiously stepped forward and peered down taking a moment to absorb the scene. Hundreds of people of various ages straining to see him high above them. All these people are dead, he thought. He felt a shiver down his spine, digital ghosts and yet it all looked very natural.

She turned to the crowd once more. "Ladies and Gentlemen, may I please present. The one and only Zigg Stardust." Blue paused and turned to Vic this time joining in the applause. As it died the music started up and everyone went back to their business. Blue took Vic's arm and walked him round the balcony. "They are all absolutely bursting to meet you, how they are keeping it all together, Heathen knows, come this way." The pair walked around the wide balcony passing small groups chatting, sipping champagne. Each one trying to steal just a glance at the caveman as they passed. There were pairs of settees and coffee tables set out at intervals. At one sat a man who stood up to greet them as they approached. He smiled, thrusting his hand into Vic's and clasped it with the other, shaking it confidently.

"Mr Stardust, a pleasure to meet you."

"Zigg," said Blue nodding to the man. "Zigg this is the," stressing the word 'the' into thee "Paul Ambrosius."

Vic thinned his lips, smiling "Pleased to meet you."

Paul nodded in a kind of salute and sat down, being careful not to ruffle his impeccable suit. Everything about Paul was crisp and clean. His perfect unblemished skin tone complimented his deep brown double breasted suit. Gold cuff links, tie and tie pin gave him a Saville Row look. He was made to measure and bespoke, unbuttoning his jacket and sitting down in single well practiced movement.

"How old do you think he is?" said Blue absolutely bursting to tell.

"25," muttered Vic.

"I am 140 years old Mr Stardust, not quite as old as your good self of course," he darted a quick look at Blue and then looked at the floor in embarrassment. "I didn't mean..." he started to explain.

Vic hadn't lost that point. Here he was in a body 22 years old and yet he had technically existed for 568 years. Something that would not have gone down well with the futures. Was this Paul fella aware of the rule change on his behalf, is that why he was embarrassed. You will be treated as 22, Blue had said. With what he now knew, that was quite significant. He was starting to feel like an army deserter, a coward or conscientious objector during the war.

Blue attempted to keep the conversation on good terms "Don't you see, we euthanise at 130, at least we used to."

"That's right, I was the first, the very first to enter the salvation project," said Paul grateful for the intervention and bowing towards Blue. "Instead of euthanasia all of my memories, personality, wishes and dreams were uploaded into V-world."

"Isn't it incredible?" said Blue "He was the first, Paul was the very first to take the Salvation option."

"It's an amazing project, I am here permanently in the virtual world. I can't die. Lots of us are here permanently now. I can change my appearance or sim anytime I like. Nothing has changed, my friends and family still log on." Vic stared blankly. He looked towards Blue once more. There was an uncomfortable silence and Vic felt he should be impressed, should question more.

"What does it feel like, not having a physical presence?" he asked at last.

"How does it feel for you right now?" Responded Paul.

Vic realised how it felt for him right now. He was not here in a 1950's hotel talking to this guy. The cigar smoke he smelt, the music he heard and the feel of the leather chair holding him up. Non of this was real and yet.... It was. I suppose that was his answer.

"But I mean you. Are you still?" Vic paused "are you still you?"

"I most certainly am still me. There's no dividing line, no change over, its continuous. I can tell you about my childhood growing up in TI's."

"2300's," said Blue by way of translation.

"Yes, exactly. I am 140 years old and before you perhaps the oldest human ever. I am proud to say I can do this, we can all do this without effecting the gene pool."

Vic wondered what he was being sold here, at least that's what it sounded like but then thinking on. No, that wasn't it. It was guilt, the man felt guilty. Perhaps I might feel that way soon he thought. Paul was justifying being alive and probably thought about the guy before him. The one who went through with it, he felt like he and everyone else in the salvation project had cheated. Vic stole a look at Blue, is that what he saw in her tone, behind those eyes? Political correctness? These people from the salvation project probably had that same deserter, conscientious objector feeling he had. Perhaps they knew it and everyone else knew it but no one would ever say it. Vic was learning fast. There was a much stronger feeling of community here in the future but it went deeper than that, more like ants. A real feeling of everyone being part of this whole freak show, as if you hurt one you hurt them all. He knew that back in his time people discussed things like humanity, society like they were real. The truth was those words were abstract vehicles to cover up their own selfishness. He always wondered who would be the first in the queue to put their baby on a spaceship to the nearest star to save 'humanity', yeah right. How many would line up to give their lives to save mankind when they wouldn't even walk to work? In his time he had always known that civil society had a very thin veneer. From what he had heard there had been no society in 2040 when the lights had gone out. Humanity just reduced to savages, ashes to ashes, dust to dust he thought. That was it, everything back to its lowest denominator.

Ashes to ashes...

It was with those words that he experienced what was to be the first of his 'incidents'. Everything faded in an instant both sound and vision moving away to allow him to think. He felt dizzy and remembered where he was. Could this helmet be malfunctioning? He saw things now, what had Blue said about the amazing Major Tom the saviour of the human race? That's the truth or something like that, you may hear other things. My mother said to get things done, you better not mess with Major Tom? His thoughts began to accelerate like a drag racer. He could see it all now, without the crutches of technology the curtain had been pulled back and the beast beneath laid bare. He wondered for a moment where that had come from? Not so much the thought but more the understanding. He felt that he understood everything completely and he knew why he understood, then as he reached out to grab that knowledge out of the air, it was gone. An enlightening deja vu feeling and he couldn't get it back. It felt like having the answer to a million dollar question on the tip of your tongue and then, poof it's gone. He tried but he couldn't get it back. He came back to reality quickly as if his life had skipped a beat.

Blue had already stood as if to leave and Vic stood to. Everything turned back up, crystal clear once more. Had he missed some of the conversation, he didn't remember standing up. "It's been a pleasure meeting you Mr Stardust," said Paul shaking his hand with a slight bow. He pulled down the bottom of his jacket and stood to attention watching them leave. Blue put her hand on her hip and made a D shape, beckoning him to link her arm as they walked down the stairs. Slowly like some historic king and queen they descended the wide staircase as the crowd parted in awe at both of them. At the bottom they took a sharp right and two people bowed slightly as they pulled aside a thick curtain covering an alcove.

As they passed through, the world became sepia and grey in an instant. The air was cold and clammy with the odour of dust filling his nostrils. The dramatic change of scenery reminded him again. Nothing is real, he thought. Then he had to whisper it as if reassuring himself "Nothing is real."

He found himself in a gothic lab like something from an old Frankenstein movie. Jars of organic material either animal or human floating in stained liquid strewn across shelves. The walls were daubed in what could have been blood or paint. Body parts lay around the floor making him shudder even after he realised they were not real, just parts of what looked like shop mannequins. Strange receptacles, tubes and instruments covered in dust were scattered on benches and tables. In the flickering shadows cast from the low hanging lamps he could make something out against the far wall. Two huge tanks of green translucent liquid stood at the far end, bubbles slowly rising. Tentatively he stepped towards them kicking and standing on rags, broken glass and other debris. An old stone stairway led from an upper level with twisted metal railings on either side. The tank on the right was empty apart from a few severed tubes floating like seaweed in a tide. Shuffling closer through the rubbish strewn floor he didn't bother to look down as he felt something soft beneath his heel. In the other tank he could see a figure, a human figure. Blue stood to one side as Vic crept deeper into the room, his curiosity getting the better of him. As he drew closer he could see it was twisted and malformed with limbs floating in unnatural ways. It was like looking at a drowned corpse beneath a thin layer of green ice. In the corner of his eye Blue was gazing at him like a child opening a birthday surprise, fingers across her open mouth. He walked closer and was able to make out the clothes on the man. A plain white shirt untucked under a dark nondescript suit floating in an invisible current, revealing the figures midriff. Ankles and elbows disjointed and twisted like a road crash victim. Is it possible that the brain can deny what it sees, as if blinking like a cartoon character will make it go away. The blood rushed to his limbs from his insides making him shake and feel sick. He bent over the table retching dry air and nothing came up. Finally looking up through the tears he could see Blue laughing, real hysterical laughter for the first time since he had known her. It was like the sound of her laughter was coming from inside a distant cave. The incongruence of the situation calmed his revulsion for a moment. He saw flashes of her and then the body in the tank through his streaming eyes as his head swam. He was sweating and felt a cold dampness inside his suit. Vic looked at Blue who was holding her mid-rift, almost unable to breath and then up at the body in the tank.

His body, his 68 year old dead body. Still in the suit, the one he had chosen to die in. Stripped of life and hanging limp and lifeless like a carcass in a butcher's van. There was the bandage on the right hand where he had covered the cannula and in it, maybe in a bizarre attempt to protect the record was the remote control. The button he had used to set the poison flowing into his veins only weeks ago and yet in that time 500 years had passed and brought him here. With what must have happened since his death seeing the remote made no sense but for some reason it was right there. But it did make sense, this was a sim, it was not real. The lifeless body had no substance to it like an animal before the taxidermist had done his work. It all made sense now as he gazed across at the empty tank next to it, slowly he looked down at his own open palms and then back again. Blue was calming down a little now and was just about able to speak.

"I apologise for laughing, please forgive me. I understand how your time may have felt very different about," she paused looking at the figure floating in the tank, and tried to find a word. "Flesh?" she said in a question.

Vic fell onto a lab stool and put his elbows on the table, head in his hands.

"Can you see now how you will be held precious Zigg? The project to bring you back began 23 years ago."

Head in hands Vic opened his fingers looking up at the empty tank. "Are you saying that this is where my new body came from?"

"It's a complex process but you were regenerated. Lots of elements from this sim came from your deepest thoughts, I had no time to tidy them up. A lot of what you experience here contains deeply held beliefs and fantasies. But yes, it took 23 years to grow the new flesh and then it was a simple transition."

Swapping his brain he assumed, spoken as if they were talking about putting a new engine in an old banger.

Vic thought for a moment, imagining his new body growing from a baby and yet never waking or leaving that tube until it was 22 years old. "So if you put my old brain in this new body," using both hands to indicate his self. Vic was still thinking his question through. "What about the brain in the young body that you grew?"

Blue flicked a wrist at him still amused at his primitive reaction to flesh. "It was never conscious," she said confused.

"I know that," said Vic "but it would have been me wouldn't it?"

"Of course not, that's a preposterous idea. It was never born. We just needed new flesh for you," she laughed at his naivety. This was going to get nowhere and he knew that. Blue was still giggling occasionally about how he had reacted to his own dead body in a jar, just flesh. It reminded him of when his cat had seen himself in the mirror and jumped in the air. Vic had laughed about that for hours. It was the same for Blue, he knew that but, seeing your own dead body.

She placed a hand on the base of his back and led him towards an outer door and as they went through he took one last look over his shoulder. 23 years or 500 years he thought, none of it made sense because what made it difficult was his own warped sense of time, like he had sat in that chair in the conference room only weeks before.

They stepped outside to where an old mini 1275GT was waiting with the engine running. Blue climbed into the drivers side and he walked around to the passenger seat. He jumped in and the door shut with a hollow clunk. He still admired the detail of V-world as he breathed the smell inside the car, a mixture of oil and leather. Once inside the accustics changed as the enclosed space sucked up the sound. Blue slipped the gear stick forwards and hit the gas as they sped off from the hotel and into the night. They both stared ahead as the landscape flew past them.

"I think that's all for today," Blue stared forwards.

The passing street lights lit up her face in flashes blinking faster and faster as the car quickened.

"Where are we going," said Vic gripping on to the seat tighter as Blue accelerated.

Blue turned and looked at Vic as a sinister grin crept across her face. Her eyes widened as he saw she was staring right at him, paying no attention to the road. The smile spread in unison with the accelerated speed. Vic looked forwards and then back at her as the engine roared, the dial on the speedometer moving steadily upwards. His heart pounded, he screamed at her to slow down but she would not look at the road, she just stared the same crazy stare. Up ahead Vic could see the street lights swinging off to the right as they approached a bend. They were getting close to the point of no return and Blue showed no signs of slowing down. Vic gripped the dashboard as the road slipped from under them realising they were never going to get round. He smelt the burn of rubber and heard the screech of the tyres as he screamed. He braced for the impact as the tree tore towards him. He closed his eyes and waited, the shattering glass and crunching metal. In a pathetic attempt to save himself he threw both arms across his face. Then nothing.

Silence and darkness along with no sense of movement. His helmet lifted but his heart was still pounding.

"Nothing is real," whispered Blue as she took her helmet off smiling. Vic quickly realised what she had done putting his hand on his heart to see if it was still beating. He wanted to be angry but he couldn't, not after he had been such an arse the other day. He took some deep breaths and laughed along politely. He seems to have discovered what makes this girl laugh. She is very entertained by his fear and remembering his cat this upset him a little. Was he some kind of pet? Cared for but not quite as important as the real people? How he had laughed at his silly cat being frightened of its own reflection.

He realised that although this stuff seemed odd to him, that's to be expected in a culture that is hundreds of years ahead of his. He would probably need to adjust and perhaps the quarantine, the trip into the V-world thing had been a good idea after all. Things had definitely changed, most people spent their lives and now their deaths in a computer game? But if he was going to live in a world where topping yourself was cause for a party and sex was no longer a physical act unless you were some kind of pervert, well he was going to have to face up to those changes. At least they seemed to be being honest with him, it's him that was faking. He was almost ready to face up to it and tell her who he really was but thought better of it. He wasn't Zigg he was just Vic, lonely and afraid and he didn't belong here. Falling in love with a person neither male nor female in a time when anyone who even knew the concept of being homosexual died hundreds of years ago. And for all this his only sense of freedom from his quarantine was running around inside a computer game.

"How was that?" said Blue dropping her helmet on the chair.

"Weird."

"Yes I imagine it was quite disorientating for you, take a moment to relax. I hope I am forgiven?"

"Only if I am," he laughed. The atmosphere seemed slightly warmer now. Could he blame her for having some fun with him after he had been such an arsehole.

"So what now, what about me? You said I was here for a reason?"

"You can see now how fortunate it was that you were on Mars when the data crash happened."

"So I am the only link to that time, the only witness?" he said fiddling with one of the helmets and wandering over to the balcony. She followed and they both stood staring out across the skyline.

"Yes, your experience of history is valuable. Major Tom and his team were the only civilised survivors of the shutdown. History, inventions, everything had to be rebuilt from their physical memories and recollections. But you are ancient, you are from a time over 500 years ago."

"But what can I tell you, everything seems cool now? Why does it matter?"

"Cool?" she was puzzled again.

"Good, alright," he confirmed.

"To most people, the history doesn't matter but we think that you can bring us back together again, ready for something amazing."

"Back together?"

"You have seen V-world today."

"I definitely have," he laughed.

"You have to understand that most experience V-world as individuals, millions of us in our own accommodation, working, playing, meeting and making love. Never needing or wanting to leave V-world."

"Is that wrong?"

"You are ancient, from a time when people interacted physically and you entertain, make music."

Oh yeah he thought I am a musician. True Vic had recorded an album and was a capable session musician. He had released an album in his youth. A head full of dreams and ideas about what he wanted from his career before he fell on his arse and it never happened. A minor novelty hit followed by obscurity. One failed flop of an album before he had crawled back under the corporate rock. Having said that he was well aware he had done a lot better in that world. It had been the success of his business ventures that had given him a good living and wealth. The very same wealth that had paid his freezer bills for the best part of the last 500 years. As for being a musician, maybe Zigg could knock out a tune or two but he doubted whether Vic Jones could. He may well be rumbled if thats what they were after.

"You can bring people out of their homes, into the street to see you," said Blue pointing outside.

"You mean to play, live?" He said following her gaze.

"Why the hell would anyone come and see me play?" he shrugged. Ok thought Vic here's a problem I didn't foresee. These futures think they have thawed out Zigg, they clearly have him down as some kind of rock star.

"You don't understand how important you are to the people of Heathen, your fame is instant and guaranteed."

His thoughts were racing into survival mode, ok he was not the greatest singer in the world but he could hold down a tune. He needed time to think this through but there might be a way he could fake this. From what he had learned all of history had been effectively wiped out and he assumed that would include art, literature and.... Music! The only reason that the futures believed Vic was a musician was his cryogenic pod record and that had become attached to Zigg's. The futures clearly had no idea what Zigg looked like or he would have been rumbled the minute the frost melted off his nose. It was also clear that they have never heard Zigg's music and neither had Vic. Something was developing in his mind and he needed time to think this through but he was becoming excited. Likewise the futures had never heard any of the music Vic knew so well. The stones, T Rex and Lennon. He grinned so hard he almost laughed out loud.

"You would like to play live then?" Exclaimed Blue who had completely misread his smile.

Vic beamed from ear to ear as he realised he had the entire twentieth centuries music catalogue to plagiarise. Looks like Lennon's on sale again he thought. He could test it out, play a few hits and see what happens but from where he was standing there was no one going to sue him. Besides, he laughed to himself, after 500 years it would all be out of copyright by now. His heart was pounding now and he imagined that second chance. Knowing deep down no matter how well he had done in his life it was always fame that he had craved more than anything.

"Your music will be a great opportunity to share your knowledge with us and help us fill the gap on our history." Blue continued.

"Let me think it over."

"You can do anything you want, everyone wants to know about the dark ages and the ancient music you made." Waving her arms in frustration.

"Understand Zigg, the world is waiting to see you." Vic was starting to think he may have got this all wrong. Perhaps he wasn't a freak after all. Mr Vic Jones might well have stumbled on a way out here, this might actually be fun.

CHAPTER 12

Touchreik stepped out of the transporter and marched across square where only weeks ago he'd had an encounter that had turned his world upside down. The memory failed to dampen his mood but every evening it crossed his mind. He was thrilled to be working with the caveman and had chosen to work in his physical presence on most occasions. They were starting to experiment with self created sims in V-world which the pair could explore together but there was no point rushing things. For the time being the job meant physical travel and returning late through the square acted like a daily calling card. A mental cue to think about things he would rather ignore. Admittedly in previous weeks it had been easy to do so as an air of normality had set in. He and his older self had settled into the routine of life together and the Professor had relaxed some of his rules. They argued less and less too, unlike the early days when the Professor would nag him about his habits or attitude.

Most annoying was the subliminal advice and warnings, when in fact it was clear that he had some kind of inside knowledge. You should think about this, or avoid that, as if they were just random thoughts. After a few days things came to a head and although unpleasant the row seemed to have cleared the air. Even the Professor had realised he was breaking his own rules. They no longer shared meals or a bed which took further pressure off the relationship. A couple of days ago the Doc had returned to discover the Professor was nowhere to be found. Admittedly he panicked somewhat, haunted by visions of his older self disappearing in a puff of smoke due to some time travel anomaly or other. The Professor reappeared a short time later shrugged the whole thing off and stormed into his room. It was clearly not the first time he had ventured outside whilst the Doctor was not around. Recently an air of tension was returning as the Professor became more aloof and quiet. As for his movements the Doc didn't ask, deciding he would share that when good and ready.

Duke had coped well with the pair, enabling instructions from either or both of them without issue. The extra waste, food and air they had consumed was gradually absorbed into Duke's schedule without fuss or question. Over the last four weeks his older self had avidly followed media broadcasts and events. He was getting used to the Professor suddenly crying out excitedly on some news item or other. Each step confirming that history was panning out exactly as he remembered it. The Doctor knew he was waiting for something, some kind of event that would signal the next phase of his plan. In the meantime there was no sense in kicking a sleeping dog he'd thought, being far to busy to worry about that.

Working with Zigg had been so exhilarating and challenging that he had little time to think about anything else, not least whatever scheme the Prof was cooking up to save humanity. He felt light on his feet, the caveman project had renewed in him an energy for his subject. Not least because it had turned his department from a remote backwater of science to its cutting edge. For anyone who was interested, and their numbers were growing, his department was now headline news. The last four weeks had flown by as he immersed himself in the 'caveman' project. He wouldn't say that in front of Zigg of course, even though he was likely aware of this nickname around Heathen. It was wise to be professional and not to upset him. If he was to get the best from him then he would need management and gentle coaxing. He always tuned in to his moods and tried to be aware when he needed to back off a little. The Doctor had been astounded at the amount of detail he was able to recollect whilst other global questions were difficult for him. He almost had to pinch himself some mornings. This was tough work mentally and not as glamorous as some thought. Questioning, analysing and comparing against many of his established assumptions, the weeks had slowly helped him realise how much of his previous theories had been right. It was going to be a long process but the Doctor was slowly building a clearer picture of life in the Moonage.

The upside down economy where humans worked for governments was apparently true. The fact they had used ancient electronics to put people on the moon was staggering. In Zigg's world artificial intelligence and robotics were so primitive as to be useless. Moonage computing power was still electronic, slow and cumbersome without any form of intelligence. They had managed to feed a population of billions. All using slow organic farming methods with no way of growing accelerated nutritions. Although there are rumoured to be small groups doing that even now it didn't reduce the impact of its reality. Leisure and learning time would have been almost non existent with their entire waking hours taken up in physical toil. Meanwhile light-age technology, the key to Mankind's future was sitting right under their noses all those years. Hidden amongst the theories and writings of a man called Albert Einstein long before it was discovered. They still bred physically like animals with a totally random gene pool. Resulting in a population that was out of control and many times the sustainable level. Zigg had confirmed his respect for what those primitive people achieved with limited resources.

There seemed to be many more ancient festivals and celebrations than he had suspected. They would celebrate their day of birth and many other anniversaries including bonding and accommodation acquirement. There were religious beliefs. The idea of a conscious being who acted for and with humans who was able to judge them and punish even after natural death. The Doctor had been fully occupied, whatever plan his older self had in mind it had drifted to the back of his conscience.

At the end of every period with the caveman there was more research and recording to do, then sleep, then repeat. He also had media and the department to keep up to date and the only time for most of that was in the evening. He had kept his work with the media very generic with very little given away.

"Yes things are progressing nicely, we have lots more to do, he is fine and well and enjoying Heathen." That kind of thing.

He was able to keep it impersonal by confirming or not various theories on pre shutdown life. The publicity for Zigg had renewed people's interest in history. Immersive filmonics based on Moonage themes such as primitive space travel and moon landings were more popular than ever, as were study and experience sims. Occasionally the Doc forgot about why the Professor had claimed to come back in time. As if by avoiding that thought it might just go away. Being engrossed in the project and finding he couldn't share it with the very person who would appreciate its allure saddened him. He was deprived of the advice, deep discussion and experience his older self could have given him. Remembering how devastating it was after that first day to find he couldn't discuss it. They could have combined their knowledge and be years ahead by now.

ϟ

The Professor placed his palm on the DNA scanner and involuntarily stepped back, jaw dropping as the panel slid away. To him it had been 45 years since she had been deactivated and looking at her now felt like a reincarnation. Ramona A Stone was standing proud and upright, square chin pushed forward with long dark lashes shading her delicate eyelids. Underneath he could detect a slight but rapid eye movement. Pink silicone flesh covered her high cheekbones. The full red lips, the long flowing auburn hair cascading across her curves like a waterfall. He absorbed every detail from the top of her clinging shimmery blue gown to her exposed painted toenails. Ramona's flush pink flesh made her look warm and alive, though she had never truly lived. Simply in hibernation mode, a standard procedure for any drone that is expected to be in storage for some time. Even as she slept her personality shone through, the part of her he loved the most. The intoxicating laugh, the tireless attention and engaging conversation. He felt his heart pounding like an old man meeting a school boy crush, a beauty locked in time. She looked as dazzling as ever. Professor Touchreik looked down at his wrinkled hands and wondered what she might make of him now. Having never felt deserving of her admiration, her attraction to him had always been a mystery.

He knew the procedure to activate her, it was very straightforward. Maybe just for a few minutes, a chance to say hello and explain. Perhaps time to apologise for something that had not happened yet. She would laugh so hard when he told her what he had done, travelling back in time. Before long they would be in deep conversation, laughing and then? Then she would want to know more and so time would slip away. As always an hour, then two. The Professor could imagine it being like it was, chatting and laughing in an endless evening of banter. He wiped away the gathering tears with the back of his hand. He regretted even coming in here now. Leaning forward he kissed her lightly on the cheek. Her flesh was warm to his lips like she might open her eyes at any moment. She didn't.

"Oh Ramona," he whispered hoarsely through his sniffles. "If there was only some kind of future."

The Professor slapped his palm angrily against the scanner once more and the panel silently closed leaving him staring at his own dull reflection in the steel door. He left the Doctors room with a sense of shame. Feeling like a father spying on a child, looking for drugs while they were out. Making his way outside he slumped into a chair on the balcony admiring the sun set over a jungle landscape. It had been one of her favourite scenes. So many years since he and Ramona had sat here together. He and the shameful secret he had shared with no one. So shameful he dare not discuss it even with his younger self. They both knew what she meant to them and that was enough for the time being. When he and Ramona had been together for the last time, no one was willing to understand. When she had been taken from him he thought he understood too but not anymore. Now he knew she might be taken away for another reason and he couldn't stop that either. When all this was over there would probably be a place for physical relationships but never with the likes of her. The Doctor would be home soon and he had delayed for far to long. If his plan was to succeed there might only be one shot and no second chances. The time for procrastination was running out. He was going to have to share everything with the Doctor. The time to do that was getting closer by the day. The thought of it filled him with dread.

CHAPTER 13

Vic pushed his right thumb and forefinger across his chest and flicked his forehead with his left hand and everything around him went black. Slipping the helmet over his head he decided to call it a night, it was getting late. He was very pleased with his work so far but maybe he could finish it tomorrow. The last few nights had been spent in V-world creating a sim of his own. Over the last week or so Doctor Touchreik had been showing him how to create virtual world environments. Working with the Doctor he had been creating scenes from his own history. Using these as templates and with his own limited skills he had developed something for himself. He wanted somewhere to relax that was a reflection of his own time.

The Doctor had shown him how the simulator that created the V-world experiences in private sims could also operate in reverse. This was how Blue had created their Lon-Don sim to provide his history lesson. It could work as a three dimensional recorder, building a world from memories, fantasy or just thoughts. Once created it could be the scene of any future adventures with its own set of rules. With a little late night fooling around Vic had mastered the equipment well enough to create a sim of his own. The sims are based on recordings of memory outputs using the same helmet in reverse mode. The real skill was eliminating the inaccuracies that came about from the intrusion of fantasy, dreams or personal bias. The subconscious mind has always struggled to determine the difference between what is real and what is fantasy. The result would be contamination of the world he was trying to create. This was not so much a fault in the software but more a fault in the human brain. Memories are never accurate and so there would be lots of things out of place or time. Vic's sim was designed to replicate his time in history and he'd done a satisfactory job. His first effort was pretty good, aware that someone from his own time would spot the glaring inaccuracies in a second. There was nothing too major though, no dinosaurs walking around or anything like that. Just the wrong car models, technology or music out of place. But seeing as the futures were 500 years out of time then they were unlikely to notice thirty or forty years either way. Anyhow who cares, no one else will see it. He enjoyed his time within a butchered version of the twentieth century. This was not for them or the Doctor anyway, it was purely for him. There were no futures going to see any of it were there?

Vic had enjoyed working with the Doctor but it could be exhausting at times. Even though he seemed to relate to Vic a bit better than most. Supposedly it was because of his job in the museum where he worked. Vic felt strange to think how he had become a living museum piece now.

Occasionally it could get boring and frustrating so they might split their time, sometimes just walking and chatting in reality or visit the reserve. It's more difficult than it seems explaining every detail about life to someone who has no idea how society works. Sometimes he sounded like an idiot, in fact sometimes Vic felt like an idiot.

Where did the money go that you gave your government? Tell me how you made food? After a while it had got deeper and more difficult.

Where there were gaps in his knowledge Vic had kept the Doctor satisfied with scenes he remembered from films and books which worked quite well. It wasn't like they were made up stories it was just easier to reference things from films and comic books. Oddly there were more problems with the real facts as opposed to the fabricated ones. When Vic explained that an actor had been President of the United States there were doubts. Politics had been a problem for him too and the questions were endless.

"Who was the king of your government?"

"Why did people speak different languages?"

"What was this and that war about?"

"Tell me about colour, racism and religion?" On and on it went.

Once Vic had relaxed a bit and started to make up the bits he didn't know then it got easier, even fun. The futures would never know whether Malcolm X and Jesse Jackson were pop stars or politicians, that was all detail. Later it amused him to think that he might be the man to literally rewrite history. It was harmless and unlikely to cause any damage. The Doc had been interested in sex and that kind of thing too. Explaining to a grown man how we made babies? Odd.

So in time came the lessons on creating private sims. Vic had become competent enough to create sims that could demonstrate various 20th Century concepts like religion and war. Mostly these were derived from memory or various war films he had seen over the years. This part came easy because he was a fan of war films but his knowledge and interest in sci-fi proved to be useless here. Not as much scope for made up stories. The weird thing was that living in the 20th century had appeared normal at the time. However, the more the Doctor questioned him the harder it was to explain. At times it was so bloody frustrating, like instructing someone to build a model whilst blindfolded.

On the upside Vic's quarantine was officially over and he had chosen to continue living in his hotel suite. Being physically moved to a new location of course but everything will go with him, including the view from the balcony. Unknown to him one or two improvements were included in the deal.

CHAPTER 14

"Manhattan Chase! Are you serious?" The Doctor had mentally committed to helping the Professor with his plan to eliminate the Humanists. He knew he would do whatever needed to be done, but to go up there? He hadn't thought it would involve going up to the Chase.

"I'm with you, I support what you need to do but do we really have to go up there? It's dangerous."

"I haven't told you my plan."

"I'm not stupid, it's obvious you have some way of getting rid of them," said the Doctor staring in to the cold store and grabbing a cooled soda. His shoulders were hunched and tense as he ripped at the lid taking a long guzzle. The Professor's jaw dropped as he looked away squeezing his temples. He hadn't considered this for one moment but of course. What else would the Doctor think? Certainly not the truth, he'd never have guessed the real reason.

"We have to talk. It's time for me to explain what happened to me in my future," the Professor beckoned him to sit down at the table. The Doctor obliged, noticing the concern in the Professor's expression. Indicating to one of the chairs at the feed area, the Doctor swung into the seat.

The Professor slid down at right angles to him.

"You're about to understand why I had to withhold information from you and why I had to be convinced that everything is happening exactly as it did before." The Professor waited until the Doctor had looked up nodding defiantly.

"Everything that is happening to you now happened in exactly the same way to me. Aside from my involvement to the exact detail as I remember mine. Everything else in Heathen is too." The Professor spun in the chair and placed his elbows on the table, hands clenched.

"I was offered the opportunity to work with the caveman just as you were. I don't need to tell you how incredible that was for me because you are experiencing it now."

The Doctor nodded in agreement.

"I can assume that everything else I am about to tell you will happen in the future," he stared downwards as if seeing what he was describing.

"Zigg had started to tour Heathen, meeting people physically. I spent a lot of time with him and Blue and was around when that happened. You're currently witnessing his popularity grow, bigger than we imagined. I had never been happier, it was a dream project." The Doctor looked up now and met his eyes.

"Was?"

The Professor continued "Is he working on his music at the moment?"

The Doctor shook his head. "No?"

"He soon will be, then announcing to the world that he is to tour with his music. The V-world tour will finish with a physical show. People physically attending his shows as they did in his time. The biggest physical live event ever. During the early shows a few of us were given some information about the Salvation project. How it was ready to go to the next level. In a few months time the backlog will have been taken up and the Migration project can begin."

"Migration Project?"

"It's the same as the Salvation project, human personalities uploading into V-world forever. The difference is that anyone can do this at any time. Young and old. Any living human can euthanise whenever they want. It's probably becoming clear to you that the caveman is becoming very influential. He will not only launch the Migration Project but be offered the chance to be the first to take it up."

"To euthanise early?" The Doctor was surprised and puzzled. Almost as if this might be a difficult decision to make.

"Known only to a small group of us he'd agreed to do this along with his partner."

The Doctor interrupted. "You mean a physical partner like they had in the twentieth century?"

"Possibly, some suspected that but it would be a natural thing for him, as we both know. It wouldn't matter anyway once they were both living in V-world permanently."

The Doctor was trying to focus on what he was being told whilst processing everything else. A physical partner would clearly be Blue.

"They will agree?"

"It happened after the very last show in the Market Square. Attended by thousands with many more thousands outside and millions watching or experiencing in accommodations. This event took the project to immense levels of excitement and the rush for places began. Over the following months and years millions took up the offer to follow them."

"It sounds amazing," the doctor was upright in his chair excited at the prospect. "So Salvation is opened up to everyone and not just those due to euthanise? Why will that be a problem?"

The Professor stared back "Maybe it wasn't?" he said thinning his lips in a wistful smile.

The Doctor worried now. "Meaning?"

"From then on after that night it was clear that many people were moving over but it all fell from my attention over time, it dropped from the media too." The Professors tone became guilty, as if he had missed something. "Some five years passed since the caveman had gone inside and he had given me permission to keep a copy of his brain trace."

The Doctor almost leapt off his chair. "Wow that's going to be amazing, you mean everything?"

The Professor ignored his enthusiasm and continued. "Of course, so as you can imagine this was a lifetimes work. Sifting through fantasy, reality, genuine and false memories to build a better picture of the ancient world. I was lost in this research for years until, around five years later something happened." The Prof looked down at his hands nervously flicking his thumbs together.

"Go on," the Doctor was fascinated now, eager to ask about the brain trace discoveries. "At the time it kind of slipped by unnoticed but Mother had announced she was reducing her reproduction of organic humans."

"Because of migration?"

"Presumably."

"It was years before any of this came back to my attention."

"What about the trace, from the caveman?" said the Doc eager to hear more.

The Professor held out a palm to silence him again. "Years later, there was an outage in my sector and it caused a few software problems."

"Humanists?" said the doctor knowingly. Sat upright now, buoyed at hearing how exciting his life was going to be. A full memory trace will be a first. He was already working on how he would approach such a mountain of knowledge from the past.

"Yes I expect so," The Professor waved a hand at him with disregard, keen to head off any diversion from the topic. "It caused a few software problems. But it wasn't just the software that started to become a little buggy. It was also my..."

The Professor looked his younger self in the eye. "My assistant, Jagger."

"Your assistant?"

"He had been with me for around four years and we had worked well together. He shared my love for the work, we socialised. But after the outage I noticed little things that were not quite right like forgetting, ignoring certain statements and repeating things. The sort of things you might not notice."

He paused before continuing. He was aware he had asked Duke to switch to private mode but he looked around all the same.

"Things you might not notice unless you had spent a lot of time with... A drone!"

The Docs eyes widened "No, your assistant was..." The Doc was stunned "that's not possible, how could you not know?"

"Very advanced, much more advanced than Ramona, without the outage I would never have known. But something had changed, I looked into his eyes and I could see.. See nothing and everything at the same time. Then I wondered, how many of us were left. How many organic humans were still here on the planet?"

"Now hang on here," the Doctor had become concerned at where the conversation was leading.

The Professor placed a hand on the doctors arm to quieten him and soldiered on with his story. "I kept quiet and carried on our work whilst I thought this through. Eventually I made my way up to Manhattan Chase, just out of curiosity," the Doc shook his head in disgust.

"It was there I met two of the Humanist leaders. Jack Halloween and Aladdin Sane, I believe you have already met one of them. When I met them they were leading the Humanists rebels, remember this all happens many years from now. They were naturally suspicious of me and over time I heard lots of stories, rumours from them. Most of it was nonsense of course but I also learned things. Things I had either ignored or had refused to hear in the past. None of us were sure if anything was going on at the time. I returned to my labs and just kept working. In the following decades I carried on as normal. Slowly over time the things I picked up from the caveman's memory trace started to make sense. The time travel device was a side project but I was having some success even though there were clearly risks. Meanwhile I had lots of time to think back about my life, time to find an opportunity to change things if I could perfect the device. My plan depended on everything happening as it did the first time around. Up until now this seems to be the case. When I arrived the first thing I did was seek out Jack, he was dubious about my story naturally, but became convinced after coming here to see you for himself. After that it was clear that me and you were actually the same person. Remember I first met him decades from now and so he had not met Aladdin and was considerably younger. I told him his future, told him they would one day work together and he was to find Aladdin." The Prof paused before looking up. "He has done that now and we have to go and meet them both."

The Doctor closed his eyes tightly in deep thought. "I am confused here, what are you saying to me?"

"This is not about destroying the Humanists. Don't you see yet? They're right."

The Doctor stood quickly sending his chair crashing into the wall "Have you lost your mind? Are you saying that all the time I have kept you here, protected and fed you, you have been involved with those savages?" the Doctor was screaming at him now "Just go now, leave," he screamed turning him away with a wave.

"Calm down please just listen to me," the Professor approached him as he backed away, waiting whilst the Doctor absorbed the information. Grabbing his elbows across his chest the Doctor hugged himself. "So your saying that Mother is trying to wipe out humanity, this is bullshit, this is impossible. We have been into V-world and met those who have been in the Salvation project, we all have," the Doctor was becoming excited again, raising his voice.

The Professor touched his arm once more speaking softly. "I am saying the opposite, I am saying that the Salvation Machine was designed to love humans, that's how it has been since the Major."

"So why would it harm us?" he pleaded.

The Professor realised he was going to have to spell this out, shaking his head. "It's the love that could kill us. I remembered what the caveman taught us about religion. My research into his trace showed how it went much deeper than that. To a desire that humans have held since they could think?" The Professor spat the word think, it was his turn to become animated now. "We have worked with the caveman. Religion was real to them."

"Which means?"

"The one thing every human being has craved since time began. Immortality! The promise to live forever. Mother, the Salvation Machine has found a way to give us all everlasting life. In V-world safe in Mothers arms forever. It's what we have craved for thousands of years and she can satisfy it. It was in the caveman's brain trace and its hidden deep within ours."

The Doctor tried to speak but he couldn't get any words out. Picking up his glass he took a large gulp and swallowed hard, gasping for breath. He pointed angrily in the Professor's face. "You have spent too much time with them they have lied to you, corrupted your mind." The Professor shook his head in frustration. "I worked for decades on those traces. That craving is a human trait, it doesn't need religion, that was just convenient. But no God had ever fulfilled that promise, only vain hopes and lies but now.... Now Mother may have realised she could do it."

"Lies, Humanist lies," he said turning away. The Professor grabbed his shoulder spinning him back round.

"Is it? The Salvation machine had stopped reproducing organic life?"

The Doctor froze as Prof continued. "Why do you think that was? Organic life was redundant and eventually there will be no one left." The Professor tasted the salty droplets of tears that had run down his cheek and onto his lips.

The Doctor stared at the floor shaking his head "This isn't true, it can't be?"

"I saw it happen, I spoke to the survivors and met some of them." Wiping his cheek with his sleeve. "I was a survivor."

The Doctor began pacing around the room like a caged animal. "They aren't survivors they're Humanists, you stupid old man, I am ashamed that I turned into you. Your pathetic. You came back here for this? You actually believe them?" The Professor didn't look up as the Doctor approached whispering into his ear. "All they want is to destroy Mother that's all they have ever wanted." Slamming his fist on the table he picked up the cup and threw it across the room. The Professor flinched, ducking involuntarily. "You have no idea how many people had gone into the project."

The Professor spoke calmly now, without tone. Wiping the spit from his beard. The Doctor uttered something as if to speak. "Let me finish please," he said holding up a palm.

"Just before I made the leap I checked and found that a lot of the systems allocated to maintenance were shutting down as the living organic humans reduced in number, there may have been very few. I had to make the leap back in time, I risked my life."

The Doctor folded his arms, studying then seemed to have realised something. "What about your age?"

"What about it?" the Professor exclaimed.

The Doctor eyed him suspiciously, arms crossed tight against his body. "Getting close to Euthanasia though, is that why you came back. Is this just a selfish plan to avoid that?"

"That's ridiculous, how dare you."

"Why?" He screamed. "Why did you come back here, you could have left me alone. Mother will take care of everything. I wish you'd never come back."

The Doc turned away but the Professor grabbed his arm and spun him back round.

"We've got five years! That's all we've got. After that humanity begins her downward spiral towards extinction. Are we going to stand by and be the last, do nothing. I know you." He pulled in close to the Doctor. "Millions of years of evolution and thousands of years of civilisation. The shutdown, Major Tom, the City of Heathen built from the ashes and humanity survived. Will you really just step aside now?"

There was a long silence before he spoke more softly. "So now what, you want me to go to the Chase with you and hear more of this rubbish?"

The Doctor stared into the eyes of an older version of himself. He could see the pain and felt it too, he felt the tears well up. Arms out stretched the Professor grabbed his younger self and they hugged each other tightly. They rocked together and sobbed for what seemed like an age.

At last the Professor pleaded, his voice broken through tears. "Come with me, please hear what they have to say, that's all I ask."

CHAPTER 15

A few days later his sim was good enough, lots of faults but they added a little spice. V-world now gave Vic access to his own reality. He craved the imperfect world he once knew. The bills he had to pay, the chores to complete, the car breaking down. He wanted to go to a movie and a dance and be back in his own time. He let himself believe that was the reason he was building his sim. Right up to the moment he invited Blue to come into it with him, he believed that. If he was honest with himself he would have admitted that maybe if they were on his turf, things might play out differently. If those physical relationships were as much of a waste of time in TVC15 then she might change her view in 2014. None of those things were thought about, all he wanted to do was be with her.

He kept it as casual as possible when he asked her.

"It's going great, I made my own sim," he said. "Heathen is cool but it's somewhere to relax, take a break." no response. "I have a few hours this afternoon, gonna give it a try."

"It sounds stimulating, have fun," she said.

Then as he was leaving he quickly turned round as if having a shot of inspiration.

"Hey, if your doing nothing why not come along?" He paused embarrassed, shoulders shrugged "If you want." Realising how manufactured that must have seemed but it was too late. By the time he looked up he could see that Blue may have been about to pass out. Her cheeks were flushed red and there were tears in her eyes. It took her a moment to reply.

"Is that a serious comment, you wish me to escort you into your simulation?" It was as if he had offered a blind man his sight back. As if Bruce Springsteen had asked a fan if she wanted to 'hang out' he almost expected her to throw her arms in the air screaming I'm not worthy, he looked her over.

She was definitely worthy.

This only added to Vic's ongoing feeling of self actualisation after a week of meeting other dew eyed futures. One by one presenting him with a shiny version of themselves way beyond anything he deserved.

Ten minutes later they were both helmeted, plugged in and ready to go. Now he was nervous. 'Nothing is real' he thought although in this case it was going to be doubly so. Had he heard that somewhere before?

⌁

Blue stood on the porch of a 1950's white wooden town house with a picket fence to match. Looking around expectantly, hands clasped in front of her. Vic rolled up at the end of the drive looking like a kid in his father's borrowed car. Unsure whether he imagined it he thought he saw the upstairs curtains twitch. His heart skipped a beat when he saw Blue looking more feminine than ever. He remembered this was his sim, his fantasy probably played a part. Her hair was lighter and slightly longer yet still cropped close to her head. Dark makeup highlighted her huge puppy dog eyes and a million freckles crowded around her tiny nose. The flesh she revealed between her baby doll red dress and knee length boots glowed with youth. Blue waved and skipped across the drive, her red dress flashing her knees as she ran and jumped in the passenger seat. Vic crunched the gears of the monstrous swaying Cadillac and Blue was too polite to say when he almost stalled it. He wore an ill fitting white dinner suit with a matching bow tie. The warm night air played with the curl on her forehead as they cruised into the suburbs. Blue squeezed his hand over the gearstick as if they were shifting it in unison and smiled. A few miles out of town he pulled off the main road and onto an improvised dirt track, scraping the underside of the beast as he did so. The Cadillac bounced along until they reached a cordoned off area. Spinning the wheel he pulled into a drive in 2D movie theatre. Rows of featureless nondescript vehicles all pointing expectantly at the large silver screen in front of them. The film was about to start as they occupied the one free spot on the back line.

Laughing and talking they payed little attention to the film itself. A senseless story to do with a space alien visiting earth in the 60's from what Vic could gather. On another day he may well have related to it but tonight was different. The pair ordered fries and cola even though they had no money for the food or the movie. This was his sim, so what.

After the film they drove giggling into the city some miles away. During the course of the drive they had managed to cross several decades as well as several countries but Blue failed to notice, he didn't expect she would. Pulling the car up outside a warehouse building to the gasps of queuing girls. There may have been guys he wasn't sure, he didn't notice them. Skipping around, he opened the door for Blue and took hold of her forearm, leading her past the nodding doormen and down the stairs. A flickering neon sign above the doorway read 'Dschungle.' The doorman had smiled slapping him on the back as he waved them inside. They hit the dance floor in fits of giggles as the crowd parted to give them room. The music played and they danced and danced till they were dizzy. Pushing through the crowds to the bar, Vic ordered two Martini's.

As he turned to hand Blue a Martini a drunken German man in military uniform nudged his arm, spilling the drink on his suit. Laughing the man leered at Blue, offering to buy her a replacement in his gruff German accent.

10 minutes later the pair were running up the stairs in the opposite direction to a line of lawmen, truncheons at the ready. A small drop of blood dripped from one nostril and on to his lip. Behind them an immense bar brawl had ensued between groups of airmen and sailors. Neither group consistent with the

time zone and neither group cared how it had all started. Leaping into the Cadillac they sped off on the wrong side of the road, the back end gaining traction as they disappeared into the night.

By the time they had reached the hilltop parking spot by the bridge history was of no consequence. In the warm night air they sat above the illuminated cityscape below. The conversation they had was million miles from any he had with the doctor. Blue was not troubled by the drama and violence they had witnessed tonight regardless of its apparent reality. These and much bloodier pastimes were commonplace in V-world sims. It was the fact that it actually happened in his time that had bothered her the most. He could understand that in his own way. He had played enough computer games in which running over old ladies gained you points. A far cry from doing it on the road. Perhaps this was the reason there seemed to be little or no commonplace violence or cruelty in Heathen. Blue reached over and dabbed his nose with a hankie. In all the time she had cared for him physically this was different, affectionate. She pulled away a little embarrassed and he guided the conversation back to their earlier altercation at the club. His shock as the drinks tray had crashed down on the man's head, before the chap had hit the floor she was dragging Vic through the crowd and up the stairs. The cops tearing into the drunken mob below as they sped away.

"Did you have family?" she said from nowhere.

"Of course." He said before realising that wasn't what she meant. She was referring to having a real organic mother and father.

"I have heard of family, it sounds nice. Like having special friends forever." she said naively.

"Yeh I suppose so" he said remembering his closest friend Nathan who must have done everything he had asked or he wouldn't be here now . It was hard to grasp the fact he would have died centuries ago.

The subject switched to relationships and particularly physical ones. Blue had asked about his, whether he had left anyone behind. Even she was talking like he was from another planet and that's how he felt. It took a humongous effort to realise that he had not moved very far physically, he was still here on earth. They were on a virtual hillside right now but up in the sky the moon was enormous. The same satellite lump of rock was still hanging in space and acting upon the hearts and minds of the earthlings as it always had. This was his world and he wanted to show it to Blue with all its faults. He couldn't explain most of it to the Doc, but where else could he go. Soaps and boy bands, wars and TV?

When they finally kissed it felt real, physical and he might have been happy with that, Blue was. What he didn't understand was whether it meant anything in here. Could the adventures in a simulation be carried into reality? Could feelings for someone be taken outside? He would soon find out, in the meantime he would go along with it, after all this was better than any game. That much was clear from his own physical reaction after he had reached across the gear shift and kissed her. In this so called computer game her warm hand on the back of his neck, the soft moist mouth were the only reality he wanted. If he could freeze time right now he would have done. Afterwards he said the L word and she did the same. He knew he felt it as deeply as she did right then.

"You like older men then?" he joked.

"What's 500 years in a relationship?" She responded

"I'd stick with you baby for a thousand years," he said and he meant it, right at that moment he meant it. He had no idea how soon those words would come back to haunt him. Despite the short lived illusion Blue really loved him but, just for a short while. The futures may as well be aliens as far as he was concerned and she was no different. But right here, right now he was head over heels.

CHAPTER 16

When Vic woke up on the first morning in his new home it felt like nothing has changed. But things had changed, he was free now and his quarantine was over. He was woken by the underlying noise of traffic from outside in the city of Lon-Don. Finally he opened his eyes and saw the balcony door was open. He didn't have the energy to move for a while but eventually rolled off the bed and padded across to close it.

He got half way across the room when a disembodied voice spoke to him. So clear it was almost inside his head.

"Good morning." It sounded male, quite camp. It came from no discernible direction.

He stopped in his tracks. "Who said that?" said Vic looking around. There was raucous laughter. Vic ran back over to the bed as if it might provide a better perspective as to where it was coming from.

"I am your religion God, you will obey me," the voice said, vainly attempting to sound deeper and more masculine followed by more laughter.

"Who's there?" shouted Vic looking up as if that where the answer lay.

"My name is Leon. I am your Intelli system," said the voice.

"Intelli system?" he questioned.

"Oh they were right, you really are a caveman aren't you?" sniggered the voice. He still couldn't place its location. "Explain please, where are you?"

"I am kind of everywhere." Another snigger as if he was being teased. Vic was slowly creeping around the room trying to keep him talking so that he would eventually give himself away. "I can't see you?"

"No I expect not, there's not much to see I can assure you." Vic stopped inbetween rooms looking in every direction. "I manage the building and I am here to offer assistance."

"But where are you?"

The voice giggled once more. "Oh you mean my physical presence? 3 deciles away at the offices of Jareth Accommodation."

Vic relaxed, he felt stupid now. Realised he had been startled by the air conditioning unit. He supposed it wasn't a huge leap to assume that the 'futures' had come up with some kind of voice activated building management system. A giant leap from having to turn the thermostat up and down. Even in his day they were doing most of that by phone. It soon became apparent this was more than an air conditioning unit.

"It's time you go hygiened and robed, we have a lot to get through and Blue will be on her way very soon. I can't imagine what she will think if I don't have you ready."

"A lot to get through?" said Vic to the ceiling.

"I have to complete your induction into the property. I calculate that your lack of intelligence might increase the time required to complete the task."

Lack of intelligence he thought, not a hint of insult or irony in the statement. It wasn't a good start if this thing was meant to be some kind of Butler. Vic's heart rate shot up and had he been here in the room instead of three deci whatever's away. He might have picked the machine up and thrown it out of the window. He wasn't going to rise to it, it probably meant no harm. "Ok, go for it," he said.

There was a long silence. "Go for what?"

Vic sighed. "So I lack intelligence?" he mumbled to himself. "Proceed with your induction," he said loudly. The damn machine even had the nerve to give a little insulted cough. "Ahem, alright. Welcome to the Jareth V9 Accommodation pod. For your convenience its initial physical layout has been set to your original plan with some special improvements. It is fully customisable and has over 40 panoramic views including 10.." he coughed again. "Ancient modes."

Vic watched as the scene from the balcony switched through very quickly like flicking through TV channels. He even felt slight changes in atmosphere as they did so. A chill then a heated breeze and different smells. Instead of differing views it was like actually being dropped in different places instantaneously. "The structural interior is fixed but also has over a hundred different customisable interior designs." Thankfully he didn't choose to go through them all but Vic got the idea. When he changed a layout it was like being in a different place. It was as if you could move house in the blink of an eye. He could spend the weekend in the equivalent of a chilly mountain cabin and flick a switch to be back home in your familiar surroundings. The building itself was just a shell. "Can you turn it all off?" Vic interrupted.

"Turn it all off?" Leon repeated.

"Yes," said Vic.

There was the pause again, he thought he was gone. Then suddenly everything disappeared. Vic found himself stood in what looked like a shimmery silver shell of a building. There were solid objects but they were made of the same material. It was as if he was standing in a 3D canvas. He took a few echoey steps around the room and looked out through the balcony window.

"Ok," he said. Hoping the machine was still there. "Put it back on." There was silence for just a moment too long and Vic was on the brink of thinking he had reset everything to zero. Like when he had reset his phone to a foreign language and couldn't get it back. He was starting to become concerned when everything started to reappear. At last he was stood right back in his bedroom.

He took a walk round the apartment and everything was just as he remembered it and then he saw it. The adjoining door, the one he had tried to open but couldn't because of the force field. Slowly he approached and took hold of the two handles in the oak panelled double door. Twisting his wrists they gave way and he pulled as both doors swung open.

The interior was no longer a reflection of his room. He cautiously stepped cross the threshold for fear of banging his head again. He couldn't believe what he saw inside.

He had stepped into a wide square lounge area with a low glass table surrounded by four sofas. In contrast to the room he had just left there was a Caribbean breeze floating through the balcony window. On the outside a wooden terrace and a beach complete with hammock and palm trees. Waves were crashing against the shore and running back down bleached white sand. That wasn't the most amazing thing. To his left and behind half glass there was what could only be a fully functioning recording studio. Sound booths for a full band and an endless array of instruments. On the far side of the lounge area was a glass door and inside what looked like a dream come true. He darted across the room and opened the door. Inside it smelled of leather and the sound was dampened to almost zero. Even his footsteps were a mellow thud. The room was rammed with an array of classic musical instruments and amps. He spotted a Marshall 200 stacked with a few others in the far corner. Stood up on one of many racks was what looked like Gibson Les Paul Lemon-burst and just behind it the Sunburst model. Holy shit there was a Custom 1957 as well as the 1958 in Gold. He slowly walked around running his fingers over their curves. There were also Fender Telecasters and much more. Picking up the the Lemon-burst he gently caressed it and picking it up fingered a few chords. When he strummed it sounded awesome, not even plugged in it sounded incredible. He felt the smile on his face stretching his skin uncomfortably and consciously relaxed.

But how? These were real but the designs, the tiny marks and scratches. Of course, they will have been plucked from his memory like they had done with the sims. If these were all built from his memory then it's likely that in this room he would have a collection of the most valued guitars in history. He looked up at the double neck lead guitar hanging high on the wall and across to the 96 Paisley Stratocaster and left the room. Dazzled he closed the door with a quiet click.

"You like those then? Musical instruments for your pleasure," said Leon.

"For my pleasure," he repeated under what breath he had left.

"If you would like to come this way." A light flashed across the floor in the main room and he walked through and into the kitchen area on the far side. An area previously unused when Blue was providing all his meals. He had always taken it that was the reason there had never been any appliances in here.

"Food prep with the latest in 4D technology," said Leon. Looking around there still seemed to be nothing in the way of equipment. None of the usual implements. There was a long kitchen style island but no sign of a fridge, toaster or kettle. Just two parallel work surfaces and a single high level oven type device and a drink dispenser.

"Is this it?" he said disappointedly.

"Sir, this is it!" said Leon stressing the word 'it'. "Allow me to demonstrate." There was that annoying cough and he put on some kind of butler type tone. "Can I offer Sir some refreshment, breakfast perhaps?" Vic wasn't keen on the idea of cooking for himself. But in light of the fact that he was retired and only had to pop next door to be on a writing holiday in Monserrat then he might find the time.

"Cheeseburger and large fries, go large," said Vic sarcastically. "I can replicate animal although it's not only immoral but it's illegal now. However my formulas still contain all the nutritional value of the natural work." Vic was relieved this wasn't a cooking lesson. Besides, they are bound to have some kind of home delivery in the future? "Oh well if your cooking then I'll have the works. Full English breakfast menu with black coffee, fruit juice." There was silence again for around thirty seconds and Vic was wondering had he offended the machine. Then a light illuminated in the cubicle and the door became transparent. He opened it and inside was his complete order, on a tray with cutlery and plates. He was sure it looked as fresh as it would be tasteless. Still you can't have everything. If he was independent now and having to be self reliant then if that meant asking Leon for something then he could manage that.

"Your views, waking arrangements and decor are all optional. You need only ask."

"Does that thing make beer?" he said.

The machine paused. "Mm do you have a formula for that?"

"Never mind," he said.

"You can get yourself steam cleaned in here as you know." A light flashed behind him. Yeah he knew how to get washed and dressed in 2515.

Finally you may wish to order items such as clothing, artwork, that kind of thing. Another light flashed and he followed it to another door which he had previously never entered. Inside there were a few chairs around a central stage, on it was a small table. In the corner a large garage sized sliding door.

"We can shop together or you can shop alone. If you want to make a purchase then I can do it for you or you can use the console. It will be delivered through here in good time. Most often within the hour." A hundred objects, real objects came and went on the stage. From bags to chairs to clothing and then disappeared.

"Cool, the very latest in home shopping and how do I pay?" said Vic realising he had no method of supporting all this.

"Pay, oh dear no," said Leon. "Who would you pay? There 'is' no one to pay," said Leon confused.

"Yeah I suppose so," he said.

"We really must get on, we need to get your AR device fitted before Blue arrives."

"What the hell is an AR device?"

Leon sighed. "Really?"

"Really," repeated Vic sarcastically. Leon continued as if unsure whether the human was having fun with him again.

"Your Augmented Reality Device. It is fitted to the back of your neck and taps into your brain stem. It enables you to access 3D menus, get loce data and media."

"What's a Loce?" asked Vic.

"Location data." The machine sounded exasperated. It tells you where you are. Where your friends are and enables you to navigate in physical space."

Vic had already switched off at the bit about brain stems. "I think I will be just fine without an AR," he said.

Leon was flabbergasted, if a machine can be. "How will you know where you are, where your friends are. How about information and media?"

"I'll just ask someone for directions." he said and walked through his bedroom and into the steamer.

Vic was finishing dressing. There were quite a few items of clothing he didn't recognise in his wardrobe. Probably some kind of futurist starter pack. He pulled out a camouflage boiler suit and cream overcoat and finished the job with a comfortable pair of cream pumps. By their standards he had dressed down but to him it was a bit extreme. Nonetheless, he felt more liberated in TVC15. He wasn't likely to bump in to the lads from the pub.

"Blue is here," said Leon from nowhere. He rushed out of the dressing room to get the door before realising that would not be necessary. Leon had taken care of that and she was already in the lounge area. As if to prove the point of how conservative he was dressed, there she was. A black and white french style top and chunk striped mini skirt. Impeccable make up with huge dark eyes and pink lips. Her high heals made her look 7 ft tall. Perched on her head with the tiniest tilt was the smallest top hat he ever saw. It was more like a cake decoration perched on her tight mousy hair.

"How do you like it?" she said looking him up and down.

"The place? amazing." He said opening his arms.

"We put some extra space in." Waving the tiniest purse he had ever seen.

"I know, the studio is pretty awesome."

"I'm sure you'll like those instruments."

"I prefer the 68 Les Paul to be honest," he said disapprovingly. She frowned in disappointment.

"Kidding, joke remember. Ha ha humour."

"I thought you might like a look around Heathen today, just us. Before the eh," she paused "The official introductions."

"Before I am paraded before the masses you mean?"

"You will never believe how excited everyone is to meet you."

"Be careful you don't lose him dear he has no AR fitted," interrupted Leon.

Blue looked at him concerned.. "No AR.?" Like he was a child refusing to wear a coat.

"Blue please have a word with him. What am I supposed to do when he leaves this building. He may as well jump down a black hole. I will have no idea where he is, I can't communicate."

"Don't worry about it ok," said Vic winking at Blue.

"Zigg it's a good idea to have an AR fitted. It can be switched off if you want. What if you got lost?"

"He will ask directions he said," interrupted Leon once more.

"Can Leon be switched off?"

"Of course I can, you only need ask."

"Then switch off."

"That's all well and good but.." There was silence.

"So what are we doing today then?"

"We have a transporter outside which will run us on the mag system over to some air transport. We can get a great view of the City from high above. Would you like that?"

"Sounds great to me, a tourist flight across Heathen."

Ten minutes later they were sat in a Quad-pod and heading away from the apartments. It was disorientating when he fooled around with the controls. With the false view up it looked like they were travelling around 40 miles an hour as the green pleasant landscape passed them by. When Vic switched it off and they could see the real landscape they were travelling at four times that speed easily.

When they arrived at the air centre it was nothing like an airport. More of a rooftop car park with the Mag pods offloading and people travelling up escalators. Still not crowded, the whole planet seemed to have a feeling of Sunday afternoon. It looked designed for crowds but never really experienced any.

The upward escalator was about ten people wide and had handrails distributed across its width. At the top there were various craft and Blue led them to a slim mean looking beast. It had no wings but he could see what looked like jet outlets half hidden in its body. A smaller craft took off quite close to them and gave off no pressure or dust. They stepped inside and made themselves comfortable.

"Where would you like to see first?" said Blue.

"Not sure really."

"Let's circle some of the residential areas of heathen." The craft lifted off and they started to get a sense of scale for the place. Although a mishmash of different sized buildings there were newer more modern areas with row up on row of residential towers. There was a wide open highway hub crisscrossing the city. These eight lane highways still held little traffic. They passed over public spaces and these were like the streets, relatively uncluttered. Then they headed out across the Nature Park which was a lush landscape which went on for miles. Blue explained they were not allowed to fly low over this area.

All in all Vic's futuristic fantasies about flying cars, robots and spaceships had been generally a disappointment. If an alien race were to arrive here they might think it relatively uninhabited.

That's until they reached the outer fringes of the City. Here he was able to witness the shear scale of the robotic machine that provided for humanity. It was so much bigger than what he had seen in Blue's V-world simulation. With the visualiser off they sped across fields with acre upon acre of crops being grown, harvested and processed.

They passed a railway system which had at least six lanes feeding into the city itself. At a certain point they would snake into tunnels, laden with parts, machinery and containers.

There were also automated voyagers which were driverless trucks. At its far reaches it seemed there were no more resources and the City ended leaving dusty roads that snaked away over the horizon. In the distance they were able to make out these mammoth vehicles the size of a mansion crawling to and fro.

They reached a far point and they were alerted to return because the vehicle could not operate further out. Although over a hundred miles across Heathen looked quite small from here.

They headed back to the air park and as they walked back to the mag system Vic was recognised. A family group were getting out of a mag transporter and made their way over to them.

"Mr Stardust, I hope you don't mind but it's an absolute pleasure to meet you." said the feminine of the group. Her companion followed suit. "Hello Mr Stardust." He said hello and they took some images. They were pleasant and spent a few moments chatting. Finally they had made their excuses and left. They made no effort to disguise their chat as they left.

"He is very nice and speaks quite well too, and seemingly quite intelligent. I am surprised."

During the course of the day they had gotten a feel for how this city functioned. The world of robotics had gone in a different direction than the visions portrayed in his schoolboy comics. There were no humanoid robots like Marvin or whatever he was called in the forgotten planet. Instead most automated tasks like waste removal and food delivery were kind of plumbed into the city and continued unseen. The machines were very discreet and designed to fade into the background or be built in to the fabric of the structures.

On the surface the city was calm and yet as he understood it, a hive of columns and tunnels kept things functioning below the surface. It was inevitable that there would be some humanoid drones for tasks that required direct interaction with people. These were a minority of course. A person would just open their fridge and it was as if someone was loading it from the back, in fact that was actually happening. 4D technology allowed them to manufacture most foods at home from basic ingredients. The replicators were like incredibly complex 4 dimensional copiers. If the machine had the right formula then it could generate any food imaginable, something Vic was well aware of.

All meat and vegetable products were now grown in simulated environments. The basic ingredients were the same for everything from a mouse to a cow, a sheep to a cat, they just had to decide what they wanted to come out at the end. He could see the attraction of V-world without a doubt. It was possible to lead an army of ten thousand men and be the only real person in the sim. This amazing technology was not the only reason that the streets were so deserted. Even for those who chose to do some kind of work could do most of it in a simulation.

At last Vic felt he had a sense of perspective for where he was. He thought about his twentieth century sim once more but maybe he would hit the music room first.

CHAPTER 17

No work, no government, all needs catered for by a computer along with a bunch of drones. As well as an abundance of food and resources. Bring it on thought Vic but the reality was proving quite different. When did he get some of that after a day working with the Doc and perhaps touring V-world as part of his education? No sooner was all that over than he was being paraded around reality too. He had spent the last two days touring the real city of Heathen and was exhausted. At last he was home and had a few moments to himself. He had almost forgotten about the note. He pulled the crumpled paper from his pocket and slowly opened it. Trying to remember where it had come from and who had thrust it into his hand.

The adjustments required to get through recent weeks had been one thing but the last couple of days were indescribable. Vic was at last seeing for himself the incredible enthusiasm for him and the twentieth century. Finally realising what Blue had said was absolutely true. He could do anything he wanted, his fame was guaranteed. Groups of people had started to physically turn up wherever he went. A few thousand wasn't many by his standards but to Heathen this was an incredible turnout. He'd spent the last couple of days being jostled and pushed around the City. Taken on a physical VIP tour of Heathen, his appearances were beamed live to media in 3d wherever he went. A Helidrone was always close by and he had assumed it was security but found out it was scanning. This meant that media clients could be in the crowd, in prime positions without leaving their homes.

The first stop had been to meet the team who had worked on the project to regenerate him. They had designed an exhibition which showed how they had grown his new body. The horror of what he had seen in V-world had softened the blow when he finally saw the real thing. At last appreciating Blue's unorthodox method of preparation, catching her eye for a moment when they revealed the tank of fluid. Still a little unnerving but a far cry from the Frankenstein scenario his subconscious had chosen to include in her sim. Thankfully he was no longer shocked at the concept and gave her a knowing grin. Blue looked like she was straining not to laugh. Probably grateful he didn't collapse and start dry retching as he'd done last time. The white coats proudly demonstrated the technology that had kept him alive for 22 years until the projects conclusion. Vic was slightly embarrassed by naked pictures of himself lay on a slab before the brain transmission had taken place.

He saw video of his second birth and time lapse of his growth. Various dignitaries made speeches and enjoyed private jokes on his behalf, relating some of his pre wake up ramblings. This was news to Vic, he had no memory of any of it. There were humble apologies from the team who had worked on the project for the slight damage to one eye. Vic had made light of it and they were grateful when he suggested it added to his mystique.

This part of the day was very light hearted and he was treated like a returning son. One or two of the nurses bursting into tears when he greeted them. His ego was being massaged at every turn and he loved every minute of it. Whilst on the facility he was asked to complete a few basic fitness tests while plugged into various bits of futuristic monitoring equipment. This appeared to be for the benefit of media rather than necessity. He was declared 100% fit by his chief surgeon who ceremoniously gave Vic some kind of certification. There were roars of laughter when he put his hand on his chest, faking a heart attack.

Having shaken hands gratefully with endless futures in white coats who had spent years monitoring and maintaining his new 'flesh'.

It intrigued him to see for the first time the inside of the cryogenic pod where he had spent the last 500 years.

Noticeably battered a little on the outside but inside the protective foam was like new. It was much bigger than he expected, more like some kind of soundproof booth. The walls lined with some kind of tubular rubbers jutting outwards. With its inner shell removed there was easily space inside for two people to stand up. The media were most excited when he posed for them in its doorway as if stepping out for the first time. Vic squeezed the hands of many more dignitaries at all levels as he made his way back to the transporter for the next leg of his whirlwind tour of Heathen. On his first official day in reality Zigg Stardust had played his part to perfection and was already winning fans.

As they lifted off from the building they waved to the crowds below and cruised low and fast across the city's gleaming skyline. Vic felt the relief at dropping the smile that had been plastered across his face throughout the day. Through the windows he admired the kind of view he had always imagined for the future. Illuminated towers, walkways and a living cityscape rushed by beneath them. It shimmered from neon lights glowing large and small. There were hundreds of people walking through brightly lit parks, malls and arcades.

He stared for a moment at the wondrous futuristic scene before him.

The deadpan look now deteriorated into an aggravated frown.

"Turn that off," he muttered.

"Turn what off?" said Blue puzzled.

"The thing, the scenery below," he said pointing out of the window.

"If you like," Blue sighed. "The life you see below exists," she said by way of explanation.

He scowled at her without comment.

"Visualiser off," she commanded. At once everything he was seeing disappeared and was replaced by reality. A grey cityscape which was a complete opposite of what he had just been witnessing.

"The visualiser is designed to offer a pleasant environment," she explained.

Vic slumped back in his chair with his arms folded and ignored her. Eventually Blue had switched it back on anyway.

He still didn't get it. They way she was in V-world and yet here in reality she was so cold? It was all the wrong way round. The time they spent together in his sim was incredible and the truth was he could easily stay. As long as Blue was there too.

They arrived at the Major Tom memorial where yet more crowds were waiting. On thinking Vic realised it was most likely here that the scrap of paper was thrust into his hand. A crowd had surged forward grabbing at him as he left the craft before he could be ushered behind a waist high glass barrier. The barrier felt like glass but it was more like the stuff that had divided his room from the next one at his hotel. He was behind a kind of waste high force field, still he was glad of it as the small but enthusiastic crowd surged forward.

He spent some considerable time admiring the stories and legends attributed to Major Tom. There were numerous artefacts and displays paying homage to his exploits. Zigg was shown the makeshift craft that had carried the Major and his crew on their perilous journey back to earth. He stopped to admire a statue of the Major in the central hallway. Standing tall in his space suit, helmet under his arm, his chest out and one leg symbolically stepping forward. The eyes slightly closed with an arrogant grin which was almost a smile. Staring outwards towards the horizon as if seeing things mere mortals would not comprehend.

They were led inside to examine records of the city of Heathen in its early years. There were also hand written notes and models which were attributed to the Mars teams outpouring of knowledge. At that time they had to record whatever they could from memory. Some of humanities greatest minds were required to tinker with well established inventions with the goal of rebuilding civilisation. Finally Vic and Blue had made their way back to the transporter and that must have been when it happened.

There had been that moment of chaos and he could see it clearer now. Feeling something thrust into his hand and looking up. He saw a face pulling away and being swallowed by the crowd like a drowning man. Wide unblinking eyes staring up at him expectantly as it sank from view. The hood hiding what could have been a clutch of bright red hair and some kind of circular symbol on his forehead. Around the mans neck hung a symbol on a chain, a lightning symbol. Where had he seen that before? It looked, no not looked... It felt familiar?

So there on the top was the same symbol, a squiggle like Lightning. As soon as he saw it he felt the 'incident' come on once more. Like an old vinyl record the incidents were like jumps in his life. Moments when things were out of place. He was having them more frequently and hadn't dared tell anyone yet. His own description of them sounded too weird. A mixture of déjà vu and understanding or an enlightenment feeling. It was here again, like the moment you work out the answer to a problem. Usually déjà vu was minuscule yet in these experiences it was continuous and unnaturally long. It was like he knew what the note would say a fraction before he read it. He knew everything just before it happened, but only just.

Since the chaos of the day he finally had a moment alone, opening the note he read.

'My mother said to get things done
You better not mess with Major Tom.
Ashes to ashes, fun to funky
We know Major Toms a junkie'

"Where did you get that?" Whispered Blue into his ear making him jump. She had clearly already read at least some of it.

"I don't know," he said screwing it up disinterestedly and throwing it to one side. Blue picked it up, reading it herself for a moment.

"I suppose it was only a matter of time," she said sadly.

"What?"

"The Humanists, this is some kind of rhyme they use to degrade Mother," she said. "It's so saddening."

Vic knew who they were. Surviving on the outskirts of the city without Mother. A group of anti technology terrorists. Without Mother's intervention they operated independently. Fending for themselves, growing organic foods, scavenging.

"A selfish agenda to return to a barbaric lifestyle, living like dogs," she had said. Vic understood the implication in her comments because Humanists wanted things to be how they were in Vic's time. They would spread gossip and rumours about the Major, claiming he had left the human race to die. Had created his own sick drug induced Kingdom on Mars.

"Is any of it true?" asked Vic provocatively.

"You have an intelligent mind, what do you see? A world created by Mother, the affection of the people of Heathen towards you?"

Vic shrugged in agreement and walked towards his room. He could feel her eyes burning into him from behind. It made him shudder and he supposed it was all to do with the frosty atmosphere between them at the moment.

He had returned to writing his own music and his enthusiasm for it was growing by the day.

"The music your making is sounding very good." No longer doubting he was heading anywhere else but to Montserrat. This was his own nickname for the beech side recording studio he had in the next room.

Vic thought 'good' was an understatement. The stuff he was writing right now was astounding. That was the interesting thing. This material was actually better than all the shit he planned to steal from Lennon, Springsteen and the Stones. He felt no humility in even thinking that because he knew it was true. He'd have one inspirational idea and then another. Then before long the songs were pouring out of him, completely effortlessly as if they had always been there. So much of it was influenced by TVC15, Heathen and his recent experiences. There was so much material to work with. Vic needed no set genre either, he was free to experiment as never before. He'd been prolific in the last couple of weeks. The confidence in being a rock star before he had written a note set him free creatively.

"Have you thought about playing them live, physically?" she said expectantly.

"I'm not sure, I thought those days were over for me," he said turning to see if she was serious.

"There's not a single person in Heathen would not come out to see you," she said. He stared at her holding eye contact for a moment. She was right, it was a matter of choice. If and when he took his music to the masses he would arrive fully formed as a rock god.

"Good night Blue," he said coldly.

He turned and went inside closing the door, still thinking. Here he was full of hormones, throwing tunes out like confetti and holding on to the underlying feeling that he was old. He had to realise he was not old anymore, he was 22 and a superstar just for smiling. It was an interesting idea.

In this moment however he was thinking about the Humanists. Why had they gone to such an effort to contact him? To Blue and anyone else he understood how vile and frightening these people would be. He was curious all the same. The general population of Heathen had an underlying feeling of conformity. They were super civilised and happy. Surely these Humanists were lunatics, fuck they had to be. Blue was right, why would anyone not go along with the life that Mother and Heathen provided. The curious thing was that they were living off grid, growing food and probably even fucking each other. The upshot was, they sounded a lot like him.

It was still a little frosty between him and Blue since her post game attitude change. The way everything in V-world was one thing and then in reality, bam it was like it never happened. How she could be so mean? In V-world they were lovers and that was a fact but once they came out? He'd do well to remember it was just for one day unless he wanted to be labeled some kind of pervert.

Vic sat down at his writing desk strewn with lyrics, ideas and songs created over the past week or so. He reached into his suit pocket and pulled out a second note.

Glancing over his shoulder towards the door he unfolded it and began reading.

CHAPTER 18

The transporter hissed to a halt indicating they had reached the limits of the maintained city. The reassuring landscape view from the windows disappeared as soon as the door had slid open and the cool air rushed in. The Professor and the Doctor stepped outside onto the pavement and the transport unit set off back towards the security of Heathen. Once it was out of sight the silence was eerie. They stood looking around nervously for a moment and then at each other before the Professor headed off up the hill.

"Lets go," the Doctor turned after him.

The atmosphere was cooler and quite misty, fog continuing to thicken as they walked further from the centre of Heathen. Because the Heathen atmosphere was manipulated the smog and cloud would accumulate here quite naturally. Manhattan Chase was a few miles further South and they would have to walk from here. It was no longer serviced by Mother or any of her automated systems. The air became moist and cold as they made their way along deserted weed ridden pavements on foot. Sunlight filtered into light greys and blues as it struggled to burst through the heavy cloud cover. The few buildings left standing were deserted and nature was winning the battle for dominance. Huge trees had taken root and ripped into the fabric of many buildings. Some had utilised the glass structures like greenhouses before punching their way through the windows reaching for the sky above. Vegetation of various kinds competed for light amongst the shade of concrete towers. Large areas of pavement were now a mixture of green moss and grey concrete. The patchy fog would shift, thicker in places and clear in others. Occasionally tricking the eye, forming figures, faces or creatures that would disappear as quickly as they formed. The Professor clearly knew where he was going, darting this way and that with the Doctor close behind. They pulled their coats tighter and marched deeper into this urban wilderness. The Doctor noticed occasional rebel lightning symbols sprayed or scratched on walls as well as occasional derogatory text pertaining to the Major. He felt like a soldier trapped behind enemy lines. Turning a corner the silence was broken by the cry of a child. The Doc felt the hairs on his neck rise in response. The Professor threw a hand out across the Doctors chest to stop him.

"Did you hear that?"

"Help me, please someone help me," the child's voice again, sounding in pain.

"This way," cried the Professor as they set off into a side road. It would once have been relatively wide but was now just a series of moss covered pathways between trees and bushes.

"Someone please help me, I hurt. I hurt so bad."

Following the sound they delved deeper, pushing branches out of their faces as they went. Up ahead a large tree was protruding between the pavement and an abandoned office block. It's trunk powerful enough to have lifted part of the pavement like an old carpet. From the other side they saw movement, a flash of yellow. Slowly the pair circled the tree as widely as they could to slowly reveal the source of the sound. The boy looked around 14 years old and was partly dressed in a yellow open neck suit with no shoes. A large metal spike was protruding from his chest and penetrated into the tree holding him in place. There was no blood but where he had the ability to move his arms and head the tree had worn away exposing the white wood below the bark. At the points of contact his clothes were torn and shredded. On the floor lay a single shoe with the foot still inside. Protruding from the severed leg were wires and metal twine of various colours. He could have been there for some time, maybe a year or more.

"Drone," said the Professor with a sigh of relief. "Come on."

The Doc stayed still, staring at the drone who attempted to hold out a hand to him, pleading.

"Don't leave me here, I hurt."

The Professor turned back slapping the Doctor on the shoulder and grabbing his collar. "Come on it's only a drone, let's go," the Professor said putting on a brave face.

Not out of care for a drone but he was slightly embarrassed that their potential hosts had shown themselves for what they were so early on. This was not going to gain any empathy from his younger self. They both knew the drone felt no real pain, it was just part of its programming to display discomfort when necessary.

The Doctor followed slightly dazed as the childish cries for help faded into the distance.

"Don't go please help me."

Making their way back to the main road they finally reached the wide open boulevard of Manhattan Chase. A hundred yards up a narrow alleyway ran off to one side up some steep steps.

"This way," said the Professor tapping his shoulder once more. By now the fog was thick and claustrophobic as they stopped by a door, slightly ajar. There was dim light coming from within and the door creaked as the Professor pushed against it, slipping inside. They found themselves in a dim narrow corridor with wall lights along its length. The deep red walls were punctuated by doors leading off at intervals. At the end of the corridor was a wide stairway leading into a large open space. It might once have been the atrium of some apartment or hotel building. The space was maybe ten stories high with windows on the left and a plain wall ahead. Cloth draped scaffold walkways filled the right wall. The glass roof was still intact and the air was noticeably warmer. They looked up and around the space seeing no one but feeling the presence of many. There was a loud clank up on the scaffold and a bulge in the cloth slithered downwards from a higher floor before swinging down in front of them. The man swung down and landed gracefully on his feet and broke seamlessly into a walk.

"Come on in, you'll catch your death in the cold," said the sneering figure walking towards them.

The Doctor had to consciously close his mouth to hide his surprise and disgust. There were subtle rebel symbols in the city but he had never seen anything so blatant and shocking before. The man before him had bright red spiky hair and the humanist symbol, a red lightning stripe was painted boldly across one eye. The sinewy man wore a white decorated one piece suit with a high collar. The Doctor felt sick and his colour had drained. The last few hours had been stressful enough but this was sickening, he just wanted to close his eyes and get home. The pair were led around a large glass tower in the centre which had obstructed their view until now. Despite its size it was brighter in one area upon a raised stage where some furniture was arranged. A table and some armchairs under some bright lights reminding the Doctor of a stage set. He had no doubt that the audience were already here, up at those windows. The whole structure was like a building turned inside out with hundreds of windows across the left wall. Looking up and around again he saw no movement. In front of them a man was perched on a table, slow clapping as they arrived. The first man raised a knowing eyebrow to him.

"Look what I found crawling down the alley," he sneered.

The Doctor was fairly sure the guy on the table was the same one who had threatened him weeks ago. He looked very different now, red high waisted dungarees and hair to match. A patch over one eye and without the shaded make up his face looked a little thinner. A tiny wine glass hung from his right hand between thumb and forefinger.

"Nice to see you again Doctor," he said taking a sip of the red liquid and trying to disguise the involuntary wince.

"This is Jack Halloween," said the Professor "and of course Aladdin Sane." He nodded towards the other man.

"So this must be" he paused "you." said Aladdin in response as they both burst into hysterical laughter. Aladdin skipped past the two visitors and perched on the table next to his colleague. Lifting one knee he put his arm across the other man's shoulder and they both stared. Maybe they could now be sure, right here side by side. The same person 75 years apart, still pretty amazing.

"How much does he know?" said Jack without removing his gaze as if the Doctor were an animal with no understanding.

"As much as anyone can know," said the Professor stepping over to the table picking up the bottle of red liquid. "May I?" Aladdin nodded his approval and the Professor poured.

"How's your history Doctor?" said Jack eyeing him closely.

"Not too bad considering it's been my career for a couple of decades," the Doctor replied arrogantly. "It's my job. Building up a picture based on facts," the Doctor stressed the final word purposely.

Jack raised one eyebrow at Aladdin in a kind of 'is he really talking to me' look.

"Is that right?"

"That's right"

The Professor took a swig of his drink and quickly put it back down on the table. "Let's get on shall we?"

Aladdin ignored him. "This is the damn point Doc. Welcome to our version of the beautiful city of Heathen. Ever wondered what that word means Mr?" He looked at them both, standing quickly he walked slowly around and in between them. Whispering in their individual ears as he eyed them both close up. Like troops being lectured by a Sargent they didn't respond "Heathenism is a state of mind. You can take it that I'm referring to one who does not see his world. He has no mental light." He made elaborate meaningless gestures with his hands. "He destroys almost unwittingly. He cannot feel any Gods presence in his life. He is the 21st century man." Aladdin spread his arms pleased with his analogy. "If you have studied your history then you will be aware of the word Heathen, and its historic meaning."

"Your point is?" said the Doctor.

"My point is that it was you who came here looking for our help. In doing so you gave us the truth and reason to be what we are."

Jack interrupted. "The Salvation Machine has to be shut down and you are going to help us do it."

"Me!" The Doctor stepped back.

"I thought he knew?" said Jack looking at the Professor who dropped his eyebrows turning to the Doctor. "We want you and the caveman with us."

"What has Zigg to do with this?" The Doctor peered up at the rows of windows, imagining the watching faces. He wondered how many there were up here. Hundreds, thousands or maybe just two? Unlikely two, but he felt like he was in a courtroom. Helping those who were up there make a decision, perhaps shifting the minds of the less committed ones.

The Professor stayed close to the Doctor trying to mentally hold this coalition together. "We are talking about shutting Mother down. No one takes this lightly but it's unavoidable. There will be huge disruption and we need people with knowledge of the past. People like you, people like Zigg."

"You think he wants this?"

"Five years, that's all. No one wants this but we have to try and help ourselves."

"People will trust him, but somehow we have to let him know what's at stake. We need him on our side and he is going to have to understand that he is finished if he Migrates anyway."

"How?"

"I think there's an opportunity to launch a virus." his throat dried up and he choked on his words like he was discussing bumping off a dear relative. "A virus into the system."

"Can't be done," the Doctor snapped eyeing the three of them.

"On one particular night we think it can," said Jack slowly walking around the table to refill his glass.

The Professor continued. "If everything happens just as it did last time there will be a short power failure on the night of the physical show, just before the interval. That will give us an opportunity to get in."

"It can't be done, the Salvation Machine is segregated by firewalls." the Doctor repeated.

The Professor looked around at them nervously.

"Usually that's true but not on this night. This is an organic live event that is being beamed to every sector of the city simultaneously. Mars will be 14 light minutes from Earth. This should give us plenty of time to infect and shut down the cloud."

The Doctor took a step back. Jack looked away scratching the back of his neck.

And there it was, suddenly this whole thing seemed plausible. It was as if the Doctor had been able deny it as long as he believed it couldn't be done. Looking at these three faces and hearing what was being said he began to see it could. The realisation that they might be able to actually do it horrified him and he felt every hair on his body bristle. Aladdin just stared right back at him. That huge reptilian grin across his face like an alligator waiting for his prey.

"You are really crazy, the lot of you," he was talking to the Professor now. "Do any of you understand what your saying? Another shutdown, is that what you want?" The Professor walked over to the Doctor, arms out as if to hold him. "I understand." He pushed him a way.

"And so this plan of yours relies on me?"

Jack was back on the table, foot up and elbow on knee chewing some kind of toothpick.

"The Migration starts with that caveman, it has to end with him." Using the tiny stick between his fingers as a pointer. "We've tried contacting him but you are on the inside. You have to convince him to help us, to tell people what's happening."

"How?"

The Professor stepped forward "Your with him all the time. He has to trust you because when the time comes he will have doubts. You have to make those doubts bigger and get him on side."

"Mother is going to blow a fuse with or without your Neanderthal friend," spat Aladdin. "Without you too if that's how things pan," he said nodding towards the Professor his eyes narrowed and his sneer slowly turned into an insincere smile that made the Professor shiver. Remembering how he had met him before, but decades from now. He will be older then and even now there were early signs of his dark temper.

The Doctor hung his head, tears forming in the corners of his eyes. "I want nothing to do with this," he said and turned to walk away. The three exchanged glances and the Professor rose to follow him.

Jack stood on the edge of the raised area and placed his hands on his hips.

"Ramona A Stone the good time drone." his words echoed across the open space. The Doctor froze in his tracks and spun round. Over the Professor's shoulder he saw the two grinning figures. The Professor staring into his eyes slowly shook his head as if in apology, the pain etched on his face. He looked older and more tired than ever before.

"Let's go," the Doctor whispered.

Shaking his head slowly the Doctor turned and continued walking, the Professor followed. He glanced over his shoulder at the two, raising his eyebrows giving a thin smile to indicate it's gonna be fine.

He knew it wasn't.

Aladdin looked across to Jack's concerned face, still grinning he shrugged his shoulders and opened his palms.

CHAPTER 19

"Zigg did you hear what I said?" the Doctor spoke a little louder. "You seem distracted."

Yes, he supposed he was distracted, had been for weeks. Even though he had worked out an understanding of what happened with Blue it still niggled him. How he had felt so passionate about her and she did him. But it was only that way when they were inside.

"I'm fine, what were you saying?" he said still in a half trance.

"President Nixon?" said the Doc. "Do you remember the President Nixon?"

How could being in love be just part of the entertainment? Fear, horror, excitement all genuinely felt real in V-world. Out here they were as real as the fear on a ghost train would feel on the bus home. The only way to remain sane was to make comparisons with what he knew. Having played violent computer games that didn't make him a criminal. So why would Blue be in love with him outside V-world? He understood that now but the incident the day after had really scarred his pride.

He'd taken her into his world and she had responded as he'd hoped. It seemed natural to him that things would be different after that. On seeing her the next day he was shocked at her reaction when he threw his arms around her shoulders to kiss her. The look of revulsion as she pushed his face away, backing off from him. She just stood there for a moment, they both did, equally horrified for opposite reasons. Blues expression of disgust like she was being molested by her best friend. Then with tears running down her cheeks, Blue had turned and run out of the room. Left standing there open mouthed Vic was clueless as to what he had done wrong. He didn't see her for a while and even after that things were a little cold between them. In that time he had considered the situation, tried to think of an explanation. Finally they had talked about it and he had been right all along. There was clearly no concept in the futures world of bringing a physical relationship from V-world into their reality. He and Blue had drawn a line under the incident and taken it as some kind of cultural misunderstanding. Little did Vic suspect that when they went back inside it was business as usual, and beautiful business it was too. It bothered him but he soon realised how he was getting better at splitting those two worlds. He still couldn't help fantasising that she was lying to herself to save face. Vic was all too aware that her culture didn't go with physical relationships because it had become pointless. Maybe that was why they had an underground culture with the drone thing. He'd heard about how these domestic humanoid drones could be hacked and reprogrammed. There were people who kept them for their own physical pleasure. It made sense there would be a market for 25th century love dolls in a twisted world where no one wanted to touch. He had seen plenty of domestic drones and he had held conversations with some. There was no doubting their realism even though they were not completely human. He wasn't sure but there was something about them. Maybe they were designed that way, to be subtly different and to stand out. In this culture any physical relationship was considered pointless. He was humiliated at the thought that he personally was the problem. He wasn't just another human, he was 'the caveman', he knew they called him that. Could he be a pet that entertained everyone like a dolphin at a theme park or a dancing bear. Would the trainer be seen to have feelings for him? Once back in reality his love was lost, that is until they went back inside again. When they were inside then it was instantaneous like nothing has changed, like a drug he soon found he couldn't resist it. If being in love in V-world was just a game then he was addicted. If that was all that was on offer he would take it for now.

"Yes, President Nixon was a King of the City of America," said Vic at last, rubbing his temples with his thumb and forefinger. He had learned by now to adapt his language to something that made more sense to the Doctor. The best policy was to keep things simple and where he didn't know the answer then any plausible explanation would do.

"Maybe we should end our session for now?" the Doctor didn't wait for an answer standing up and folding his tablet. Vic was pleased, he had a lot on his mind.

Over time Vic had sunk deeper and deeper behind the mask of Zigg Stardust. So much so he wondered if he could ever take it off and be Vic again. He could do no wrong as Zigg and the futures adored him. He wasn't crazy about brazen publicity but this just made him more aloof, desirable. If he was expected in any public V-world sim, he would be mobbed by admiring fans. As a result he had security and paparazzi following him around when he visited public areas. This disturbed him a little because he had learned how V-world sims could be quite revealing. Adventures contaminated by hidden wishes, dreams or fantasies. Since the last time he was in his twenties he had wanted to be famous. He now had the fame he always dreamed of. When that shitty album he made went tits up he was pushed in another direction. He smiled to himself, realising how naive it was in comparison to what he was writing now.

Ironically, as famous as he was he found most peace in the real world. Here he could wander freely and almost at will. Not because the fans had no interest in him but because they were simply not around. Reality was a very quiet place on the whole and when he did run into real futures they would either be too polite to acknowledge him or be in small groups which were quite manageable.

In a way that's why he liked it, the real world was almost devoid of human existence in certain places. The Doctor seemed not to mind reality so much either, for a future that is. On many occasions they'd travelled outside together. Heathen was vast by any City standards, maybe hundreds of miles across. With the visualiser off he would spend hours soaring across huge expanses of land. It was here that the shear scale of automation could be appreciated. It was like travelling around inside a huge clockwork machine or being inside an engine. There were numerous signs of life but it was not organic human, merely humanoid drones going about their tasks. These were the ones whose role put them in contact with humanity. It was these that gave him some comfort that he was not touring a long dead metropolis. There were humans of course and he saw many of them but they were different in some way. He could recognise them against non human drones easily. He wasn't sure how, they were just less human he supposed. Maybe a look in the eye or some subconscious connection, he couldn't put his finger on it.

Then there was Manhattan Chase, having travelled to its outskirts on many occasions. The transport would not take him that far and so he went as close as it would. Vic would sit and stare out into what looked like a lifeless ruined city. Mist constantly hanging in the air and without going outside it looked damp and cold. In places the man made structures had been almost completely overcome by nature. In others it soon would be as powerful trees had lifted curb stones and distorted pathways. The transport would travel slowly across its boundary without daring to cross an invisible line.

'My mother said never to play
with the gypsies in the woods,
and if I did she would say
naughty girl to disobey'

He still had the paper given to him by the strange character, the one he later found out was a Humanist. It was very cryptic and he'd done some discreet research to make any sense of it. Maybe that had been the intention, to encourage him to find out. If not for Blue's reaction, and then other people's he might never had investigated further. When they subtly questioned his sanity he felt it best to drop the subject altogether. They were too dismissive he thought, overly dismissive. The other reason was his own compulsion as he called it.

The 'incidents' it was the best description he had so far. In one of them he had seen those same words given to him in the note but differently written. He knew there was some kind of connection. On bad days Vic questioned whether he had ever been thawed out at all. Whether this was some kind of coma, delusion or such like.

'My mother said
To get things done
You better not mess with Major Tom'

Any everyday future he had mentioned it to had reacted quite strongly, particularly the Doc. The Major was the centre of attention for these techno terrorists and they relished insulting him. In his research he found that they held an opposing view of this national hero. Spinning tales of how the Major was not the hero related to in common folklore. How he left humans to become virtually extinct before he intervened. Enjoying drug fuelled orgies whilst humanity ate itself almost to extinction back on earth. Finally they say he returns to feed off the scraps. There are even crazier conspiracy theories about how if there is any life on Mars its him. That dead planet is not just a giant server room for everything that goes on down here. Of course this is nonsense unless he is a few hundred years old but it adds to the mystery. Vic wanted to stay realistic and not get drawn in by mischief making stories and nonsense. He squinted into the gloom thinking he saw movement, a shadow in the mist perhaps someone watching him, but no maybe he is mistaken. They are out there somewhere, he thought but after a couple of hours he would usually go home. There's no sign of life, certainly not human life up on the outskirts of the Chase.

Vic was dragged back from his trance as the door slid open and Blue marched in unannounced.

"Hello," she said sheepishly "Busy?"

"We are all done, I am just leaving anyway," said the Doc snatching his case.

"Ok see you later," said Vic.

The Doctor looked across at Blue grinning, he never got bored of this ancient dialect. Shaking his head he walked through the door, smiling at Blue as he passed her.

"See you later too Zigg," he said comically shaking his head as he stepped past Blue, aware it was unlikely he would see Zigg later?

Blue leapt across the room as soon as the door closed, clearly excited about something. Vic heard the Doctor chatting with someone outside as he was leaving but couldn't make any of the conversation out. Clasping her hands together she opened her mouth to speak but didn't manage to get the words out before the interruption. From outside came the sound of a booming voice, presumably someone who had come in with Blue.

"Where is he? The second greatest star in Heathen is not here to greet me. Where is the great Ziggy Star-dust" the voice said breaking up the word stardust. Thunderous deep laughter followed, filling the air outside the door. Blue was beaten to an explanation as the door crashed open.

"Ziggy this is.." uttered Blue. A giant of a man stood in the doorway made even bigger by his extraordinary attire. Even by TVC15 standards this was exceptional.

"I am Pierrot my good friend." The huge figure powered towards him. Before he had any chance to acknowledge the man Vic was gripped in a bearhug just below the shoulders. With arms by his sides he was picked up with the same regard as a baby picks up a puppy. Arms splaying out from the elbows, defenceless as he caught the eye of Blue who watched helplessly. At the point where Vic thought he might pass out the man held him at arms length by his shoulders as if admiring a shirt, albeit with the Vic still inside. It was the first opportunity that Vic had to observe what had intruded into his life so abruptly. At first glance he looked like a giant clown from a childhood nightmare. A towering man with a smile painted on his lips across a white mannequin face. An electric blue frilly one piece suit cut off below the knees and elbows. Metalic socks and plimsoles with a pudding hat finished it all off. Vic was suspended in space for a moment before this giant of a man finally put him down, slapping him hard across the shoulder with enough force to rock him on his heels. This resulted in another burst of laughter that filled the room.

"Pierrot will be hosting the final show of the tour," cried Blue above the laughter.

"Hosting? Tour?" Vics eyes narrowed inquisitively.

"Ziggy its up to you it really is but I know you will.."

Blue was flushed again, breathless and clasping her hands together in front of her lips.

"Explain," said Vic regaining his breath and his composure.

"It's amazing, but you can think about it," she shrieked.

The monster in the clown costume came back to life cutting her off once more.

"We have plenty of time for that my dear," said the clown pushing between them. Blue was clearly excited about something but he could see she had given up on getting that out for now. The giant continued. "But let's take care of business. The two greatest superstars on Heathen are to share a stage. The biggest physical event in history." Flamboyantly spreading his arms.

Vic unconsciously backed off towards the wall.

"That's right my dear friend, you are going to be on stage with the great Pierrot."

On stage, with him? What the hell thought Vic.

"I am going to be hosting the event in the Market Square and if your going to be on stage with me, we need to do something about your fashion sense."

Pierrot stood back a step or two with his arms outstretched as if giving Vic a chance to clearly admire his own style. Vic did, and it was the least of his worries at this moment.

"Don't worry, I have brought my own people. We will need to do something. You look like a goon in all that 20th century get up."

The giant clown clicked his fingers and a group of around three or four futures burst through the door and lunged towards Vic.

⚡

So that was how it happened. There were no publicity or A & R meetings, contracts signed or album sales analysis. It was that simple. Blue had explained about the idea and then held her breath.

"Will you Ziggy, will you?" She waited whilst the grin spread across his face. Smiling in unison she almost leapt to the ceiling when he said yes. It was worth it just to see Blue so happy. What he didn't know at the time was, she wanted to see him play but that wasn't the only reason she was excited about a tour.

So now aside from everything else going on in his life he was preparing to go on tour. The plan was to do a handful of shows in V-world and then the climax being the live physical event. A live gig in Vic's world was no big deal but in Heathen it was all turned on its head. Pierrot, Blue and everyone else were convinced they could pull the biggest crowd in memory. Bigger then 83, bigger than the Isle of Wight festival or Woodstock. They were talking about filling the Market Square stadium with over a hundred thousand people with many times that outside. Still, since being here Vic had seen no more than a couple of thousand in any one place. Pierrot believed there would hardly be a human on the planet who didn't experience the show live in some way. Would these people actually come out of their homes to see him? Everyone thought so, Blue was absolutely ecstatic at the idea and that was partly the reason he agreed to do it.

So it was on and Ziggy needed to get a band together very quickly. Strangely that turned out to be the easiest part. Pierrot had some great contacts and they pulled together some amazing musicians almost straight away. At least they seemed to be? There was so much electronic musical enhancement he was unsure whether you just needed to hum and electronics did the rest. Zigg had told them time and again to switch it off. It was a great system for getting an idea of what you wanted but it was way too perfect to play live. Ziggy and the band spent a lot of time together early on but he broke away as the shows got closer. They had the show nailed as far as he was concerned. Pierrot turned out to be a great professional and he was right about the clothes. Ziggy and his band were fitted out with foil jump suits, platform shoes and the most dazzling stage attire he had ever seen. They had designed a stage set to match.

If they were right then this was going to be the biggest show ever. As show time approached he decided to relax a little and maybe give some thought to the band name.

CHAPTER 20

Vic could feel the building rumble beneath his feet at the shear power created from 100,000 human beings stamping and screaming. They chanted his name Ziggy, Ziggy! almost in sync with his pounding heart. The stadiums house lights went down sending the crowd to higher levels of ecstasy. As the stage lights came up he felt a cool breeze across his face as Weird, Gilly and the 'Spiders' ran past him onto the stage waving to the audience as they did, sending them into further raptures. Zigg had finally found a name for his band, his own private joke. He had remembered a conversation with some computer geeks at his office about algorithms they have in search engines. Spiders or crawlers or something like that. They were robotic computer programs that could help you find what you were looking for. Finding himself living in a world that was run by a computer not least a computer on Mars it was perfect. He had named his band the Spiders from Mars. They were Ziggy's band, Ziggy Stardust and the Spiders from Mars. Now he would have everything his way, the way it should have been all those years ago when he had his first crack at fame. The last time he had put his music out it resulted in utter disappointment. He wasn't surprised of course, not with what he knew now. Looking back he had no idea how forced and naive his music had been in those days. As the lights came up and the crowd roared Vic thought back to the night he quit music. Feeling like the only musician who had ever gone home and cried like a baby seeing their dreams shattered like broken glass. Never in those wildest fantasies could he have foreseen this.

He had fully adopted the name Ziggy by now. It was the name Blue used to address him and so he had decided Ziggy it would be. He had demanded his show promoters change everything associated with the tour, every single reference to his name was to be changed.

"I don't give a shit how difficult it is, just do it!" So it was done, like everything else he asked for was done. As the shows became closer the mask of Ziggy had welded to him so much it was hardly a mask anymore.

At last the people of Heathen would get the chance to see their hero in the flesh, to almost taste him. Cameras projecting onto huge screens caught a glimpse of him back stage. Just a momentary glimpse of him in his woollen leotard and feather boa. It was now, it had to be now as the guitars struck up he marched confidently towards the microphone. That was when it happened. As the band finished the intro to the first song he missed his cue. Instead Ziggy just stared into the crowd as if in a trance.

The band attempted to reconfigure the song and start the intro again, sensing something was wrong. They got as far as the opening lyric for a second time and still nothing. He was frozen, like a rabbit dazzled by the lights. The crowd, realising something was wrong slowly hushed and the music died. Finally a hundred thousand faces just stared up at him, wide eyed. They were almost silent as he just stared, the only sound the occasional uncomfortable shuffle of feet or involuntary cough. Every tiny sound echoing across this cavernous concert hall. The Red, yellow and blue spotlights circling the stage seemed pathetic without any musical accompaniment.

It was another of his 'incidents', this one was strong, powerful. He was aware of why it felt so right to be in front of 100,000 fans. He was Ziggy Stardust and his band were the Spiders from Mars. He was no longer Vic Jones and never had been. He could see his past and he could see the future. He knew everything that had happened and everything that would. It had all been staring him in the face, plain as day. He didn't need the Humanists to tell him what to do because he already knew. All this he realised in that instant.

Then, as quickly as it arrived... The realisation he had a few moments ago was gone, everything he had known only seconds ago had disappeared and he could not get it back. Like waking from a dream, where he knew what it was about but could not recall its detail.

Ziggy raised his hand to block the bright lights from his eyes and gazed at the ghostly faces staring up at him.

Shaking he clasped half a fist across his chest with thumb and forefinger outstretched and flicked his forehead with the fingertips of his other hand. Everything disappeared from his vision and he reached up onto his head and pulled the V-world helmet off. The screaming crowd, the stadium and the band all gone.

Finding himself back in the real world rehearsal space. He was no longer in the private rehearsal sim they had designed for the tour.

"Fuck it," he screamed throwing the V-world helmet at one of the futures. "Rehearsals over."

"Hey Man!" the future looked nervous, in despair.

"Don't you fucking 'hey man' me. It's Ziggy, get it." he screamed into his face stabbing the man's temple with his finger. "Your using that electronic thing again."

The futures had been artificially enhancing his music and voice with some gadgetry that resampled every note to perfection. He had already demanded that this all be taken out of the recordings.

He was angry about that but in honesty, it was all just cover for the incident. He dare not tell anyone, more over he was concerned it could happen on the night of the show. He felt it better to keep it to himself for now until he had some idea what was going on.

"But every note..?" said the engineer.

"I don't give a shit about how plastic you want this, I want my music to be real."

"The notes are great, we are not.." Pleaded the man.

"It's off, forget it. This show is not happening. Leave me alone."

Vic stormed out, slamming the door.

That had been a week ago, the show was off. Fuck'em he thought. He was happy to stay in Montserrat and write. Admittedly over time he had calmed down a lot and no one had approached him about the show. This amused if not concerned him somewhat, clearly they had been unaware they were supposed to beg him to come back, pacify him whilst he begrudgingly accepted. This had not happened and he was becoming increasingly concerned especially as the quality of his writing increased exponentially. He was absorbing this new environment into his songs both in reality and V-world. Everything in TVC15 provided limitless new themes on which to write his music, coupled with numerous genres from his own history. He borrowed from jazz, techno and rock to produce a sound that had been long forgotten in time and he knew the futures would love it. Not that he wrote for them, he would have no need to do that. He was aware that anything he produced would be lapped up regardless of quality. Even the Doctor hadn't seemed concerned that the shows were cancelled or even questioned him about it. He had expected that the Doctor if not Blue would be chosen to make the plea but none came.

It seemed that the Futures had decided if he said, that's it then that was it. If this kind of behaviour continued he may well have to consider begrudgingly relenting after all. No matter, he was ready anyway.

CHAPTER 21

The Doctor had made it clear he had no intention of going back up to the Chase. In his anger he had requested a more neutral meeting place for this meeting. Eventually suggesting Sector S036, a subliminal insult to the rebels which had backfired when they agreed. The Doctor had isolated his location from Duke and expected the Professor would have done the same. Being off grid was one thing but having to explain why you were in Sector S036 was an entirely different matter. It was one of the grubbiest sectors in Heathen sitting on its outer fringes. By physical human standards it was busy, physical being the reason most people were here anyway. It's narrow, dimly lit streets hid a multitude of sins. If Manhattan Chase was Heathen's human sewer then S061 was its overflow pipe. There were plenty of bodies milling around, few of which had a legitimate reason to be here. On the surface it bustled but it wasn't always clear how many of these people were organic. If the whole place wasn't lit like a cave it might be easier to tell. Truth is there were people here who didn't want to know who was and who wasn't organic. The Mother system allowed certain immoral activities to go on provided most people were willing participants and in sector So36 this was most definitely the case. A large number of hacked drones for sale or hire boosted the visible population on the streets. The Doctor felt a hint of hypocrisy in his distain for them considering his relations with Ramona but that was different. They had not lowered their relationship morals to crawling down alleyways. At least So36 was serviced by Mother which meant it was possible to catch a Magpod into the area. The upshot being you only have to endure it's depressing stench once you hit the street. Neon signs reflected in the puddle strewn pavements washing yellow and purple hews up the dark damp walls. Disembarking at his destination there was no such signs, instead a worn plate on the wall read 'Cafe Exile'. The

Doctor stepped from the transport and clunked down a narrow stairwell towards the muffled beat of music. At the bottom he pushed a dark heavy curtain to one side and the odour filled his nostrils. It smelt damp and musky like a derelict building. A bar ran across the far wall and a row of dimly lit booths ran along the right hand side. The bearded man leaning across an under illuminated bar was looking straight at him. The place was empty except for three figures sat in the only occupied booth and he nodded in their direction. The barman stood upright as he approached, drying his hands ready to take his order. The Doctor ignored him and as he passed the man leant back on his elbows and began reading. The monotonous beat of the music faded in the confines of the booth as he spread his legs and pulled a stool between them. Aladdin stared straight ahead, his smile too wide as if holding back a laugh, eyeing the Doctor sideways.

"How's it going?" said Jack. At the end of his elbow a glass dangled from thumb and finger. His head shot back as he took a large gulp of the red liquid, slamming the glass down on the table. Dragging his sleeve across his mouth like a pirate causing his lipstick to smudge a little. He looked around nervously, much of the confidence for the last time they had met was gone. We're in no mans land now the Doctor thought, feeling the power had shifted just a little. Jack looked different again, none of the shadowy make up and definitely no blatant Humanist symbols. There were hints of grey hair but still the eye patch over his right eye.

"How's what going?" said the Doctor knowing full well what he meant.

"The caveman, everything going as he said it would?" Nodding towards the Professor. The three waited for his reply and he paused purposefully, looking up in thought and then down at the table.

"It's been a week, he has cancelled the show." There were looks of concern around the table as the three men waited for a response from the Professor.

"Tomorrow or the next day," he paused. "Just as last time, he will change his mind." The Professor simply nodded in acknowledgement and the two sighed with relief, sitting back in their chairs. Aladdin threw a look at Jack.

"It looks like we are on." Scrunching his lips, picking up Jack's glass and taking a slug in acknowledgement. Not for the first time the Doctor wondered about these two. Whether they might be physical? Who knows what goes on up there in the chase, you hear stories.

"It's no concern, we keep to the timetable, 7 days. It will happen." said the Professor. Having no wish to rub salt in the wounds for his younger self. Perhaps a neutral location may not have been a good idea. The Doctor caught the eye of Jack looking over his shoulder and spun round to see the barman staring at them.

"It's ok," said Jack. "He's with us."

The Doctor narrowed his eyes at the word 'us' hoping Jack hadn't noticed his contemptuous stare.

He did, and smiled to himself.

The atmosphere was still very tense between the Doctor and his older self. Even though they had ample opportunity to talk about the implications of their actions, last night had been particularly venomous. The veiled threat to blackmail him by exposing his relationship with Ramona hadn't gone down well. Something the Professor had not seen coming but under the circumstances he supposed it was natural. There had been no resolution or reconciliation and an atmosphere of mistrust still pervaded. The Doctor was feeling the same way and all along both of them had to keep reminding themselves that they were the same person, just years apart. It had taken the Doctor longer to grasp how wide that gulf was. Not just physically but in mental attitude, to see in real time what he would one day become. Cooperating with the people he loathed and conspiring to kill the thing he loved most. He knew the word kill made no sense and yet that was what they were planning to do. He had grown to like Ziggy and working with him had increased the Doctor's knowledge of the Moonage. The more he knew the more this whole thing terrified him. How could the people of Heathen survive in that world if Mother shuts down. The Caveman had asked about the Humanists some time ago and he had told him the truth. They were savages, unstable and dangerous and yet he was expected to turn that on its head and convince him to join 'us'! His experience with these scum had not changed his opinion one bit in fact it had served to confirm his opinions. He had said as much last night to the Professor as they had argued long into the night.

"What if they are using you? Have you thought of that?" he shouted at him.

"In what way?"

"Surely you don't trust them, you went to them with your idea, a theory of what happened or what is going to happen and they grasped it. They don't care what's true as long as you help them shut Mother down."

"I told you what's going to happen! a reduction in organic life support systems, I was working with a drone and didn't know it."

"So on that evidence they'll encourage you to help them achieve what they have failed to achieve in hundreds of years," screamed the Doctor.

"It organic life that matters, you've learned a lot from the caveman but remember I've studied him for decades, sifting through his memory cast, building Sims of the Moonage."

"Organic life matters, yes I agree but what about those who live in V-world permanently? Those who have gone into Salvation?" pleaded the Doctor.

"Not again, they are already dead," said the Professor in despair. "They died a long, long time ago."

"What's going to be left for us? Living like the caveman."

"We won't be completely isolated, we'll still have manual technology, electricity and there's lots of people like you and me who can help rebuild a manual system."

"Physical work? Physical relationships? Living like animals?" The Doctor stared, challenging the Professor to explain how they could go back to that.

He paused "Yes," he said looking at the floor. "There's no other way."

"Mother could help us if we were to reach out to her."

"Don't say that, it's a Machine."

"It? You already sound like one of them." holding his gaze, probing for a reaction to his venomous insult.

The Doctor just wanted his life to be the way it was going to be, he wanted to continue with his life and his work. He didn't want to meddle with time, he just wanted to wait and see for himself when he reached the Professor's age, maybe with hindsight it could be different? But to destroy the Saviour Machine? He still found it hard to believe he was sitting here now with these two.

"Shall we run through the whole thing while we're together? We won't meet up until after it's done," said the Professor as the two scumbags nodded enthusiastically.

"At the moment we still have confirmation that everything is happening as it did. Let's assume that'll continue to be the case. On the night of the final show there will be a power failure in one of the sectors attached to the Market square. It should be just before the interval, Jack are you able to get in?"

"That's the easy part, once the power goes down we will be able to lock in every sector. No matter what happens, any sector that opens up to that broadcast stream will be locked in, we have the off button." He emphasised the point by performing a slow karate chop on the table.

The Professor turned to the Doc. "You realise what this means? We then control the broadcast and it cannot be switched off. When the time comes we'll need Ziggy to announce to the world that Mother is closing down. To tell them what they have to do."

The Doctor just looked up like a lost child, he had no words. The Professor continued. "Once we have that then the virus can be uploaded?"

Aladdin tapped his breast presumably to indicate he had the card on him.

"Will it work?" said the Professor.

Jack thinned his lips "We have used the virus before and it's tested but.." Aladdin interrupted. "It's never done much damage because of Mother's firewalls."

"This time it's different right?" The Professor dipped his head staring up at them both in unison. Aladdin presented as confident, over confident thought the Professor but this was all they had. "I told you, if what you told us happens. If that show goes out live to every sector then we can get into Mother's main system on Mars."

Jack sipped his drink once more. "We've checked the coordinates, on the night of the show Mars will be 14.38 light minutes away. That will give us a window of 14 minutes to hit her and 14 minutes once she is hit to come for us or drop the firewall, by then it should be too late."

Aladdin laughed falling back in his seat. "Way too late baby, by the time she realises her system has been infected she'll start blowing fuses, boom." Aladdin widened his eyes making a slow explosion gesture with his fingers for effect.

Not for the first time the Professor was slightly embarrassed and waved it away dismissively. Aladdin made it quite clear that the gesture was aimed at the Doctor. This snivelling little man who was afraid of surviving without a machine to look after him. He was right too, the Doctor was afraid, maybe because he knew a lot more about the Moonage than these lunatics.

There were times when the Doctor had wondered which was worse. Maybe to allow humanity a graceful end, oblivious to its fate. The alternative was a return to the caveman's time, racism, physical war and struggle. To send our society back to that was a travesty, maybe better to just let it die a natural death.

"This is where you come in," said the Professor to the Doctor. "It was during the break that I spoke again to Ziggy about the migration. He was concerned about what he was about to do and so I reassured him."

The Doctor was aware that they were all staring at him intently, trying to read his thoughts. The Professor continued. "I explained that he would be living in a whole new world within the cloud. I supported his decision. His every desire catered for and he would be with the love of his life forever."

There was an involuntary snigger from Aladdin that the Professor ignored. "In the past he had become confused within V-world about emotions etc. In the end he took my advice and well.... The rest you know."

"I suppose that changes now?" said the Doctor without looking up.

Aladdin replied for him "Because of what he did, because of his endorsement the Migration project flew." He poked the table hard with an outstretched finger.

The Professor held up a hand as the three mentally crowded in on the Doctor like they were trying to coax a child? "You will be there, you need to explain to him that he should not do it, I should have done it when I had the chance but with what we know now it's even more important."

The Doctor wrung his hands under the table, rocking back and forth nervously. "What if he ignores my advice and goes ahead?"

"The plan is in place, by the time you speak to him." the Professor nodded to the two men.

"It can't be stopped but more than that, he will have the ear of Heathen. The cloud will not be able to shut him down. Whatever he says will go out. He has to warn people."

"You will have to tell him the cloud he is about to go into and live forever is about to blow a fuse!" Aladdin laughed again on his own.

"Once the power is restored and that sector is back on line then it will be inevitable, the cloud will be shutting down for good." The Professor threw a glance towards Jack before continuing. "We really need him on our side, you know what happened last time. We can't have that happen again, genocide, the years of the Diamond Dogs. Humans scavenging like animals."

"Some of us still are," he said looking at Aladdin.

Before anyone knew what was happening the Doctor was on the floor with Aladdin's knee on his chest and a loaded ray gun pointing hard into the side of his head. He had never seen anyone move so fast, none of them had. Experience was probably the reason Jack remained calm.

"Not now Aladdin," he said calmly without moving from his seat. It was hard to know how he could have heard him, it was as if they were telepathic.

"If you kill him," said the Professor. Holding out a shaking hand. "you might kill me too."

Aladdin froze, spinning to look the Professor in the eye, his chest heaving with the anger.

The Prof shook his head slowly. "We just don't know." The end of the ray gun pushed hard into the Doctor's temple and beads of sweat ran down his forehead. The barman casually looked up for a moment. Making no attempt to intervene as Aladdin slowly returned to his seat and replaced his gun in a single smooth movement. The Professor helped him up and they sat in silence for a moment before Aladdin finally spoke as if in explanation for his actions.

"We don't need him," he said pointing into his face.

The expression on Jacks face didn't go unnoticed by the Professor. He could see the worry as the veins still bulged on Aladdin's neck. "Let's remain calm," he spread his arms across the table. "Everyone is needed if we are to make this work." He knew this wasn't strictly true but he did want to come through this voyage with all hands accounted for.

Jack continued as if nothing had happened, cracking nuts and popping them in his mouth. "Myself and Aladdin will be amongst the crowds on the night. Don't worry about us, we'll get in." he said with a nod.

The Professor stared him out, he didn't flinch, then he slowly turned to the Doctor who was adjusting his clothing back into some kind of order.

"Ziggy will have doubts when he comes in, that'll be an opportunity to explain what's happening. He'd be a lot more use if he stays out here. We could do with people like him."

"I'll do my best," mumbled the Doctor.

Aladdin opened his mouth to speak until Jack squeezed his hand.

"We need him on side man," said Jack. "He's a dog, one of us."

The Doctor was deep in thought, working though the plan in his mind. "You know if we convince him not to Migrate," he glanced downwards, distracted as Jack gently massaged Aladdin's manicured hand. Their thumbs and fingers in identical deep red nail varnish wrestled with each other on the table top. "Have you thought about Blue. They are close, what if she wants to go inside?"

"I'm thinkin she does," chuckled Aladdin in some kind of comic voice, looking knowingly at Jack.

The Doctor looked around the faces, glances darting between them. "What do you mean?"

Aladdin laughed. "Doesn't he know yet?

The Prof squinted his eyes at the two. "I haven't had a chance," he said between gritted teeth.

"What about Blue?" The Doctor was concerned, noticing the fleeting look of guilt on the Professor's face.

Aladdin started laughing hysterically, head down on the table. Banging and thumping and every time he looked up at the pained expression on the face of the Doctor he laughed more. The Professor shrugs his shoulders and cocks his head, Jack offers a wry smile of embarrassment. They wait until he composes himself as the barman regards the group once more.

"It's decades before anyone finds out," said the Professor.

"Finds out what?"

"Blue," he whispers. " It sounds silly now, it should have been obvious." He made eye contact with Jack.

"Blue, as in Blue Gene?"

The Doctor grimaces then as he realises what the Professor is saying his eyes widen. He glares at the three of them, for a moment he feels so foolish. Perhaps it's a joke? He laughs nervously, shaking his head. "No."

This sets Aladdin laughing furiously once more.

"Yes. I am sorry I couldn't tell you sooner," said the Professor uncomfortably over the laughter of Aladdin. "Can you imagine the position it would have put you in. If I had revealed everything right off?"

"So what else is there? How many other surprises have you got in store for me?"

"That's it I promise, this will all be over very soon."

The Doctor stares at the table top. "Blue Gene?" he whispers in a question to himself. "She can't be."

CHAPTER 22

Over the last week or so since that meeting, the Doctor had looked at Blue in a whole new light. Once or twice she may have caught him studying her intently whilst pretending to do something else. He was trying to see behind her eyes, looking for anything that gave her away. Bringing up subjects in conversation that might give any kind of clue but without success. She was a perfect specimen and ironically it was her imperfections that made her special. Neither stunningly beautiful nor highly intelligent. He noticed how she might laugh uncontrollably, make mistakes or forget things occasionally. He knew his Ramona was a wonderful example of a drone but it was her perfections that gave her away. The knowledge that she was not human was reassuring, with Blue this was impossible to determine. He sympathised with Zigg, would he have felt the same about Ramona if he actually thought she was organic? If all goes to plan then Blue will certainly be a victim. No one knew more than he how painful that was going to be for Ziggy. Whether a partner was organic or not they can become woven into your life. He will be as heartbroken as the Doctor was right now. Sadly, Zigg will never know what his destiny could have been had they chosen to leave history alone. He may well have never known that Blue was non-organic. The pair would probably have gone into V-world and lived in ignorant bliss forever. However it did reveal the extra motivation Blue had for convincing Ziggy to Migrate with her.

The Doc had decided to appear unannounced at Vics but he wasn't around. Doing so was an unusual practice in Heathen but Vic had explained that this is how it used to be. He called it 'old school' just turn up and hang out? There had been no loce devices or quality communication in the 20th century. He was making a habit of being off grid, finding Blue at his place she was equally mystified.

"Do you know where he is?" the Doctor said casually.

"No, he likes to explore alone, you know that. He goes off grid and returns when he returns." Blue was glowing today and increasingly so in recent weeks.

"Don't you think that's strange?" The Doc thrust his hands in his pockets frustrated.

"You would know better than anyone. He is from the Moonage, being offline is natural for him."

"The V-world shows have been incredible," said the Doc trying not to show any urgency.

"Yes, he needs his own time to relax. Even though they are V shows it's been very demanding for him, he is still writing and adding music for the physical show."

"He must have been a huge star in his time, he doesn't talk too much about that," said the Doc.

There was a pause, why were they having this inane conversation? They each wanted something. She stood up nervously, he even saw a bead of sweat on her brow. What amazing attention to detail.

Blue stood quickly. "Would you like a drink Doctor?" She didn't wait for an answer, walking round the bar and taking a glass from the cupboard. He caught sight of her shapely form under large maroon baggy slacks and an almost transparent yellow patterned top. She had metamorphic features that could display masculinity and beauty at different times, today it was the latter.

"Thank you," he said as he stood leaning across the other side of the bar. Blue poured and slid a glass across towards him. He was conscious of their hands touching for a fraction of a second, perhaps accidentally. Placing a hand on her glass without picking it up she reflected his body language. He felt the heat below his collar, wondering could she detect his emotions? Their eyes met and he studied the detail of her skin, imperfect and blemished with an organic beauty. She just had to be organic, and yet the Professor had worked with a very advanced drone without knowing for years. She returned the look, dark eyes and large pupils piercing into him, holding a moment too long.

"I am glad we are alone at last," she said softly looking down, fingering the condensation up and down on her glass. The Doctor felt flushed as the blood rushed up from his neck. Leaning on her elbows her small breasts appeared more ample across his eye-line.

"Really?" he said sipping the cool liquid from the tumbler as his hands shook ever so slightly. Without moving her head those huge eyes flashed up at him.

"It's about the final show. All that remains is the the Market Square performance. This is different and I am worried for him."

"Worried?"

"You must have heard the rumours? About the announcement?"

There was an uncomfortable silence before she took a sip and continued. Dabbing liquid from her deep red lips with the back of a finger she coughed nervously. "Ziggy trusts you, having worked together a long time now."

"Yes, likewise yourself," he said feeling the heat and unbuttoning his jacket.

"Our relationship is virtual of course. You know that?" What was she suggesting, that he was accusing her of being physical or simply confirming it wasn't?

"Of course," he acknowledged indicating some surprise she might even need to say it.

"I have to discuss something with you, it concerns Ziggy. It concerns us both and I need to know I can," she cocked her head and flashed an embarrassed smile. "Rely on you?"

Speaking the last statement in a question she was unusually vulnerable and evasive. He wanted to take the stress of this from her. If he was being manipulated by a well choreographed performance of impishness it was surely working.

Then just as the Professor had predicted she would, Blue went on to explain about the Migration project. How it was about to be launched, how it was such a wonderful opportunity for everyone in Heathen. The Doctor did his best to be surprised and excited at the prospect as he would if it was the first he had heard of it.

She continued with how it had transpired that it would be launched on the last night of the tour. The night of the live performance in the Market Square. Blue and Ziggy having the opportunity to be the very first to Migrate and in effect be together forever in V-world. To be together and set an example to everyone.

"I think it's a wonderful opportunity for us both don't you agree?" Clearly a probing question.

"It sounds very interesting," Remembering this was allegedly the first he had heard of the project.

"Myself and Ziggy, we have a very strong relationship in V-world you know."

This wasn't a question, this was a statement.

"I have told Ziggy about this opportunity and he naturally has a lot to think about. We have to remember he is from a very different world to ours. It would be natural for him to have concerns and he will probably.." she nodded at him involuntarily as she sipped from her glass, shaking slightly as she did so. Once more the Doc was impressed, nerves? From a drone?

"You think he may come to me? Is that it?" how perceptive I am, he thought even though the Professor had already made it clear this conversation would happen.

"What would your opinion be of such an act?" She looked concerned now. Would he disapprove, accuse them of being physical. He had no idea whether Blue was even aware she was a drone, that is if she was? It was a ludicrous notion but it appeared her feelings for Ziggy were genuine.

"In what way?"

"Would you support such an action?"

"I don't know much about the Migration project," he lied. "It sounds amazing and as for the two of you, yes I would certainly agree it would be a great idea to take it up. A historic occasion."

She slowly looked up as the smile radiated across her face and her eyes lit up in relief. She almost leapt across the bar to hug him. She grabbed him around the shoulders and his face pushed into her neck. He could smell her hair and feel the warmth of her flesh. He thought he felt the pulse of a heart beat as he was pulled against her. He was starting to doubt what the Professor had told him. This was really just too much, he shuddered at the physical contact and yet it gave him pleasure at the same time.

He pulled away and she still held him across his shoulders. "I should go now. I think it's a wonderful idea and I can't wait to hear more about Migration."

Blue watched him leave, hands clasped in front of her face glowing like a bride on her wedding day.

Sitting in the Magpod on the way home he got to thinking. Let's say that Blue wasn't a drone, that she was actually organic. It would serve the Professor and the scum if they could convince him she wasn't. Being much more likely to help shut Mother down if they could get him as paranoid as them. Blue might be organic, if so then she and Ziggy could go into V-world. But Aladdin was right, it's over anyway. Like plunging a knife into a sleeping baby they would drop the virus into the cloud whilst Mother was defenceless.

The show in the square was going to be the biggest real world event in memory. If it wasn't for that then there would be no reason for Mother to open up across all sectors. The show

166

would have to be cancelled before Mother could defend herself and there was little chance of that.

Moments later as he walked towards his block an idea started to form in his mind. Something the Professor had said when they first met. The more he worked it out the faster he walked, loosening his tie his pace quickened in line with his thoughts. His excitement grew until he broke into a run, his overcoat waving in his wake like a cloak.

First he needed to get home and then he needed to find Ziggy. He had one last thought for Blue. Seeing in his minds eye how happy he had left her. The realisation he would never see her again filled him with regret.

CHAPTER 23

Vic stared out of the transporter as it crawled along the outer limits of the city. The final show of the tour was in two days. After that, and ironically not for the first time he would die and be reborn. He considered the words of Paul, the first to go inside, something like "it was seamless," but couldn't shake the feeling there was unfinished business here. The incidents weren't helping either, coming at different levels at different times. What was so frustrating was that in those moments he knew the answers. After an incident it was like he forgot, he simply couldn't hold the information. Like being given the winning lottery numbers only to find the memory had faded away later.

Since the note there had been nothing from the rebels. Vic wanted to judge for himself, see them eye to eye. Security had been tighter since the V-world shows but if there was a message he didn't get it.

The Virtual warm up shows had been an incredible experience and in two days time it would be the real thing. Amazing to think that it will feel exactly the same except it won't be the same. The 'futures' are more aware of that then he is. "Nothing is real," had been the mantra and yet in two days time 'Everything is real'. To the futures, being in reality by default entailed some form of risk. Whatever happened in V-world, crashing a car for example would never hurt you but in reality it was a different matter. He let out a little giggle at the memory of Blue's little joke that first time in V-world.

It had become habit after the shows to log into his own private sim to relax. The reality show had closed in fast and he wanted the time alone, time to think.

Earlier in the week there had been a proposal from Blue. It made him realise how lonely he was, how different to everyone else here. There was a huge decision to be made without anyone 'normal' he could talk to. What Blue had said sounded like a fantastic idea.

As his experience of V-world had grown Vic had understood something. It wasn't just the reality of V-world that made it so amazing, there was something else. Blue had said how pain is limited and other emotions could be accelerated. Maybe it was that or maybe it was just that feeling you get when everything goes your way? Which it always would if you wanted it too. It was as if emotions were deeper and more powerful. He knew this was a quirk of the system but it could be quite subtle. That was one of it's addictive properties. It was ironic to live in a world where the possibilities were endless only to find it was the simple things that gave him the most pleasure. In V-world emotions were in technicolor and Blue had chosen just the right moment to open up about the Migration Project.

The two of them had gone inside to another sim after the show. Cruising across miles of dusty desert roads in an open topped Cadillac, music blaring and not a soul for miles. The horizon rippled in the heat of the sun as it belted down on them both. They had pulled off the road and arrived in what looked like a dusty Australian town.

This was a public travel sim, designed for adventure and exploration. The Cadillac slid to a stop in a pool of dust outside what looked like the only bar around. A road-train cattle truck passed covering them in a layer of dust. Hopping over the doors and passing a lone tethered horse the pair made their way inside. There were around twenty or so people chatting along the bar but in a place like this it could have been the entire population. A few locals eyed them from bar stools and Vic had ordered at the bar whilst Blue checked out the jukebox. Being an open sim these were live residents and not automated bots, it was clear that they had recognised them. Being polite enough to keep that to whispering amongst themselves the pair were left to their own devices. Vic thanked the lady and carried the drinks to a table nearby. As he did so a record clunked into place and the music broke the silence of the place, covering the gossip between a couple of older looking gents on stools at the end.

"Let's Dance," she whispered taking each hand and pulling him towards a space on the floor.

They were already hot and baked from the desert sun and Vic's bronzed face glistened with sweat. Blue looked cool and relaxed despite the heat as her light frock dipped and span in time to the music. Dancing for a while they had provided a source of entertainment for the locals. One or two occasionally mimicking them at the far end of the bar to the amusement of the others. At last they collapsed onto chairs around one of the old wooden tables. Vic was hot and the air felt stuffy, the ice crystals clawed against his throat as he drank. He had never felt better in all the time he had been here, he laughed to himself for thinking of this being somewhere else. He was staring through the door at the haze rising up from the dusty road whilst some mischievous local kids eyed his car. Knowing how he was always completely safe in V-world made him feel an internal warmth.

Blue leaned across him, looking up into his eyes as if to answer his thoughts.

"What if you could?"

"Could what?" he said surprised pulling his head back to look down at her.

"Love me, for a thousand years?"

"I meant it," he whispered, kissing the side of her nose. Remembering for a moment her complete lack of sexuality in the real world. How strange and natural it was that in here he absolutely loved her. She was a complete and beautiful woman in every way.

"I mean it too. But I am not talking about just in the sim."

"I am not sure what you mean?" he said melting into those huge eyes of hers.

"Do you mean reality, physical?" Vic said excitedly. Was it possible that she had been suggesting a relationship in the real world. A physical relationship? It turned out that what she was suggesting was the exact opposite.

"When we are back in reality then our love ends," she explained. "We go back to reality," she looked down, as his smile and excitement ebbed.

"But this is good isn't it?" he said. "being here right now, the two of us?"

"It's the most wonderful thing."

There was a long pause as they both stared through the doorway at the kids fooling around his car, taking turns in the driving seat.

"The Salvation project, when the time comes would you?" whispered Blue.

He thinks, looks at her. The audience at the bar losing interest now and returning to their own conversations.

"Would I choose this over reality? Is that what your saying? Or this over death?"

"Yes," she said deliberately.

"Right here now, being together? With you I would choose this forever." When he said that he meant it so sincerely, but like a hasty drunken promise he was having doubts now. He wasn't drunk when he said it but he was drunk on the emotion of that moment.

"Then what if we could do it now?" said Blue sitting upright.

"Euthanise? Now?" Vic was puzzled. He guessed they were a similar age. Vic had planned on enjoying his extended life here in the future. Believing the need to top himself was some way off.

"I mean the Migration project, the project that is being launched at the reality show in the Market Square." Then he realised. His live show was going to be the launch of the new project, the next stage from Salvation. It will allow anyone to go into V-world at any age at any time.

"Your not thinking? We could actually do it right now?"

"We could and what's better is that we can be the first, if we want to," nervously she waited.

He thought, eyeing the line of characters at the bar who like them could log out in an instant.

"So we go and live forever in this ga.." he stopped himself from saying the word game.

"In V-world."

"You said our love was lost when we are back in reality, but it never would if we were to stay," she smiled at him.

"A thousand years?" he said almost to himself

"Maybe more."

He had thought about it before saying yes but not for long. Did any of it matter anymore, really? His shows were a success and he was a superstar in both worlds and that meant something here. His final show was days away and would play in front of thousands of real live organic humans and then what? He was becoming one of them anyway, he even dressed like one after Pierrot had brought in his Goon squad to help him with his fashion sense. In V-world he was still very much a twentieth century boy. Out there in reality he dressed in future clothing, a full range of what would have seemed futuristic? Now with thanks to Pierrot he had a show that would be the icing on his musical cake. With Pierrot's choice of costume for him and the Spiders from Mars it looked like nothing he had ever seen in his own time.

Pierrot may have fallen in the personality barrel as a baby but that's why he was Heathen's biggest presenter. His loud voice and louder personality had enabled him to be at the top for decades. Right now Ziggy Stardust and the Spiders from Mars were the biggest act the planet had seen in living memory. Pierrot was not threatened by Vic and he had told him so.

"Ziggy my good fellow, music has a short lifespan. Your my favourite flash in the pan but I have been around for forty years and will be around for another forty," he had confidently boomed.

Vic took that as a compliment, not least because he said it with a tiny hint of concern.

So in V-world with Blue, looking into those eyes of course he had said yes, absolutely, but now he was not so sure.

What was out there in the mist? Is there a question unanswered, an itch he needed to scratch before he did this. Vic was running out of time. He was going to live in Virtual reality forever and this was a big decision. He had said yes but really aught to speak to someone. Since that day in V-world his brain felt rammed, like a warehouse with no room to spare.

He stared out once more in vane, nothing.

"Home," he whispered and the Pod pulled away.

CHAPTER 24

Twenty minutes later Vic was pulling up outside his accommodation. It had been another long day and he was mentally shattered. He slumped out of the transport and sauntered towards the block entrance. As he walked along the short public area between the towering buildings he became aware of a presence behind him. It could have been a waste drone or suchlike but something made him feel uneasy. Vic didn't look back but suddenly the world closed in and darkened, he felt very alone.

These people had seemed non violent to him but he couldn't be sure. Every race has crazies, his fame might be too much for them. On top of that there were these humanists, maybe they had found him after all, perhaps they were dangerous? He felt the figure had dropped out of the shadows and was walking directly behind him. His heart was pounding, recalling images on his mind of those before him, left for dead for no reason other than fame. It takes just one lone headcase. Lennon, Kennedy and Reagan could tell you that.

There was no reason to target any particular area because this was no affluent part of the city. Heathen just didn't work like that, there was no real segregation because any affluence that existed took place within the homes rather than the outside. Relatively speaking it was possible to live next door to a high spec accommodation or average without knowing. The main front facade of any apartment pretty much looked like any other, there was no way of knowing what lay behind it. He had certainly heard rumours that one or two people suspected he lived here but they would never expect to find him in the street, alone. Suddenly he felt so stupid for leaving himself so exposed. He heard the footsteps behind him break into a trot as he lunged towards the DNA scanner. His only chance was to get behind the security of the block and ask questions later. He reached out placing his flat palm against a plate on the door which simultaneously read his DNA and unlocked. The door gave instantly and Vic stepped across the threshold as the figure bore down on him. Knowing that no unauthorised person could follow him across the doorway boundary he stepped inside. The scanner would have detected any unauthorised organic bodies and set off the security. The hairs on his neck seemed to bristle as he crossed to the safety of the interior.

"Ziggy!" A familiar voice shouted.

He made sure he was across the door line before spinning round to see the Doctor standing in the centre of the path illuminated in the yellow light. He held out a palm to stop the door closing but stayed inside.

"Fuck man. You scared the shit out of me!" he screamed in annoyance. The Doctor looked breathless and sinister in the darkness. "Apologies, I had no intention," he stuttered. He had stopped a few yards back from the doorway as if not wanting to come closer.

"What the hell are you doing here? How come you didn't broadcast or something?"

"Old school you call it?" said the Doctor nervously grinning, "Just stopped by to see if you were interested in some real world travel?"

Vic laughed. It was probably one of the reasons he really liked Dr Touchreik so much. He would really tune in to stuff. Having spoken a lot about how things used to be with Vic telling how people would physically interact, call round to the house and hang out. He'd explained that's how they did things 'old school'. It was typical that the Doctor would try and please him in that way. Vic had been off grid for a long time and Blue would want to be able to detect him soon.

"It's kinda late now, the shows and everything?" he said slapping his forehead.

"The thing is," said the Doctor taking a step closer.

Vic waited, looking up the stairs knowing that Blue might be concerned about him.

"I hope, you don't mind, I just wanted to talk?"

Wow this was kind of unusual, not just for the Doctor but for any of the futures. In fact it was outright odd that any of them would use that language at all. Zigg took a single step outside, letting the door close behind him with another whispered whoosh. Late as it was, maybe the Doctor could help him out a little too? Why not?

Pausing he, glanced upwards and stepped forward. "Ok, let's hit the road," he said stepping outside as the door closed behind him.

They grabbed a Pod and headed out towards the edge of the Natural History Park. Modern transport was not allowed inside and so, as they often did they began walking amongst the dark wooded area. It was illuminated by false moonlight and would be almost completely devoid of organic life on the fringes. This area seldom drew crowds in the daytime and so now it would be mostly deserted unless you travelled a lot deeper.

"So, what's it about?" They strolled along the wooded path amongst the trees, some areas almost pitch black whilst beams of bright silver light broke through others.

"Blue told me about the Migration Project, how you were planning to go inside early," he said nervously.

"You know about that then? I wanted to talk to you about that."

"Oh."

"Yeah, Blue thinks it's a great idea, I was interested to know your thoughts?"

If Blue is a drone then it certainly would be a good idea for her. Perhaps she is, but even if he told Ziggy he'd never believe him, no one would. He'd studied her intently and found nothing that would give her away. Whichever way things went in the coming few days whether Blue Gene was actually non organic or not was going to make little difference. The Doctor felt a deep affinity with this primitive man in the time they had worked together. Some of the Doctor's views drifted towards Moonage and that's natural in light of the work he did. He could not publicly condone the principles of physical relationships but he understood them. Given how things must have been in those days what option had humans but to behave as animals did.

"I think I might miss you?" he said finally

"We can continue our work in V-world can't we?"

The Doctor looked away, grateful for the dim light. Anxious not to show the tear that was pooling in the corner of his eye.

"Yes we can," he whispered. "I think it's a good thing, if you have the opportunity to Migrate then you should." He realised that with these words he had reached a tipping point, his decision had been made. He was going against his older self and the Humanists. He was deciding to follow his own agenda. The Doctor really cared for Ziggy but as so often is the case, the discovery of a rare species will often result in it's destruction.

"I have been thinking, once your inside, it's going to be like your euthanised and there's still a lot for me to learn." said the Doctor as his fingers clasped tighter at the device in his pocket, feeling the cold metal in his palm. He rubbed his fingers across it's form, feeling it's power run into him.

"I never thought about that," smiled Ziggy.

"You know what this project means to me?" becoming conscious he took both hands out of his pockets and clasped them in front of him.

"I suppose I do."

"There's a way I could continue my work after you go into V-world. Without ever bothering you so much."

"I don't mind, if you want to continue in V-world."

"It's not just that, its, well it would be easier too. I mean I would visit you socially."

"How would you be able to continue without me?" Zigg was puzzled and intrigued.

"Simple really. A complete trace of your brain has been taken. They had to do that so that you can still be the same person in V-world. You have to take every experience and memory with you."

Ziggy laughed nervously. "That's one of the things that scares me, my personality now exists in a hard drive somewhere," he said waving upwards as they reached a fork in the path, taking them in a circular route back.

The Doctor laughed. "Oh don't worry it's not activated until you go inside. It all very straightforward."

"Well I wasn't too sure about the technical aspects but I suppose so."

"I thought, with your permission I could access a copy of that trace, I could continue to work on your memories and all the other information that is inside there."

Vic stopped walking and looked at the Doctor. The night had darkened under the trees and he struggled to see his expression.

"Fuck, so you would kind of have a copy of my personality?"

"No not in that way. It would just be data, a lifetimes work to interpret. It would mean I can continue to help the people of Heathen rebuild their history, those that care." The Doctor set off walking and Zigg followed. Vic thought for a moment and then realised how ridiculous his mental objection was. Here he was planning to spend the rest of his known life in a giant Xbox and this bothered him? It didn't take long to see this wasn't a much bigger step. After all there's a lot of nutcase things gone on since he thawed out.

"No comebacks, no secrets revealed or anything like that?" he enquired.

The Doctor smiled "Every single secret revealed I am afraid but no comebacks, I promise that would never happen and I would never share it."

"Well if it's as cool as you say, let me talk to Blue."

"Your going to do it then, Migrate?"

"Why not? I am happy there and it's as close to home as I want it to be."

"Home," smiled the Doctor, realising the irony of that word.

"I'm an earthling just like you but I really do feel like an alien."

"It's ok I understand."

"Ok well," he sighed. "I never thought I'd say this but if you want a copy of my brain then. God help you." They both laughed once more and shook on it.

"You seem to miss your time and yet from what you have told me it seemed a difficult life, why do you want it back?"

"Conditioning I expect. It's what I know."

"Can I ask you something?" said the Doctor stopping once more and plunging both hands into his overcoat pockets.

"Sure."

"What if we had a choice, right now? If we could go back to how things were? If we could switch everything off?"

"What like no Mother, no Cloud? Are you crazy?" Ziggy laughed. "No way. I miss my world but not that much. You guys wouldn't stand a chance. No offence but your all just too soft, even softer than the first time it happened." The Doctor had known the answer to that before he even asked it but still. Here it was coming from an ancient being who had experienced both worlds.

Vic continued. "It's funny but it's not like I am dying in a couple of days, it's like I am being born."

"Your both very lucky."

"Soon you'll know everything about me."

"Well it's not that straightforward really, remember you told me about written books all stored in rooms like paper servers."

"Libraries," Zigg corrected.

"That's right, well it's a little bit like ripping all the pages out and throwing them out of a window. In a storm," he added. "I will have to build the data into something. It will be a lifetime's work."

"Wow, sounds pretty awful."

"It's what I do, it's very exciting to me."

Vic was unsure about asking what he wanted to know again but it seemed like a good time, maybe now.

"Ok but if your having all my secrets, I want to ask you something I have asked before. Could I ask you a second time about the Humanists?" he said inquisitively.

The Doctor felt himself redden in the cheeks, glad of the cold draft in the air. This had caught him out and he took a moment to steady his nerve. He needed to be calm here, act natural.

"Sick people. Everything bad you ever heard about them is true."

"Have you ever met one of them, spoke to them?"

The Doctor stuttered a little, did he know? Is this why he was probing because he knew about the plan? Suddenly he felt unnerved. He had to keep his trust, get his hands on that memory trace.

"It's hard to say, you would not always know. They range from hardcore lunatics to general sympathisers. Their venomous messages, sly symbolic references are around but, spoken to one of them? I don't think I could bring myself to knowingly do so"

He said that with complete honesty, the Doc's feelings for them remained unchanged regardless of the position he found himself in.

"Are you worried about the cloud! Once your inside?"

"No I am just curious."

"Forget them Ziggy. They can't harm you. In a couple of days your going to have the greatest night of your life. You and Blue are going to be very happy."

Doctor Touchreik understood even more what a terrible dilemma he was in, he had to decide who he would betray. He held the world in his hands like it was something he could buy and sell. He was glad he had spoken to Ziggy, he knew now what was right.

"Thanks Doc."

"My pleasure and thank you. I am very excited about our project and can't wait to get home and start working on the data. You should get a permission request later."

Vic smiled. "Dr Touchreik requires permission to access your brain," he said in a comical voice.

The Doctor took a long hard look at the caveman. Unconsciously he was fingering the device in his pocket once more. He was genuinely going to miss him.

"Come on," said the Doctor. "Lets get back."

"Will you be there? At the reality show? He said as they parted.

"I sure will." he said squinting in the darkness to see his friend.

"Yes I will," he said. Walking away, he waved to Ziggy for the last time. He wouldn't be at the show and neither would Ziggy, he had decided it was for the best.

CHAPTER 25

Everyone knew that tonight was different. A physical show brought it's own unique challenges. Ziggy and the band would have to physically get to the stadium to perform for a start. As it was going to be the busiest place on the planet they had arrived very early in the day. Since deciding to reinstate the tour Ziggy and his band were well rehearsed and it was all about waiting now. They had been told that rumours were already out about tonight's announcement. Most guesses as to it's nature were uncannily close to the truth. Live tickets could have allocated many times over and the Market Square would act as an overflow, this too would be filled to capacity. The performance would be shown on huge 2D screens outside and there were virtual 4d facilities available. Donning a headset would enable many to be in the crowd just like the lucky ones without leaving their armchairs. There would be over a hundred thousand real physical people crammed inside later with similar numbers outside. It is estimated that 95 percent of the population would experience the show live in some way. It was going to be beamed into every sector of Heathen.

The dressing rooms were incredibly plush and better than most modern day apartments. Huge white leather settees, entertainment systems and soundproof bedrooms. Vic's suite housed a sauna and jacuzzi as well as entertainment, games and a fully stocked kitchen with waiting staff. Three of the walls in the main lounge were glass offering a choice of views, one across the City another over the Market Square and a third which was high on stage left. The tinted glass would hide anyone from those who cared to look up from the excited throng below. There was no sign of Pierrot but he wasn't particularly expected as they had made no plans, they would surely all get together after the show instead. Pierrot would have his own suite anyway so there was no need to disturb him. There was a small army of security and drones to attend to their every need. Blue and Ziggy had spent the afternoon relaxed and chatted excitedly about their plans for the future.

Weird, Gilly and the rest of the band were in the adjoining suite enjoying their own time before the performance. He still hadn't told them his plans to migrate and only now considered whether he should.

Ziggy hadn't expected the Doctor to arrive as early as them but it was getting late. The doors to the stadium were open to the public and already the streets looked busier than Ziggy had ever seen them. From the window he could see the five sided tower situated in the centre of the square outside. Huge screens blinking and going through tests then flipping back to generic support performances and chat. At one point he recognised one or two of the team who had regenerated his new body being interviewed. Although a permanent fixture in Heathen the tower had never been used for it's intended purpose. Small groups of people were standing and chatting below, most looked like vendors of various kinds. There were flags and banners as well as high tech memorabilia such as Ziggyworld sim access and virtual avatar codes which would enable users to imitate the Ziggy style. All be it a style that had to be credited to Pierrot and his goon squad. There were still teams of engineers confidently making final checks on screens which would occasionally light up with enormous audible and visual countdowns. Groups of revellers would join in count along and sigh in frustration when it abruptly ended at three or two. Sudden and deafening sounds would occasionally crash out of the sound system causing people to jump in fear. Ziggy felt no apprehension about tonight, it was natural to him and he was concerned. Not being nervous can be a bad thing in his experience and many performers agreed.

"Is the Doctor here?" he said to Blue who was relaxing on one of the bed like sofas. "He's not on grid, hasn't been since this morning"

Zigg scanned the milling bodies below as if he might spot the Doctor down there somewhere, which would be an impossibility from here. Unseen and behind them was the main stadium and stage area. At last the sound of rock and roll filtered up from the distance and it never failed to get his heart racing. The distant thud of drums and the echo of guitars during sound checks. One, two.. Two.. Two. The dressing room apartments were amazing but he knew that once he was outside he would smell it too. Rock gigs had a particular smell and sound that even five hundred years would never change.

7

Jack Halloween had distributed members of the group around the Square in readiness for tonight's event. Only those who were dedicated to the cause at the higher levels had been briefed. All the others would appear and fall into line after tonight's success. Like soldiers who were working under cover they hid their rebel symbols beneath civilian clothing. Lightning symbols and red attire buried under hooded tops and shirts until they could reveal themselves. Jack for one was both excited and apprehensive at the possibility of finally being able to reset the clock. Being on the brink of freeing humanity from manipulation by technology. The reality of how difficult this was going to be had already hit him. There was going to be a great deal of responsibility upon the Humanists to complete this bloodless revolution. To bring everyone along and ensure they were weaned off their reliance on technology. This was the end game and he knew that now was the time to be on his guard. This was not a time for being stupid or impulsive. Jack was exposing some of his most dedicated people here in the square. With his entire hierarchy within a hundred yards of this spot he felt exposed. Still he was proud to be at the head of this battle being seen leading the group come success or failure.

Sitting here waiting for the time to move, his mind drifted. Of course he'd considered whether this whole thing may have been a trap and so had some of the others. But the prize on offer was too big to turn down. He had been cautious in his dealings with the Professor ever since he had arrived in the Chase. Willing to listen to his story of time travel and the horrific news from the future. After meeting the Doctor it was clear that they were one and the same. The Professors predictions had to be proof he really had come from the future. Trust him? he didn't, however he trusted him a lot more than he trusted the Doctor. They were two sides to the same coin but without a doubt the Doctor was the most dangerous. Jack still had concerns about Aladdin too. He remembered how it was the Professor who had suggested he seek him out, telling him how in his future they would become close friends. Having done so he had given Aladdin who was almost a stranger a short cut to the heart of his organisation. If it wasn't for the fact that Aladdin was so unstable and undoubtedly dedicated to humanism then that too could have aroused his suspicion. On the positive side he had been offered a silver bullet that could shut down Mother for good. Hearing that the Humanists were right all along may have diminished his normal sense of caution. The rebels had no idea how or why the reliance on technology would be so harmful in the long-run. It was more a sensitivity, an awareness of what might be coming. In all their assumptions he remembered none who predicted that a machine that loved might one day smother it's own children. This opportunity was too good to miss, too tempting. Regardless of tonight's outcome he was right here in the thick of it. He stared up at one of the huge screens on the tower. It had just finished another mock countdown to the cheers of the crowd before returning to a huge digital display.
To performance,
4 HOURS 32 MINUTES 45 SECONDS 44, 43, 42..

CHAPTER 26

It's going to be a long night. The Professor had multiple channels of media coverage on in the life area. This was the only news in the world right now and no media channel dared talk about anything else. The whole city is almost on shutdown in preparation for the biggest single live event in history. He couldn't help thinking of the last time he was here in these moments. Experiencing events in history for a second time but from a completely different perspective. The first time this night had occurred he was already at the stadium with Ziggy and the rest of them just as the Doctor is now. It was a powerful memory of an incredible night in his life. He could remember the excitement at having secured the data trace from Ziggy's upload. He smiled at the enthusiasm he had, feeling like pushing Ziggy out the door so he could get started. Desperate to get to work deciphering the memory trace and the treasure trove of history it contained. Completely unaware of what he would discover in the decades to come. So much has happened since then, decades of work, the Ramona incident and all his other achievements. Ramona entered his thoughts once more, like she was calling him one last time before she was finally gone. Ramona would be another one of the thousands of victims from tonight's actions. All the times he remembered sharing with her from this day on, she would never experience. As a precaution he had hibernated the Duke and it felt quite lonely here just waiting. It would be four hours until the event actually started and even longer until the power failure. After that it would be a short time before they could know if they had been successful. From then on a new challenge for mankind would begin and he wondered for a single moment, did they have the right to make that choice for them?

Too late for that now.

His younger self would not return until way after the performance tonight. To a new world in which humanity would survive once more as it had done in the past. That's when he started to think that maybe he could reinstate Ramona just for what little time remains. He knew the codes and she was right down the hallway. Just a few hours with her would be amazing, to be able to explain what he was doing. Surely this would be better than letting her shut down whilst she is in hibernate mode. It felt like putting a cushion over the face of a lover while she sleeps. What harm could it do to laugh with her once more? She would understand, he desperately wanted to feel her against him one last time. Ramona was his, wasn't she? Him and the Doctor were one and the same.

The Professor stepped cautiously into the corridor, still unsure where he was going as if his body was on autopilot. Behind him the sound of Pierrot's voice dimmed and echoed across the media in the life room.

The Professor stopped for a moment and stared down the hall before continuing on to the Doctor's quarters. At the moment he pushed the door there was a huge roar from the crowd as if in response. The door instantaneously detected his DNA imprint and allowed him access. His excitement gathered pace at the prospect of seeing her open those beautiful deep eyes and smile at him one last time. He opened the wardrobe and slid back the clothes hanging there. Punching in the code he stepped back in shock as the buff stainless steel panel slipped open.

The Professor almost screamed out at what he saw, covering his mouth he began shaking like a child. His eyes widened as tears poured down the back of his hands. His Ramona, his beautiful Ramona was..

He reached out to touch her cold dead cheek with his shaking fingers. He stroked her long flowing hair and located a small panel under her right ear. It was flipped open and the tiny drive inside had been removed and lay on the floor in front of him. Clearly crushed by the heal of a boot.

Why?

He dropped to his knees holding his head and sobbed. He thought he might be physically sick but resisted the urge. After a few moments he shakily got to his feet and dropped backwards into a sitting position on the bed. He stole himself to look up at her cold dead form.

Wiping the tears from his eyes he looked around the Doctor's room and for the first time noticed something at the end of the bed. A pile of clothes as if someone had stepped out of them. He felt dizzy and took a moment to question what he was seeing but knew it was true.

That was when it hit him.

The urgency of what was happening brought him back to life. He jumped up and running into his own room he ripped open the wardrobe. Pulling out a holdall he threw it on the bed and tipped it's contents out.

"Shit, shit shit!" he said in frustration.

It was gone, it was definitely gone.

He ran into the life area where the media channels seemed to have gathered in volume and excitement. The biggest show in living memory was about to begin and Pierrot was already on screen.

"Duke activate please," he said.

"Good evening sir, how very exciting it is don't you think?" Duke had always reactivated as if he had never been away. It was like he was unaware he had ever been placed in shutdown mode.

"Duke can you show me some holographic security media from earlier please," said the Professor trying to remain calm. He was sweating now and his breathing increased. He knew what he was about to see and wanted to be wrong.

"Sure, where and when would you like to review?"

"The last couple of days at triple speed."

"Of course."

The Professor ran into his room and sat on the bed. After a few moments a holographic blurry image entered and began whizzing around the room.

"Rewind five minutes and then normal speed," said the Professor.

A hologram of the Doctor entered his room and began searching the various storage areas. He followed him until finally pulling the bag from the bottom of the wardrobe. Peering over his shoulder he could see that the Doctor had found what he was looking for. The back up time travel device which he quickly placed in his pocket. He rummaged around some more before returning the bag to it's rightful place. Presumably he was trying to find the other device, the one that the Professor had with him.

He left the room and the Professor followed him into his own room. Then as he left the building with the device in his pocket.

"Stop please" he said and went back into the Doc's room and sat on the bed opposite Ramona. "Today Duke, quad speed," he knew what was coming and could hardly bring himself to watch. It wasn't long before a high speed hologram of the Doctor appeared in the room and approached the wardrobe.

"Single speed."

The Professor watched in horror as the Doctor opened up the door behind the wardrobe. He winced and turned away as the Doctor opened up the sync card space in Ramona's head, kissed her and then crushed it beneath his boot.

He then went over to his desk and started to examine some data on his screen. It was clearly the data stream from Ziggy. Looking over his shoulder the Professor could see he was focusing on a tiny area of memory. He would not be able to interpret the data fully but he didn't need to. Having found what he wanted he took out the time travel device and input a destination date. It was clear he didn't know exactly how to use it but being as it was effectively a prototype it was simple enough. The Doc's hologram then stood over the pile of clothes and he pressed launch. He disappeared and the non organic portion of his clothes remained in place for a second before falling to the ground. The hologram and the real clothes piled on the floor becoming one.

"Stop. Thank you Duke."

The Professor stood staring at the place where the hologram had stood seconds ago.

"Is there anything else?" said Duke calmly.

"No," he said in a daze.

The Professor went back into the main area and even though he wasn't taking in any media he felt it's tone was building. The stadium was filling and the Market Square was busy too. The mere sight of so many people physically in one place was mind blowing. He tried to calm himself, he had to think clearly. He knew the plan was in motion but what could he do? Communication was risky but he had to warn Jack. He tapped his AR communicator but there was no signal. Of course they were off gird, why wouldn't they be? Firstly to protect against Mother but he imagined it would be a safeguard against a double cross.

He paced around, had to think.

There was nothing else for it, he would have to get over there. He ran around the house throwing items into his bag and started towards the door. As he was about to leave he stopped and turned around.

"Duke."

"Yes sir."

"Close down and hard delete please," he said.

There was a long pause. "Could you confirm that your instruction is for a hard delete?" He questioned with some concern in his voice.

"That's correct."

"Are you aware a hard delete is unrecoverable?"

"Yes I am aware, carry out the instruction," he said frustrated.

"Certainly sir." said Duke calmly. "If you would be kind enough to DNA scan I can do that for you right away. I am obliged to inform you that the company cannot be held responsible for any loss of data or services associated with a hard delete. Shall I proceed?"

The Professor opened the panel near the front door and placed his hand on it. "Proceed."

"Thank you," said Duke cheerfully. "It's been a pleasure serving you."

The Professor picked up his bag and left through the open door. It remained open and he was way down the corridor before the lights went out and apartments systems started to shut down.

Out in the street it was clear that things were already very different in Heathen. The transport system was in no way capable of coping with so many people actually being on the streets. It had ground to a halt and there was no alternative but to walk. He needed to find a way of getting to the busiest location in Heathen and warning Ziggy and his friends. His only consolation being it wasn't more than a few miles and if he hurried he could still make it in time.

CHAPTER 27

Jack had felt exposed arriving so early but they had soon been absorbed into the growing crowds. Becoming more and more anonymous amongst the masses as the time grew nearer. As a precaution they stayed in visual contact so there was no need to be on grid or have communicators on. The Square had filled up quickly as people streamed in from the surrounding alleyways and streets. In no time at all this enormous space started feeling quite claustrophobic. As the excitement grew so did Aladdin's tension, his eyes darting around rapidly. After hours of waiting the unmistakable figure of Pierrot had appeared on all five of the screens enabling them to relax as all eyes switched to tonight's host. The footage had begun with 2D cameras shadowing his movements backstage. There was no sound just the over the shoulder shots, smiles and backslapping as the crowd shared the back stage preparations. The loudest cheer had come when Pierrot had knocked on a dressing room door which was answered by a smiling band member. Gilly had waved to the camera before ushering Pierrot inside leaving the camera and 200,000 audience members outside waving back. After a few moments Pierrot had theatrically opened the door, waved to an unseen figure inside and continued his backstage tour. After numerous similar scenes he had given a final thumbs up into the camera and was clearly heading for the stage. There was certainly sound now as the larger than life figure of Pierrot took to the stage to the loud approval of the crowd. Heathen had never seen anything like this, for organic humans to physically gather together was both incredible and nerve wracking. Jack was warmed by the idea of people physically being in each other's presence once again. Pierrot's voice echoed from every corner of the square.

"Good evening people of Heathen, where have you all been?" he said followed by his trademark booming laugh. The crowd roared in approval. This whole thing was just as exciting for

Pierrot. He was without doubt the biggest entertainment host in Heathen and yet people had seldom seen him in the flesh. Most often he would have been on screen or holographic form.

"Where did all these people come from?" He put his hand across his eyebrows as if looking into the distance. "I thought there were only ten people living in this city?" He exclaimed and once more they screamed.

It was time.

Pierrot continued to warm the crowd, teasing and cajoling them ready for the big event.

Jack gave a subtle nod to Aladdin and the pair started to push their way towards the centre of the square. The tower that held the screens was so big that it was impossible to see any of the screens close up and so as they got nearer the crowd thinned out. There were random groups of people underneath getting some temporary relief from the people around them or meeting others. The two Humanists were well rehearsed in guerrilla action and didn't hesitate. They marched confidently across the 100 yards or so towards the maintenance access gate. Both wore just the trouser portion of grey boiler suits with the empty arm sections hanging limply by their sides. On top their open neck black shirts were open to the chest. There was nothing official about their dress but it was as nondescript as they could muster. As they approached Aladdin pulled out a laser slicer and cut through the lock in an instant movement. Even if anyone had been looking directly at them they might barely have noticed what he had just done. Jack pushed the gate open with his backside and rolled inside followed by Aladdin who slammed the gate behind them.

Up above the echoing voice of Pierrot continued toying with the crowd below and they were responding with vigour. The tower was a little like a lighthouse structure except it widened at the top to accommodate the screens and looked more like a gigantic chalice shape from a distance. One more locked door at the base and they were inside the inner core. Dim lights illuminated the dusty air and highlighted a spiral stairway that disappeared into the darkness above. Their boots echoed on the steel steps of the hollow tubular structure as they ran endlessly upwards. Finally they reached their goal and pushed the door open into the unmanned control centre at the top. They were now below the screens and were able to see the real scale of the crowd spread out below. Tens of thousands of eyes on the outside all seemed to be staring up at them when in reality their gaze was fixed 20ft higher. Every last one mesmerised by the face of the greatest entertainer in living memory, Pierrot.

Jack surveyed the crowd below with no fear he would be spotted in the darkened room. Aladdin went to work pulling panels out from under the control desk. He produced an old Palm sized physical interaction computer from his bag and opened it up.

Jack smiled. "Wow, where did you get that?" he said laughing.

Aladdin narrowed his eyebrows insulted. "Code man, that's how it used to be done. Real code"

He put a small torch between his teeth and started to carefully examine various wires before unplugging one and attaching a lead from his own machine. He stared tapping away at the keys and two of the desk top screens came to life. They showed the images of Pierrot on the screen then a green screen of digits. Finally they settled back to the original images. The screens inside were now showing what everyone else on Heathen was seeing.

"Is this it are we on?"

Aladdin was too busy to answer, entering code, looking up and back again.

"Oh what kind of magic spell to use?" he said to himself before gracefully tapping one last key and then standing up to bow like a ballerina.

"Slime and snails or puppy dogs tails. Phase one complete comrade," he said with a sigh of relief.

"Is that it?" said Jack surprised at the speed he had operated at.

"That's it," said Aladdin standing upright and joining Jack as he surveyed the crowd.

"Are we in?"

"I think so."

Jack sighed and shook his head, thinning his lips. "What now?"

"This sector is locked into the broadcast in every sector. It's going out to all sectors and they can't switch us out of the grid."

"So now what?"

"Now we wait," said Aladdin with a proud smile admiring the view. He grabbed Jack around the shoulders with one arm and squeezed. "Once the power fails we can start administering the virus. They cannot turn us off locally. That will need a command from Mother on Mars and she is 14 light minutes away." He pulled Jack close and kissed the top of his head.

4

The Professor was still some way off and the crowd was getting tighter around him. With so many people on the streets the transport system was incapable of moving at even a walking pace. The closer he got to the stadium the bigger the flow of people, like a mountain river it gathered pace. In some places there were physical parties where the group spilling onto the road intended to stay put. They were watching on media screens locally and so only served to cause log jams on the pavements. Even those who found automated transport were giving up, because it was programmed to allow pedestrians right of way. The smart option was to get out and walk. The Professor did his best to move slightly quicker than the flow of the crowd but it was difficult. As he approached the stadium from the east side most people who intended to enter had done so which meant the crowds thinned out somewhat. By the time he arrived at his destination the outside was almost deserted except for small groups of stragglers. He stood and looked up in awe at the towering grey walls of the stadium before him. Anyone intending to be in the Market Square for the performance was on the opposite side of the stadium by now. He could hear the echoey roar from inside as he skirted around in search of the stage door.

He ran around the outer edges of the structure trying doors until finally he found what he was looking for. Finally approaching the security console where a young man was watching the events on his own 2d screen he looked up irritated as the Professor approached.

"My name is Doctor Algeria Touchreik," he lied as calmly as he could.

The man hardly looked up at him. "You listed?" he said.

"Yes," said the Professor. The man simply nodded towards the door, knowing the DNA scanner would soon pick him up if he wasn't. Of course it was the Doctor who's DNA scan was on the guest list so he wasn't really lying. The Professor placed his palm on the unit and the door buzzed open. 'Straight up the stairs," the man said as an afterthought before returning to his screen.

There was another distant cheer from the enthusiastic crowds. This time it shook the building as he heard not so much the words but the tone of Pierrot's final announcement introducing Ziggy and his band. The Professor leapt up the stairs two at a time, following the signs and partially his memory to the main dressing room. Finally at the dressing room door he composed himself and calmly placed his palm on the panel as it hissed open.

He stepped through into the plush hallway and walked forward into the lounge area. Now he felt like he really was travelling back in time. He hadn't seen Blue for over 75 years and there she was. She was so engrossed in the spectacle she was witnessing below she hadn't heard him come in. She had her elbows on her knees and was leant forward as if watching a movie. The seams of her dark flowered dress tightened across her shoulders. Through the glass in front of her a hundred thousand humans were crammed into a single space. The Professor purposefully coughed to gain her attention above the euphoria she was witnessing. At that moment Ziggy had taken to the stage for the first part of his performance. Blue spun round, startled and almost jumped to a standing position her back to the window behind her.

"Oh my, who are you? How did you get in here!" She made a dive across the settee and lurched towards the room controller to press the button for security.

"Wait!" called a familiar voice "Just wait. It's me."

Blue had her finger on the button as she slowly climbed upright from the couch to look at the figure in front of her. Studying his features intently the realisation spread across her face as she calmed, throwing her hand up to her chin in shock.

"Holy mother. Doctor, what happened to you?" Recognising the face of someone she knew well but who seemed to have aged maybe 60 or 70 years in a matter of days. This was the Doctor, there was no doubt of that, even the voice.

"Doc, is that really you?" slipping her hand from her open jaw and craning her slender neck forward as if the few inches might give her a better view.

"Sort of," he whispered still panting heavily from the rush up the stairs. The distance he had covered on foot had been impressive for a man of his age and had left his clothes feeling sweaty and damp. He was still trying to contain his breathing and reduce his heart rate so as not to appear over anxious.

Blue looked confused, her pretty face wrinkled. Her attention was torn between the spectacle behind her and the sight in front of her. Doctor Algeria Touchreik had aged almost over night by decades, she had seen him only two days ago. Not just his features but the posture, the skin and eyes were greyer. His crisp long hair now dangled lifelessly over his face.

"What happened to you? Ziggy was wondering why you were not here," she managed to say.

"What do you mean?" he said as she followed his gaze over her shoulder.

"You look," she paused. "Older."

"How old are you, Blue?" he whispered stressing the word 'you' as he regaining his breath. She shrugged her shoulders and gave out a quick breath, almost an involuntary snigger. The Professor detected a slight look of concern on her face, again she glanced over her right shoulder as if looking for support from the people outside, maybe from Ziggy himself?

"I asked you a question," she responded with a matron like tone, cocking her head slightly. The Professor approached her speaking gently once more.

"I want you to tell me your age," he said firmly

"I think you should leave." holding up the controller with her finger poised over the security button once more.

This threat unnerved the Professor, if she pressed that button he would be thrown out without any chance of explanation. He knew he had to persist if he was to gain access. Letting her see the doubts, letting himself see the doubts if there were any. Casually walking around the room, deliberately putting more distance between them. "When Ziggy came cut of quarantine you were the only one who was allowed physical contact with him for some time." her eyes were darting around nervously. "Why do you think that was?" He continued.

"That was my task for Heathen, why would that not be?" a slight throaty quake in her voice.

"Have you never wondered why it was you?" he paused. "in light of the possible germs, microbes you might have been exposed to?"

"I am best qualified to look after him," she said confidently

"What were those qualifications?" he walked around with his hands clasped behind his back under his overcoat like a giant bird. He even faced away from her so he could keep her talking without making her feel threatened in any physical way.

She spoke out deliberately loud but it came out as false confidence. "I think you might leave Doctor, I think you are unwell. Maybe the citizens?.." she did have doubts, he could see it, he had to try.

He interrupted her. "I want you to repeat something for me." As pools of tears welled up in her eyes. She slowly shook her head and mouthed the word 'no' but there wasn't any sound came out, she looked into his eyes pleadingly. Raising both hands to her mouth in horror.

"I don't want to," she whimpered through them like a child at bedtime. The tears formed enough to run down her cheeks and she rubbed them away with the back of her hand. "Don't make me."

The Prof stopped and spoke directly to her. "They are just words."

"We discussed this only last night, you know how I have true emotion." Yes they had discussed it, he remembered that conversation and to him it was decades ago.

"You don't know do you Blue?" slowly shaking his head.

"Know what?" Blue wished she didn't know what he was talking about but maybe she did? But even so, would it really matter in a couple of hours? Soon it would be over and Blue would never need to know because she would be with Ziggy in V-world. Able to be free and together forever just like they had planned.

Him as a boy and she as a girl. They had talked about it so much, he would be King and she would be his Queen.

Blue spoke calmly and slowly as if addressing her executioner. "Doctor, don't do this, please," she pleaded. "It doesn't matter now does it? You will have what you want. Ziggy has agreed to give you his mind trace."

The Professor steadied himself, he was hurting too. He had liked Blue and had always found her pleasant and if he chose to admit it very attractive. He gathered his thoughts, of course she was attractive to him, thats how she was programmed to be.

He turned and shouted at her. "Repeat access code initiation." stopping abruptly her eyes glazed over. "I love Ziggy, I have real emotion for him." she said. "Wait before you do this." Holding out her palms in defence. "I will do anything, absolutely anything. Think of Ziggy, you are friends and whatever your thinking I want you to stop. Just please give me a chance to explain."

The Professor began, his bottom lip quivering.

"Victor, SF 8287," the Professor said loud and clear.

"Victor, SF 8287," she repeated her hands still out pleadingly, shaking all over.

"Mercury, Gemma, 6052, 011," he said.

"Mercury, Gemma, 6052, 011." Her body stiffened for a second and her eyes blinked rapidly and then she switched back to normal as if nothing had happened.

"8446, 94483, 3853" she said nothing.

"How old are you?" said the Professor.

The pain and fear he saw in her only seconds ago was gone. "I am 2 periods and 7 months old beginning operations in TVC13," she smiled, looking down as if caught out in a white lie.

"Can you understand you are a drone?" he said.

"Of course I do, thank you," said Blue in a matter of fact way as if not a care in the world, she grabbed an electronic Vmag from the table and slumped down on the chair.

"We don't have much time. There's something you need to know about me."

Blue looked like a spoilt child turning pages rapidly as if looking for something. Trying to make it quite clear she didn't want to listen. He began to speak but everything went black and they were plunged into darkness, he paused. The lights flickered as the power was restored and the emergency system took over seamlessly.

CHAPTER 28

The vile speech made earlier by Pierrot only served to enforce the feelings Jack had about how far humanity had fallen. Even if everything failed tonight this was surely the end of the human race. Whether the Professor was right or not didn't matter anymore because out there were hundreds of thousands of people who were celebrating their own demise. He was too young to remember how men had become slaves to machines and to hear Pierrot, it was machines that were worshipped now. How had we allowed a human invention to govern our lives. To Jack Halloween it looked like a hundred thousand condemned men celebrating their execution. Aladdin had been so engrossed in the spectacle below he hadn't noticed his stare. He'd proven to be a valuable if not volatile ally in the battle for humanity. The Professor had arrived from the future claiming that they would eventually be future leaders and friends. No doubt their paths would have crossed at some point even without his introduction. Those people out there were not the only ones whose destiny was being changed tonight, his was too. If the old man was telling the truth he had met them both in TVC50, 35 years from now. By then he and Aladdin would be leaders of what was left of the Humanists. Meanwhile right under their noses the entire organic human race was being coerced into living a virtual existence inside a machine. What might have happened to them next gave him goosebumps. If as the Professor described Mother stopped reproducing organic life then they could eventually have been the last. All of this had proven that they had been right and had to succeed tonight. Jack Halloween may be young but he wasn't stupid, he knew this could be a double cross to root them out but that was a risk he would have to take. Jack had become lost in his thoughts having watched the fat clown whip them all into a frenzy. Explaining how tonight was special and tonight's announcement would take us to the next level. The great Ziggy Stardust was here physically, and the crowd felt it as if in the presence of a god.

At last the moment all of Heathen had waited for had arrived. Pierrot finally left the stage and the lights dimmed. Pierrot's voice echoed across the cavernous space only just heard above the screams.

"Ladies and gentlemen," drawing out his words. "please," another pause. "Welcome," longer this time. "Ziggy Stardust and the spiders from Maaaaaarrrsssss!" He screamed with the crowd. In the darkness on stage there was movement, figures.

Suddenly in an explosion of colour and sound the caveman appeared on the stage. A hundred thousand souls jumping in unison to worship at the church of a man. His ora and charisma were contagious and almost physical both inside and outside the stadium. The opening music and song were electrifying and Jack felt the hairs bristle on his arms. The pair were not immune and from their own vantage point were mesmerised by the performance they were witnessing. The event had relieved some of the tension and shortened the wait. Jack even had time to daydream about the future whilst under the caveman's spell. If all went well he would soon meet him, they would be kindred souls for sure. It was not lost on him that the pair had some affinity with the distant past. If the caveman did join them and become part of what they were trying to achieve then they might all replace the Major. It was they who could be heroes. They would be able to destroy the Major Tom myth and replace it with the men who really saved the world. After an incredible performance lasting maybe forty minutes Ziggy announced they would be taking a break after the next song. They had only played a few chords when it happened.

The pair were slapped from their individual trance as the power failed and everything went dark, seconds later the emergency backup kicked in.

"Was that it?" shouted Jack.

Jack leapt off the desk excitedly as Aladdin got to work.

"Me thinks so," his fingers stabbed at the old interface he held in his palm. Numbers and letters of code overlaid the screens inside the tower with show proceedings outside providing a background. None of this was visible on the outside main screens, at least they hoped so.

On the monitors the caveman had begun singing an acoustic tune whether as part of the program or not who knows but the people were enthralled and mostly unaware of the brief power failure.

Meanwhile Aladdin went back to work. From inside his jacket he produced a tiny fingernail sized memcard and inserted it into his device.

He pressed a few keys then frowned, looking up concerned. After shaking the device he went through the whole process once more. He took the card out and for a third time he did the same things in succession.

"Fuck!" he slapped the small handheld device. Jack didn't need telling, he could see the overlay on the monitors around the control room.

FIREWALL: SUSPECT FIGMENT DENIED

"What?" screamed Jack knowingly.

"It's fire-walled!" the reality of the situation hitting him like a slap in the face.

"How the hell, you said you could do this?" Jack screamed angrily slapping his forehead with the heal of his hand.

Aladdin's eyes seemed to spin in their sockets and he exploded with rage. Jumping up he had Jack pinned against the wall by his throat in an instant.

"You said the system would be open." he growled through gritted teeth.

Jack put both palms up in submission, spit dribbling from the corners of his mouth. "Calm down ok, let's try again," he croaked, struggling for breath.

"I know what I'm doing, the firewall is up. We have been crossed," he spat the words in his face. He opened his fists and released Jack who slid down the wall allowing the full weight back on to his buckling legs.

"No it can't be a cross," Jack straightened his shirt and began rushing around the windows trying to see outside. He didn't know what he was looking for, perhaps the citizens arrest of his comrades? This was a pointless exercise, he would never make anything like that out from up here.

"We wouldn't have got into the signal would we?"

"Of course you fool, that's local. We need to get into the cloud fella." He was right, they had got into the feed and hopefully had frozen it so it would continue to broadcast but with a firewall up there could be no virus upload.

"The citizens could come for us, sat up here like rats with the rest of our people out in the square. I aught ta gut you and that Professor."

Aladdin lurched forward again with incredible speed but Jack was ready for him this time. Using the split seconds advantage to fend him off with an instinctive hard punch to the midriff. He stumbled to the floor coughing and gagging for breath, shocked that his violence had been countered with such a calculated move. He reached inside his suit and pulled out his ray gun as if expecting another attack.

"I am on your side remember," said Jack tapping the side of his temple. "Lets just think for a moment." Opening his arms he slapped his upper thigh and turned his back on Aladdin as he observed the crowds below. The hairs on the back of his neck bristled as he waited for the shot.

None came.

Aladdin lay on his elbow clasping his lower body and spitting onto the dusty steel floor.

Jack thought for a moment. Turning his back on him had worked to diffuse the situation for now. "It's over, grab the device and let's get out of here, we need to get everyone back up to the Chase." Jack was already out the door and heading for the stairwell.

Aladdin slid the weapon back inside his clothing and rolled onto all fours still panting.

↲

The roar of the crowd rose and died in unison with the opening and closing of the door as Ziggy burst through. He was mid sentence before he noticed the Professor standing over his lover.

"Holy.. Holy did you see..?" looking up his voice trailed off as he froze in his tracks. He looked the Professor up and down intently. Ziggy recognised him immediately but it was as if he had aged considerably in the last 48 hours. The premature wrinkles were intensified by the distressed look on his face. The opposite was true for his lover who sat below him in the chair. A wide eyed childish grin on her face like a 12 year old on barbs. Sweat was still pouring down Ziggy's exposed pounding chest, the adrenalin rush fading fast, realising something wasn't quite right. He'd expected to see her jumping up and down with pride after what she had just witnessed. The situation was incongruous and the atmosphere in the room heavy, like he had disturbed something private between two people. It clearly was the Doctor, but the way he looked? Sitting on the chair still staring straight ahead, blue hadn't even acknowledged him.

"Are you alright?" She clearly wasn't. The Professor looked down at her, "I'm sorry," was all he could think of to say.

"Doc is that you?" Squinting as he strode forwards to be sure of what he was seeing. It really was the Doctor but something was amiss. His long overcoat hung across his slumped shoulders and his posture was less imposing. He wore a scruffy unkept beard below his red tired eyes. The exposed skin below his white shirt was greyer as were his wrinkled hands.

"Yes," he said watching Blue intently. "I'm Doctor Algeria Touchreik but perhaps not as you remember me," finally turning to face Ziggy.

"You can say that again, what the hell happened?"

The Professor looked him up and down, thinning his lips as if in pain. "We don't have much time. There's a lot to explain and almost no time to do it."

Ziggy ignored him, pushing past he crouched down beside Blue, shaking her by the shoulders. Aware of the odd role reversal, a flash of memory from when he was first thawed out and she had cared for him.

"Blue speak to me," she looked at him but there was no expression she simply stared.

"What the hell is going on here? What's wrong with her and what happened to you?" he said anxiously.

After what Ziggy had experienced in recent months, the odd culture, the experience of V-world, situations like this were especially unnerving. Along with the 'incidents' there was an odd palpable atmosphere now, of blurred reality as if the different worlds overlapped.

The Professor looked deep into the eyes of his subject from all those years ago. An interesting subject in the beginning but as time passed Ziggy had become human and later even a friend to the young Doctor. The years he'd spent sifting through the memory trace had increased his respect for Ziggy. In time understanding he was a real person just like everyone else.

"Do you remember a conversation we had recently? We spoke about the Migration Project?"

"Of course I remember," said Ziggy keeping one hand on her shoulder in concern as he stood.

The Professor braced himself. "To you that was days ago, to me it has been over 75 years." Ziggy looked confused and kept glancing down at Blue.

"He came back in time," she blurted and began laughing hysterically then gripping her sides rolled sideways on the chair.

"Look at me," shouted the Professor urgently trying to snatch his attention. Ziggy's head shot round and their eyes locked, Blue slowly regained a little more composure, reduced to random giggles squirting uncontrollably through her nose.

The Professor continued slowly and purposefully. "What I am about to say to you will.." The level understatement was mind boggling but he had to try. "It will sound crazy but please believe me. There will be time for explanations later. The person you had that talk with days ago was a younger version of me." The Professor swallowed and considered the ridiculousness of what he was about to say. "That was the person who belongs in TVC15." He paused but there was nothing in Ziggy's face he could read. "I don't belong in TVC15. I have travelled back in time. I belong in the year TVC90."

There was along silence, Ziggy looked closer at his old friend then back at Blue. She smiled vacantly up at him. "If that's true then where's the Doctor?"

"He's gone, he stole the other device and went back the same way I got here," replied the Professor.

"So your saying there were two of you?" He was interrupted by another childish snorted laugh from Blue. "Where has he gone?" Correcting himself. "When has he gone to?"

"That's why I am here tonight and not him. Because he went back" The Professor ran his fingers through his tired greying hair. "To your time, the same way I travelled back from my future."

"You are the Doctor but." Ziggy trailed off then took a moment to realise he laughed at the idea. "Ha, you travelled back in time to see him and he has now done the same?" Ziggy shook his head. His real concern was for Blue. "So there's two of you?, an older and younger version?" Ziggy wondered about the citizens, perhaps Blue was on some kind of drugs.

The Professor sighed. "There was, the Doctor you knew has gone back to the year 1967."

"Is he ok?"

The Professor appreciated the concern for the Doctor because by default it was concern for him but now was not the time. Ziggy stole another quick glance at Blue. "Thats before my time?" Looking outside and then to the door as if he might walk through at any moment. "Why would he do that, he liked it that much?" Ziggy knew it was his experiences here that allowed him to even ask such a bizarre question.

"I expect he has gone." The Professor paused swallowing hard. "To kill you."

Those words hung in the silent air and they felt the stadium vibrate under their feet.

"Kill me? He has no reason to kill me?" he said

"He wants to stop you doing what you might do tonight." Ziggy looked around in surprise, opening his arms. "It's just a show man, he was excited about the show, we all were."

"It's not just a show anymore," Ziggy followed his eyes as they both contemplated the waiting masses outside. "I came back in time because of what I saw in the future. The reason he probably went back was to prevent you doing what we need you to do."

"You are not making any sense?"

"I don't know how much time we have, or what the consequences are. He has gone back to your early life, presumably to kill you before you could come here. Thats why he has accessed you brain trace so that he will be able to intercept you easily at the other end."

"He used my memory to find a way of killing me? But you said," the Professor interrupted him.

"It's the most likely explanation. In June 1967 you released your first and only music album as you call it, he will find you easier during your brief flirtation with fame," he paused "Vic!" Ziggys blood froze at the use of that name. How utterly stupid had he been? Of course his memories were bound to reveal everything about him and he had never stopped to think for one moment. He had been faking it for so long and in light of his success maybe he lost track of its importance to the Futures. The fact he was Victor Robert Jones and not Ziggy Stardust had become meaningless.

"You know then?"

The Professor shrugged his shoulders. "I know lots of things, I spent decades on your trace. There's other things I can't explain but none of that's important right now."

"So what happens if he kills me? Do I just disappear?"

"I am fairly sure that won't happen, there's something my younger self was either unaware of or ignored." The Professor felt a twinge of guilt for even involving the Doctor now. "All my experiments seemed to show that it isn't possible to travel outside ones own lifetime."

Ziggy spun. "So you don't know for sure?" he said. "I might just drop dead or disappear?" He was becoming more excepting now. Perhaps he was genuine, he certainly looked to be willing to accept what was happening.

"There is no exact science here, no certainty. In all likelihood there's more chance of that happening to me. Lets suppose he has already killed himself by going outside his own lifetime. We still don't know how that will effect me. Myself and the Doctor are the same person remember, ok we are made of different stuff, different molecules but who knows. My early experiments with the device seemed to indicate that some very basic laws of physics come into play when using it. Matter can be neither created or destroyed only transformed. There's a finite amount of matter in the universe and we are all made of some of it." The Professor tried to dumb down the science as best he could. "It was possible to steal a few billion, billion atoms from another time without too much disruption. Go too far or outside of your own lifetime and it quickly falls apart. As if the bits are not there waiting for you at the other end." There was another stupendous roar from the crowd outside and it sounded like Pierrot was leading some kind of chant or singalong.

By now Ziggy was considering these consequences, amazing himself at how easily he was excepting this story. He was overcome by a deep feeling of destiny, like being in a film that he has seen a thousand times before. The fellow standing in front of him was claiming to be an older version of his friend the Doc and ridiculous as it was, he knew it to be true.

Ziggy was starting to feel like an actor running through his lines in a play. "What is it I might do that would make you want to kill me?"

"It's not me it's the Doctor." he stressed. "You have to remember we are different people."

Ziggy looked confused, he walked over to the window rubbing the back of his neck and stared down at the crowds below. The Professors words echoing and overlapping in his head.

"In the future I experienced, you went into that machine with Blue. However in time more and more organic humans followed you until there are very few left. After around five years Mother ceased to produce any more organic life. The Migration Project was the beginning of the end. I was witnessing the elimination of humanity through natural wastage. Homo Sapiens were obsolete."

"Isn't this Machine of your's supposed to be reliable, to love humanity?"

"If anything the Saviour Machine is too good. It thinks its what we have always wanted. It's a primitive desire that has existed in humans since they could think."

"What is?"

"To live forever, eternal life, immortality call it what you want. Mother believes that inside V-world the Migration project will provide that for us."

Ziggy flicked his hair and dragged down the zipper on his red and green body suit to cool himself.

"What's this got to do with me?" he said turning with his hands on his hips. He knew the answer to that question before he asked it but could never express it. He needed to hear it said, had to wait for his next line.

"I don't know for sure but it's possible that your brain trace was confirmation of that desire. You are more primitive than us." The urgency of the situation didn't allow the luxury of subtlety. "In around ten minutes time you are going out there to launch that project and effectively set in motion the destruction of humanity. We cannot allow you to do that."

"We?"

"The Humanists."

Realisation spread across Ziggy's face, he nodded.

The Prof continued. "Right now as we speak a virus is being uploaded to her servers on Mars. The red planet is 14 light minutes away and every sector is open for tonight's show, we can ensure it stays open. Mother is closing down and if you go inside then so are you."

"Holy shit, so that's it?"

"Nothing can stop it. Your one of us, an organic human being. We need you to go out there and deliver a different message"

"Which is?"

"To explain that everything is going to be ok, that Mother is being shutdown and we can," he paused. "We will survive this." How sure he was of that he didn't know. "We've got five years, that's all we got. After that the decline of humanity begins."

"So what's left for us?" said Ziggy stabbing his chest and pointing at Blue. Becoming angry as he realised the implications. "You crazy bastards are destroying everything.

We are going to be the first, tonight. This fucking nightmare was over for me. We are going to live in my time in V-world and now your just going to turn the lights off?" he said raising his voice and glancing at the door.

"The virus is already on its way." The Professor stared down at Blue and Ziggy followed his eyes. "Whether you decide to go or not there's something you need to know." He swallowed hard. "Something you need to know about Blue."

The Professor's mind flashing back to the cold empty features of Ramona he had witnessed earlier. He knew in detail the pain felt in losing a physical partner.

"There's no easy way to explain this but Blue is not organic, she is a drone."

"No. That's ridiculous," Ziggy said pleadingly "That's not true I would have known." Even as Ziggy said those words he had doubts. It was true they had shared their lives but how much had been in reality? The memories from their time together in V-world felt real but they weren't. Blue's lack of any discernible sexuality, her lack of physical interaction with him were both completely normal for TVC15. Despite all that he had grown to love her right here in the organic world too. Blue had always been open about how she was androgynous, Ziggy had always placed her in his consciousness as a girl. Was it because he felt foolish that he protested against what he knew to be true?

"We are in love, we love each other," he said looking down at her, his eyes moistening.

"I am sorry, so sorry but," he nodded over his shoulder towards her. "That's what she was programmed to be, to be the person you would fall in love with."

Ziggy surged forward and grabbed the Professor by the lapels and threw him onto the settee. The frail old man fell backwards, looking pathetically up at him, elbows up to defend himself. He wanted to hit out but what was the point, who else was there to blame but himself?

214

Ziggy walked over to Blue and grabbed her shoulders, looking into her eyes but what he saw frightened him. As if she could see right through him. He shakes her lightly as if she might snap out of it but she's gone. The Blue he fell in love with wasn't there anymore.

"What have you done to her?"

"I accessed her intel, she is functioning in a safe mode."

"Thats nonsense, have you drugged her or something?" He walks over and is towering over the Prof's face now and that's when he sees. Unblinking the Professor looks back at his old friend and recognised the realisation in his eyes.

Ziggy unclenched his fists and walked back to her.

"Blue," he whispered quietly into her ear. She looked up at him sharply as if he had screamed, looking like a frightened child her eyes stripped of any of her personality. The Professor pulled himself upright and touched Ziggy's shoulder. Time was running out and he could already hear the distant roars as Pierrot wound up the crowd for part two of the show and the special announcement.

"Do something, help her. I won't do this without her."

"Ziggy see sense, she is just a drone and that's it. You can't love her and she certainly can't love you." He didn't truly believe that, remembering a time he almost confided in Ziggy about Ramona all those years ago.

"So now what?"

"The virus is on its way to Mars. In minutes her automated systems will shut down. The people of Heathen trust you. They need your reassurance."

Ziggy squeezed his temples with thumb and forefinger as he considered his options. The Professor opens his mouth to speak but is interrupted by Blue. "Firewall down, virus blocked!"

"What did she say?"

The Professor approached her. "Blue what did you say, whats happening?"

She giggled a little. "Mother has blocked the upload."

"Oh no," whispered the Professor as he collapsed into the chair that Blue had been sitting in, putting his head in his hands, shaking his head slowly.

"What does it mean?" asked Ziggy.

The Professor ran his fingers through his straggled tired locks. "It's over. The Humanists are right. Even if we were to try and warn people they would either not hear it or not believe it."

The situation started to fast forward for Ziggy and he felt a kind of synergy with what was happening. The Professor jumped to his feet pacing up and down pushing his hair up across his forehead and standing between them both.

"How?" he was asking himself but Blue answered him all the same.

"Doctor Touchreik had sent a communication to a drone called Ramona A Stone, its trending."

"Of course, I never thought of that," he said "The Doctor, the younger.." he paused so he could make himself clear. "The younger me, the one you saw recently has sent a message. He knew it would never arrive but it would eventually share and trend before warning the citizens and Mother." Hand on one hip, biting his thumb he continued to pace, trying to work out what the implications were. How much danger were Jack and his comrades in, how much danger was he in for that matter.

Blue burst into hysterical laughter "Its failed," she screamed out to the sky.

"How does she know?" Ziggy asked.

"I am plugged into Mothers grid aren't I?" That familiar matron tone again. "The fix is on its way and the entry point has been detected."

"Holy Mother!" said the Professor into his hands. It sounded like the Humanists have been found, it wouldn't be long before the citizens were able to pick them up. If only he could have warned them but he was probably already too late.

"What does it mean for us? If Blue and I go inside then your friends will always be on the outside trying to switch Mother off?"

"How can we know? It's possible that the world will revert to a version of the future I knew. It can't be exactly the same now, but close." The Professor needed time to think but there was none.

"I need her back, can you get her back? We had plans, we were going to share a life in a twentieth century sim, but now?"

The Professor tapped his communicator, still nothing. Pacing again he continued rubbing his chin frantically.

Ziggy was still confused. "She is gone isn't she?" he said looking at her vacant expression.

The Professor still ignored him, he had a lot to work out now. He had never considered what would happen if this plan failed. He needed to get out and warn the others.

"Yes you would be safe." he replied "In fact with the likelihood of the rebels succeeding in another attack being zero who knows how long you could both live in V-world. Maybe Mother is right after all? Humanity may well migrate into V-world and exist for as long as the servers are functioning on Mars." For a moment the Professor even allowed himself to imagine a time, thousands of years from now when the residents forgot they were not real organic beings. 70 million humans living on Mars and not a single soul to be seen. Then he dared to ask himself the question, would it really matter. Perhaps the existence of organic life wasn't as important as he imagined.

Ziggy made a decision. "I am going to finish the show. To carry on." Ziggy turned to leave. "I am taking Blue with me tonight and we're going to migrate."

The Prof grabbed his arm "I don't think that's wise." He said. "We need to go, to find a way out of here."

"But why?"

"The Doctors message. Who knows how much he has implicated us. We should find that out before the citizens catch up with us."

"If what you say is right, the Doctor is toast way back in 1967," said Ziggy unblinking he stared into the Professor's tired red eyes. "I only wish he had taken me with him," he paused. "I suggest you leave." He turned for the door.

Then suddenly it hit the Professor, something that had bothered him for decades.

"My Heathen that's it," said the Professor his eyes widened and he was grinning like a madman.

"The Doc in 1967 is toast. But you wouldn't be."

"What do you mean?" said Ziggy turning at the door.

"Your right, he could have taken you with him. It's starting to make sense now. The problems I had with your memory trace."

"I have to go."

"Wait."

The immense difficulty he had in pulling Ziggy's brain trace into any kind of order. Falsities, gaps and pure fantasy had made the job incredibly difficult. He had even been forced to put false placeholders into the gaps in his life and in many instances there were multiple, duplicated memories. In short his deep memory had been a mess.

"Of course now, it might make sense," he said at last.

The crowd in the stadium roared once more as the building vibrated. "What does?" The amber light flashed in the dressing suite to indicate two minutes to stage time.

"In your trace there are memories that didn't belong there. Deep and hidden but I had put them down as just fantasy. What if they weren't?"

"What kind of memories?"

"Memories of you, Ziggy Stardust performing," he paused still trying to make sense of his theory. "Performing in your own time," he finished.

"That's not possible?" Quieter he added "I am not Ziggy, I am Victor Robert Jones?" looking down at the stage and seeing the figure of Pierrot waving and agitating the crowd. It would not be long now.

"Block theory!" he yelled clicking his fingers in the air.

"What the hell is block theory?"

"It's an ancient idea, completely unprovable. But if it's true then it might be an explanation." His mind was in overdrive now as he pulled everything together. The more he explained the more it made sense. "We naturally think that time runs concurrently. The day starts in the morning and ends at night, days years and months pass us by. But block theory says that it's just an illusion."

Ziggy turned and furrowed his eyebrows as he continued. "In actual fact the future is as fixed as the past. Everything that has ever happened and ever will happen exists in a single block of space time. There is no future or past. We can only experience the moment and so we believe we are moving through time."

"That's clearly not true, I have a choice?" said Ziggy "I could choose to go on stage or not too," he said pointing to the door.

"You think you have a choice." he said pushing the tips of his thumb and fingers together in front of Ziggy's face. "But you don't because the future already happened, we are just experiencing a tiny slice of it right now. Then tomorrow another slice and another until?"

"What's this theory got to do with my memories?" said Ziggy frustrated and looking up at the flashing amber light.

"What if those memories in your trace are real? What if you are going back to your own time. Taking your new body, your new music and.."

The Professor went almost white, his heart pounding "maybe even our influence?"

"Your not making sense."

"Don't you see? Look around you at our clothes, our style, our culture then look at yourself. Those things are all influences from the past." He could hardly breath he was so excited.

"Ziggy!" the Professor had an insane look in his eyes putting his face close up to his. "What if it was you who was that influence upon us? What if I was to send you back to your time, say 1968 and you lived your life in a different way. Wore the clothes played the music?"

"That's nuts, I would remember." Ziggy could hear himself saying the words. But he had remembered hadn't he? He was remembering now. What if the 'incidents' were snippets of those memories? He hadn't told anyone about those but he knew there was something.

"Wouldn't I have to go back in time for that to happen?" He laughed. "So your saying I take influences back in time and then those influences are still around 500 years later, then I arrive and take them back again?"

"Block theory," snapped the Professor.

"There's no beginning and no end?" he said puzzled.

"Take this and put it on," said the Professor excitedly.

"What is it?"

"My time belt." Unbuckling it he swung it around Ziggy's waist. He fiddled with what looked like a combination lock on the oversized buckle. "It's all set and will take you back. Don't you see? Only you can go back five hundred years and still be within your own lifetime, you will be completely safe. Back before any of this ever happens, your 22 year old body can do it all again. You have the cure you came for and can relive your life."

"But what about?" Ziggy was playing the scenario through in his head. "What about Vic?"

"Honestly, I don't know but I lived in the same space with my younger self didn't I?"

"If what your saying is true, the block thing then I would come back here and do all this again?"

"It's already done and has been done, you could have lived this life a thousand times before for all we know."

"So whilst most people live in a single slice then mine will repeat itself forever with no beginning and."

The Professor interrupted excitedly. "It's as if your slice of space time is creased or folded"

Ziggy paused and stared upwards. "That means no end, no death?"

"It's never over for you Ziggy. You will sacrifice your death to save humanity every time. You will be back I am convinced of that and everything will happen in the same way. You will meet Blue and fall in love again and again. Both of us have travelled in time therefore we have experienced the slices in the wrong order."

Ziggy knew it was true, he had lived this life so many times before and would do again.

He was unsure whether it was the emotion he felt that had pushed him over the edge but the 'incident' he was having now was powerful. Everything harmonising in a single moment. He could make sense of everything and this time he was desperate to keep that knowledge. The 'incidents' were giving Ziggy his memories back in full but only for short periods. He saw his lives, every one of them. He was going back to when he was twenty two just like he had done a thousand times before. He also knew that this 'incident' was going to end soon and when it did this knowledge would be gone. Drifting frustratingly away like cigarette smoke in the wind leaving him with the feeling he had known something. Whilst this knowledge was here he knew what he had to do next. Ziggy rubbed his eyes hard with the back of his hands and saw the symbol of the lightning stripe, deep flashes of red.

"You have to go Ziggy, go now before its too late." The Prof reached over to press the button on the belt.

"Use me," whispered Blue to herself "You could use me."

The Professor looks up now, frozen with his finger hovering on the button. Slowly the colour returning to his cheeks. "What?"

Blue spoke out again. "I am connected to the grid, you can use me to upload the virus."

Ziggy was still in shock. "What do you mean?"

The Professor becoming more animated, perhaps there was a chance. "Holy Mother she is right, she is connected to the cloud. She would have to.."

Blue answered his question "I would have to switch to manual and drop my firewall," she said in a matter of fact tone.

The Professor laughed and grabbed Ziggy almost jumping for joy. "She can do it as long as it's voluntary, Mother would always assume her data is clean because of her local firewalls."

"What about Blue, it will kill her. We can't do that."

"Understand, Blue is just a non-organic machine, we are talking about the human race here." he said angrily.

"I love her."

"She can't love, don't you see she is just a drone?" Clenching his fists in a prayer motion as if to hammer home the sense of what he was saying.

"Then why am I willing to self sacrifice Doctor? Offering my life for his? Isn't it because I feel 'emotion' for him?" Blue smiled mischievously revealing a tiny peek of the personality that lay within. The Professor was dumbstruck, she was right. He had no answer, Blue was effectively offering herself to save them all. He looked at Ziggy and then at the floor. Some error in programming perhaps, too much love not enough logic but who cares now. It was their only chance.

It couldn't be done here that's for sure. It would be too easy to trace the upload. Perhaps under the circumstances the opposite was true? Maybe if they had too many signals it might shield them long enough. He would need to contact the Humanists in the tower if they weren't in the hands of citizens by now.

Ziggy turns to Blue and grasps her around the shoulders for support as his legs buckle.

"So it's true," he cries into her ear.

"Yes."

"I know what I have to do now but trust me. we will be together again."

"My emotion is true," she whispered as if begging him to believe her. The Professor turned away as she physically kissed him.

"I know," Ziggy smiled rubbing her cheek with the back of his hand. "It always is."

The Professor was forced to interrupt the pair. "If we are going to do this we have to move fast," he said stepping in between them." He touched the belt "When the time comes just press, it's all set. We have to get Blue into the crowds so we can upload without detection."

The buzzer sounded for stage time and Ziggy made his way towards the dressing room.

"Give me five minutes, there's something I have to do." He disappeared inside.

The Professor turned to Blue. "Do you have access to the public areas in the Market square?"

"Yes."

"Go there and wait, I will send you a loce to meet my friends."

She made her way towards the door without a word before the Professor shouted her. "Blue!" She stopped and twisted her waist to look over her shoulder.

"Thank you," he said in a whisper.

Without any acknowledgement she turned and was gone.

The Professor tapped the side of his head and finally Jack answers. "Thank Heathen."

"You better," said Jack pushing his way through the crowds with Aladdin close behind. "Keep your mouth shut and stop squawking, I'm coming for you."

"We had a problem with the Doctor, I haven't got time to explain."

"You said.."

The Professor cut him short. "I know what I said."

Aladdin is raging and has hold of Jack's shoulder indicating he wants to communicate but Jack waves him away.

"You need to get out of there as quickly as you can, I don't have time to explain just do what I say."

"Oh really?" Jack replied ironically. "Could that be because it's fire-walled? Don't worry we did, and it looks like mama is coming for you too."

"I know she is. But I have another access point, straight in. Get down to the market square and into the busiest part of the audience. I am sending you a location for a drone, she will have yours."

"No way man. No way are you giving my loce to a drone are you nuts?" Screamed Jack, attracting attention he lowered his voice. Aladdin was shaking his head furiously on hearing this.

"It's a fix up, there ain't no drone gonna drop its firewall, it doesn't happen," said Jack rolling his eyes at Aladdin. "Believe me we've tried."

"We don't have time for discussion. This ain't 'no drone'" he said mockingly. "It's Blue." Jack's silence was enough to know he understood. "Now get out of there and into the crowd, find her. She will allow you to upload through her port. Mars already knows we have locked all the sectors in. The fix and instructions are on their way back and you are being picked up locally. I need you in a crowd understand? That's all we got, take it or leave it. Yes or no?"

There was a long pause and the Professor was catching his breath, resisting the urge to say anything further he waited.

Jack stared at Aladdin knowing the seriousness of this decision. It was all or nothing, high risk and high reward. This was leadership.

"Yes," came the reply.

The Professor hung up his communication and forwarded Blue's Loce. There's a whoosh from the door as Ziggy appears from the dressing room behind him. The Professor turns to speak but is immediately silenced. His jaw drops in shock at the sight before him.

"Ziggy!" he says "Oh by holy Heathen!. What have you done?"

CHAPTER 29

A hundred thousand human beings were physically in the stadium and a similar number were outside in the Market Square. The millions who weren't physically at the show were watching in 3d simulators and virtual representations. There were physical gatherings taking place across Heathen using old style 2D silver screens. There was barely an organic human on the planet who would not experience tonight's show in some way. The bringing together of so many people was not without its problems, resulting in a small number of casualties. Mainly through those who had partaken in behaviour which might ordinarily have been safe enough in V-world. In the physical world however, falls, bumps and in one case attempted flight had real consequences. In light of tonight's announcement it was ironic how humanity was revelling in the experience of physically being together. The word was that Mother was opening up the Salvation Project to everyone and that Ziggy along with his V partner were to be the first. Behind the scenes the heart of Heathen continued to beat as the robotic infrastructure continued its work. Where humans had gathered the atmosphere was electric and the hysteria created by the first part of the show had still not died down. Ziggy's music had blown their minds in its complexity. It was in awe that they heard songs written by a human who was over 500 years old and yet his music was about them. He had gained an incredible perspective on their lives within his lyrics. His music and songs reflecting his experiences in their time since he was thawed. A buzz was going around the crowd as they realised Ziggy was late returning. Possibly a ploy, some said to help build the tension before the finale.

At last on the huge 2D screens there was some movement and a roar went up before it was quickly drowned in the groan of disappointment as Pierrot walked on to the stage.

"Ladies, gentlemen and drones," he screamed and the crowd laughed along with him. "Are you ready for the final part of tonight's performance?"

From the noise they made it was clear they definitely were. "Please be patient, I am told that Mr. Stardust will be with us very soon." The announcement was followed by further groans and sections beginning the slow hand clap. Pierrot carried on with his improvised entertainment in an attempt to fill the unscheduled void.

"Hey, I can't believe Ziggy is late either," he said with arms spread in genuine concern. "They told me he was 'Early Man'" at this Pierrot's laughter almost fed back the sound equipment it was so raucous. Sections of the audience beginning to re-engage with him whilst others continued their own conversations.

Aladdin had stopped in the crowd until Jack gave him a sharp dig in the back. They cautiously moved deeper towards the executive area where special guests could enjoy the clearest view of the stage. According to the Loce she was close and would be just on the other side of the invisible barrier in front of them. At last they spotted her but Jack grabbed his shoulder and pulled him back.

"He was right, she don't look like any drone," he whispered in his ear.

"Let's find out," said Aladdin shrugging him off and approaching her from behind. Blue didn't look round as the pair positioned themselves behind her. "Hello Blue, nice to meet you," he whispered into her ear. She didn't respond and just stood staring up, sniggering at Pierrot's jokes. Aladdin looked over at Jack and reached inside his pocket pulling out a small knife. Jack moved closer so as to block the view of anyone stood around them and opened the blade. Quickly looking around Aladdin put the tip under her right shoulder and pushed it into the material. Sharply shoving the blade upwards he tore a hole in her dress big enough to slip a fist into. Blue didn't react as he put his hand inside and began fumbling around inside her clothing. He took a wire from his small handheld device and pulled the end inside her dress. Pinching a piece of skin under her right breast he popped out a receptacle and plugged in. He tapped a few keys on his device and nodded to Jack. He dropped the device into an inside pocket and pushed up close.

He tapped his head to check the time. Mother knew the sector was locked in and if that was the case they would be working on a fix to break free. If that happened then they were screwed and their virus would remain local. Calculating the light time to Mars there's a chance that the fix is already heading back and could hit Earth at any moment.

That was when people started to look around suspiciously at each other and were becoming more agitated. Aladdin and Jack comically mimicked this behaviour in the hope of buying a few minutes. One or two citizens were grabbing at each other and they would soon zero in on them. Locally there was a fix on the signal but with so many people compacted into a tight space they could not pinpoint where it was coming from, for now. Jack silently applauded the stroke of genius from the Professor in sending them here.

Aladdin stood behind Blue with his arm appearing to lean on the barrier. Jack sensed the agitation around him but tried to appear enthralled by Pierrot and his humour. He spoke to Aladdin through gritted teeth "How long?"

He laughed loudly and said, "Nearly there."

Aladdin looked at the device in his pocket as two or three citizens on Blue's side of the barrier began moving in their direction.

"Come on," whispered Jack to himself. One of the men pointed at Blue and they began pushing through urgently towards her. She continued to look up at Pierrot laughing at his poor humour. The men were only yards away now and beckoning to people around her, pointing but to no avail. One man was shouting something but it was drowned out by the cheers of the crowd. At last Aladdin pulled the wire from inside her torn dress and kissed her on the cheek. That definitely did get a reaction as he pushed backwards and disappeared into the crowds followed by Jack. One or two had seen the physical kiss and grabbed at him as he pulled away.

Pierrot continued improvising. "Mrs. Pierrot wanted me to be more caveman in the bedroom, wait till she see's the pictures I painted on the.." He didn't finish his punchline and he didn't laugh, he fell silent as he stared stage left. His eyes wide and his jaw gaping, for once in his life Pierrot was genuinely speechless. At that moment, along with everyone else Jack and Aladdin stopped dead and could only stare in wonder at what they saw on the stage. As the crowd followed his gaze a wave of silence filled the stadium and no doubt filled Heathen. The whole City and by default almost every human being stared in utter disbelief. There were pockets of nervous laughter but only from the few who hadn't picked up the message trend the Doctor had sent to Ramona. The Doctor's lost message had done its job in providing warning of what was to come should he fail in his attempt to kill Ziggy.

At first there was disbelief that the figure who nervously walks onto the stage was actually him, surely not their Ziggy. If only it was a joke or parody or perhaps an imposter.

The screams and cheers quickly turned to shock and tears as the man they have worshipped steps towards the microphone for part two of the show. He stood before them as a living breathing insult to every decent human being on the planet. Slowly they see it actually is Ziggy under the bright red spiked wig. Painted across his face is the red lightning stripe that symbolises the Humanist movement. It couldn't be clearer where his allegiance lay, even if in jest it was in very poor taste.

As if broken from a spell the media and news networks burst into life. Broadcasting pointless news flashes to the mere handful of residents who were not witnessing this event live. The media too are starting to trend the message from the Doctor. One of the news guys wept as he told how the Earth was really dying as mentioned in the Doc's message. By now almost everyone knew that this was part of the evil, plotted by the rebels. Random screams, tears and shouts of anger spread across the crowd both inside and out.

Ziggy slowly raised a hand and a wave of silence swept across the crowds except for occasional outbursts from individuals. Their feeling of betrayal insurmountable.

The confusion was as strong as the shock. Why is this happening? Why has mother not shut this down?

Aladdin stopped to admire the view first looking up at the screens and then around at the faces. He wanted to jump for joy and scream out. The smile on his face said it all, it was the most beautiful thing he had ever seen.

Ziggy paused at the microphone and if it were possible for an entire planet to hold its breath, then it was now.

Finally he spoke. The world listened.

"Everybody.." he said nervously. "this has been one of the greatest tours of our lives. I would like to thank the band.. I would like to thank our crew. I would like to thank our lighting people."

They waited, he waited.

"Of all the shows on this tour, this particular show will remain with us the longest."

Silence.

"because not only is it the last show of the tour, but it's the last show that we'll ever do. Thank you."

Someone in the crowd screamed out "No!"

Ziggy looked tiny and isolated as he began strumming his acoustic guitar, playing his final song to tears in the crowd and all over the City. A song he had written to celebrate the new life that he would have been starting with Blue. A song that had a complete new meaning now.

7

Ziggy had said what he needed to say and as he now knew, what he always said. The Doctor's message had informed everyone of the consequences of tonight but it was for Ziggy to offer the reassurance. To try and explain that in his time humanity had thrived in the physical world and had spread across the planet. His words may have fallen on many deaf ears for now but he hoped that they would offer comfort in the years to come. He was sorry he had never had a chance to meet the people who had made this happen but he praised the Humanists. He was going back soon to start again and would never know how he might effect the future he found himself in. If the Professor was right then that could be the reason he was going back?

Sadly, Ziggy was also aware of what would become of Blue. She would shut down once the virus hit Mother along with all the other automated systems. The virus was now on its way to Mars at light speed whilst the fix headed in the opposite direction.

Ziggy had walked from the stage to an eerie silence, able to almost hear his own footsteps. His head hung low and he headed off stage, ready to go home. As he walked back into the dressing room suite the very last person he expected to see was standing right there in front of him.

"Blue!"

"It's done," she said. "I wanted to say goodbye."

She had always appeared more masculine in reality but now she looked more beautiful than she ever had. Ziggy knew it wouldn't be long until his 'incident' faded completely and robbed him of the understanding he had. The way he felt, he wanted it to go right now. He wanted his ignorance back so he wouldn't know any of this. He was going home and when he did he would lose the knowledge just like he did every time. The future he had experienced was about to be shut down but he knew one thing for sure. He was going back to another slice as the Professor called it. Back over 500 years to live the life of Ziggy Stardust. After centuries had passed the Doctor would be born and Blue would exist. Eventually, just as he always did Vic would be thawed and he would fall in love. Like all the times before it would end with him being right here, knowing block theory was not a theory, it was real.

When he got back to 1968 he would have no idea that in the future humanity would build a machine that loved. That machine would build Blue and a single human would travel forward in time to love her. She would give her life for him and humanity, whilst ironically he must give his death.

"Thank you," he whispered and they kissed physically and despite everything they had shared as lovers, it was the first time.

"See you in a thousand years," she said, her lips touching his ears as she spoke.

"I'm so thankful," he said hoping she would understand. "We'll be strangers when we meet." There were tears in his eyes as he held her against him.

"Why?"

"Because we can do it all again, like we always do."

Blue felt a shudder as the virus ravaged her circuits. "It's worked," she said. "I am shutting down."

Ziggy wanted more time to explain, to tell her how he felt. In their first physical embrace he felt her slender fingers slip inside the front of his belt.

"I love you," she whispered and pressed the buckle with her thumb.

The non-organic parts of Ziggy's outfit fell to the ground in a heap and he was gone. A second later Blue's legs folded and she collapsed in the same spot on top of them. Although she was physically still there.

She was gone too.

EPILOGUE

There wasn't another vehicle in sight when Nathan Adler swung his Jaguar into the labs empty car park. The admin block was situated in a large four story Victorian building upon a small hill. The smell of pines along the landscaped path was always incredibly up-lifting. There had been numerous additional buildings added in the seventies. For some reason these were semi buried beneath large grass slopes and at ground level the windows made them look like giant staring eyes.

Although the remembrance service was some weeks ago he had known there could be no real closure for him until today. Once he completed this final act then perhaps his sleep would settle down again. Nathan was unsure whether it was illegal or whether any law even covered it. Even if it was a crime then anyone who might be a victim would be long dead before or if it was ever discovered.

He unlocked the front door and went through the motions of unsetting the alarm before shuffling up the wide staircase to his office. He passed the boardroom on the right where some weeks earlier he had arrived to find his dearest friend slumped in a chair. Whilst doing so he thought back to the words he had offered in his memory.

"There are some human beings for whom their ullage writes itself," it was with those words that Nathan had proudly opened.

"Victor Robert Jones will be remembered as a great man in both life and death." he said projecting his voice towards the packed congregation. "A man who took control of his death in the manner he controlled his life, with absolute certainty and commitment. He chose to leave us because the time was right for him and it was no selfish act on his part." Nathan's voice breaking up as it echoed through the church's towering space. "In his early life he had shown great talent as a musician, something he was very humble about." There had been good natured sniggers from one or two who remembered the song that has brought Vic what might be more notoriety than fame. "This in itself had been a blessing and had allowed Vic to pursue his other passion, physics. Vic's success in business and technology made his company a household name but had never delivered the prize he sought above all else. I believe he hoped to find a way to see his dream a reality. He has provided his company with the remit and finances to pursue light processing technology. His wish to be held in Cryogenic suspension was certainly a measure of that belief and gave him the hope of one day being able to witness that success."

Comforting words to colleagues and relatives but he knew them to be true. Still he had tortured himself that he had provided the means for his dear friend to do what he did. Being a director of a cryogenics laboratory Nathan had been enthusiastic about its potential. After it had all happened he had carried out his friends instructions to the letter, except this final one.

Nathan's computer fired up and illuminated the dim wood chip walls. As is his habit he went next door and put the kettle on whilst it slowly booted into life. Returning with a steaming mug of tea he felt the chill of the room. Running a hand across the bulky Victorian radiator he felt a hint of warmth, it was early but the place would heat up soon. He tried sipping his tea but it burnt his lips and he dropped it down on the desk. Nathan pulled a well creased piece of paper from deep in his wallet and opened it up on the desk. On it were two hand written words

'Zigg Stardust'.

Within a few dozen mouse clicks he had opened up two cryogenic pod I.D's. The first was his good friend Victor Robert Jones and the second was a musician called 'Zigg Stardust'. He jotted down both pod numbers on his pad and proceeded to swap one for the other. A moments pause before he closed the windows and a small box popped up.

'Save changes? - Yes/no/cancel' it said.

Nathan hit yes and the windows closed.

He ripped the scrap of paper from his pad and crushed it in one hand. Standing he pushed the chair with the back of his knees and walked over to the window. He peered through the steam rising from his cup out towards the main gate. The morning mist was clearing and the sun was struggling through the grey cloud. He could almost make out the lake from here.

"It might well brighten up later," he thought as he raised the steaming mug to his lips and dropped the crumpled paper in the basket.

ABOUT THE AUTHOR

Michael J Dawson is a writer, producer and presenter from Cheshire in the United Kingdom. He is the author of numerous the award winning stage plays including 'Jesus is a City Fan' and the controversial 'London 7/7'

His script for the radio play and film 'Second Life' reached the final of two separate national TV writing competitions. As well as his stand up comedy and live presenting endeavors he wrote and produced the 'Gloria Swanson Fan Club Radio Show' for 10 years and was a finalist in the European podcast of the year.

His latest book 'Life On Mars' was originally conceived as a rock opera inspired by the work and characters of David Bowie. setting out to test the strength of the story he has written it in the form of a novel and is currently working on the stage production. Michael has written a number of other non fiction books as well as a fictional work under a pseudonym.

AUTHORS NOTE

"I think you should write something based on Bowie, maybe a musical like the last one." I had been a writer for many years and my brother a dedicated Bowie fan for many times that. Like most writers I already have eight or nine books or plays sitting on my metaphorical desk waiting to be written.

"Why would I?" I said surprised. "Your the Bowie fan, why don't you do it?"

He never did, but we threw the idea around on occasions when we met up. One night whilst sitting around chatting I started to develop a story. It was about a thousand year love affair and a man who would sacrifice his death and not his life (as is often the case) for humanity. It wasn't a Bowie story as such and my intention was to develop it further at some point. In the months that followed it begged to be a Bowie story and as the weeks passed it screamed louder and louder to be written. There was ony one way to shut off the noise. Over the coming months I had sketched out the complete idea for the stage musical version and loved it. The references and nods to Bowies work became subliminal and on occasion I would wonder were they written in on purpose. On other occasions they were in songs I had never heard before? Little wonder then, that this story was going to barge its way to the top of the queue. I wanted the story to come first instead of the songs and there was only one way to prove it. That was to write a novel that could stand up on its own without any knowledge of David Bowie. It had to be an enjoyable story for those who had never heard of him whilst being seeded with codes and references to his work for the real fans to decipher. I think it achieves both and now I hope that within these pages is a story that will intrigue rock audiences one day on the stage as well as in these pages.

I hope you enjoyed it.

Contact:

www.michaeljdawson.co.uk

info@sourgrapeproductions.com

For news on the upcoming stage show register at:

www.lifeonmarsbook.com

This book references names and places associated with the work of David Bowie. These are used for inspiration and in no way suggest any association or endorsement from David Bowie or licencees of his work either in the present or past.